continued . . .

"A prim heroine with a fiery core and a haunted, searching hero who thrives on the rush of adrenaline join with an abundance of quirky characters to drive the classic plot of this funny, spicy romance to a satisfying conclusion. With her typical sense of humor, Linz has given readers another joyful, laughter-filled story to savor—and another view into the charming Pennsylvania town she has created."

—*Library Journal*

"A worthy addition." —*Romance Reviews Today*

"A fresh romance that has both snap and sass . . . May Cathie Linz continue writing such wonderfully smart romance!" —*We Write Romance*

Big Girls Don't Cry

"The characters spring to life, and readers will be thrilled to find that individuals from Linz's earlier novels pop in and out like old friends. And kudos to Linz for creating a heroine who looks and acts like a real woman."

—*Booklist* (starred review)

"[A] sweetly charming, splendidly funny and supremely satisfying contemporary romance." —*Chicago Tribune*

"Another winner." —*Fresh Fiction*

"Another keeper." —*Contemporary Romance Writers*

"A must read. Top pick!" —*Romance Reader at Heart*

"Definitely one for the keeper shelf." —*Genrefluent*

Bad Girls Don't

"Cathie Linz gives her beautifully matched protagonists lots of sexy chemistry and some delightfully snappy dialogue, and the quirky cast of secondary characters gives *Bad Girls Don't* its irresistible charm." —*Chicago Tribune*

"Linz, known for her fast-paced, snappy romantic come-
dies, once again sparkles in this heartwarming, funny tale.
And her secondary characters . . . make an already excellent story exceptional." —*Booklist* (starred review)

"Linz's characterizations are absolutely wonderful. I fell
in love with the protagonists from the first page . . . It has
always been a pleasure to read her books, but I must say
that this one is a fantastic novel!" —*Rendezvous*

"Totally delightful." —*Fresh Fiction*

Good Girls Do

"Humor and warmth . . . Readers are going to love this!"
—Susan Elizabeth Phillips

"Cathie Linz is the author that readers of romantic comedy
have been waiting for. She knows how to do it—characters
with depth, sharp dialogue and a compelling story. The
result is a charming, offbeat world, one you'll hate to leave."
—Jayne Ann Krentz

"Sometimes even good girls need to take a walk on the
wild side. Linz deftly seasons her writing with her usual
delectable wit, and the book's quirky cast of endearing secondary characters adds another measure of humor to this
sweetly sexy, fabulously fun contemporary romance."
—*Booklist* (starred review)

"Sexy, sassy and graced with exceptional dialogue, this fast-
paced story is both hilarious and heartwarming, featuring
wonderfully wacky secondary characters and well-developed
protagonists you will come to love." —*Library Journal*

"Lively and fun, and you won't be able to put it down."
—*Fresh Fiction*

"A fun contemporary romance . . . Fans of *You Can't Take
It with You* who like romantic romps will enjoy this funny
family tale." —*The Best Reviews*

Berkley Sensation Titles by Cathie Linz

GOOD GIRLS DO
BAD GIRLS DON'T
BIG GIRLS DON'T CRY
SMART GIRLS THINK TWICE
MAD, BAD AND BLONDE
LUCK BE A LADY

Luck Be a Lady

. . . .

Cathie Linz

BERKLEY SENSATION, NEW YORK

THE BERKLEY PUBLISHING GROUP
Published by the Penguin Group
Penguin Group (USA) Inc.
375 Hudson Street, New York, New York 10014, USA
Penguin Group (Canada), 90 Eglinton Avenue East, Suite 700, Toronto, Ontario M4P 2Y3, Canada
(a division of Pearson Penguin Canada Inc.)
Penguin Books Ltd., 80 Strand, London WC2R 0RL, England
Penguin Group Ireland, 25 St. Stephen's Green, Dublin 2, Ireland (a division of Penguin Books Ltd.)
Penguin Group (Australia), 250 Camberwell Road, Camberwell, Victoria 3124, Australia
(a division of Pearson Australia Group Pty. Ltd.)
Penguin Books India Pvt. Ltd., 11 Community Centre, Panchsheel Park, New Delhi—110 017, India
Penguin Group (NZ), 67 Apollo Drive, Rosedale, North Shore 0632, New Zealand
(a division of Pearson New Zealand Ltd.)
Penguin Books (South Africa) (Pty.) Ltd., 24 Sturdee Avenue, Rosebank, Johannesburg 2196,
South Africa

Penguin Books Ltd., Registered Offices: 80 Strand, London WC2R 0RL, England

This is a work of fiction. Names, characters, places, and incidents either are the product of the author's imagination or are used fictitiously, and any resemblance to actual persons, living or dead, business establishments, events, or locales is entirely coincidental. The publisher does not have any control over and does not assume any responsibility for author or third-party websites or their content.

LUCK BE A LADY

A Berkley Sensation Book / published by arrangement with the author

PRINTING HISTORY
Berkley Sensation mass-market edition / October 2010

ISBN: 978-0-425-23783-0

BERKLEY® SENSATION
Berkley Sensation Books are published by The Berkley Publishing Group,
a division of Penguin Group (USA) Inc.,
375 Hudson Street, New York, New York 10014.
BERKLEY® SENSATION and the "B" design are trademarks of Penguin Group (USA) Inc.

PRINTED IN THE UNITED STATES OF AMERICA

10 9 8 7 6 5 4 3 2 1

Dedication

This book is dedicated to Donna Jean Simon, a dear friend who has become family. I couldn't have completed this project without you stepping in and keeping me sane. You went way above and beyond and I appreciate it more than I can say.

Special thanks go to Cathy Yarmoski, Head of the Literature Unit at the Harold Washington Library Center, Chicago Public Library. You patiently answered my many dorky questions with concise answers and information. Thanks also to my local librarians Susan Gibberman, Head of Reader Services, Schaumburg Township District Library; Karen Toonen and Kathleen Longacre from the Naperville Public Library; Dianne Harmon, Associate Director for Public Services, Joliet Library; Fran Gilles, Reference Librarian, Helen Plum Library, Lombard; the gang at Lisle Public Library and the librarians and library students on my Facebook page.

As always and with much love, thanks to the Chilibabes—Susan Elizabeth Phillips, Lindsay Longford, Suzette Vann and Margaret Watson for your brainstorming wisdom and friendship. Ditto for Jennifer Greene and Julie Wachowski, who will never acknowledge how good they really are no matter how many times I tell them. A special hug goes to Jayne Ann Krentz, who has been there for me year after year. Thank you, dear friends.

Thanks to the Berkley team starting with my editor extraordinaire, Cindy Hwang; as well as Leis Pederson; my publicist, Kathryn Tumen; and Dominique Jenkins (we'll always have ALA, Dominique!). My agent, Annelise Robey, already knows how much I treasure her.

Last but never least, a huge thanks to my readers who have supported me over the years—none of this would be possible without you.

Chapter One

· · · · · · · · · · ·

It was the perfect day for a wedding. Thank God the groom showed up this time. Megan West couldn't deal with a repeat of her cousin Faith's last attempt to get married, when the groom took off.

But that was then, and this was now. A new groom made all the difference in the world. Now former Marine Caine Hunter would be at Faith's side. Megan was so pleased Faith had found Caine—the man of her dreams.

"You were smart to come here to Las Vegas and have a small ceremony with only a few close friends and family," Megan told Faith as the two of them completed their final preparations for the big event. "And having it here at the Venetian was brilliant."

Faith grinned. "I thought so."

Megan was determined that everything go right this time around. And the magical location sure helped. The instant you entered the Venetian's lobby, with all the mosaic Italian marble floors and the colorful fresco ceilings, you knew you were somewhere special. And that was a good thing, because Megan fiercely believed that Faith deserved the best.

Faith was like a sister to her. They'd been born two days apart and grew up two blocks apart. Even now, back in Chicago as adults, they lived within walking distance of each other in their Streeterville neighborhood. But now Faith was going to become a married woman. And Megan wasn't.

Megan told herself it was natural to be emotional leading up to today. Not that she gave any sign of what she considered to be her inner wimp. That wasn't her way.

Instead, she focused her energies on making this day the best of Faith's life. And after that . . . well, there were plenty of things for a non-gambling librarian like Megan to do while here in Vegas. Plenty of things for her to do right here at the Venetian—the unique stores, the singing gondoliers, the gelato, the Hermitage art museum adjacent to the lobby. Megan would be able to check them all out later this weekend. First she had to make sure Faith was safely married to Caine.

"We're actually a little ahead of schedule, if you can believe that," Megan said as she checked her appearance in the wall mirror. She and Faith were waiting in a small room designed for brides just off the wedding chapel area. Like the rest of the hotel, it was elaborately decorated in creams and gold.

"The Venetian was one of my favorite places when I lived here in Vegas and worked at the library," Faith said. "And since Caine and I met in Italy, it seemed like a nice vibe to add to the ceremony without having to return to the Amalfi Coast. Not that I wouldn't love to go back there. But this time we're honeymooning in New

Zealand. And I'm not honeymooning alone. Not that I was really alone last time because I met Caine there. I'm babbling, right? Yes, I'm incoherently babbling. I babble when I'm nervous. But I'm not really nervous. Should I be nervous? Are you nervous?"

"I'm not nervous," Megan said.

"Because you're not the bride and you're the optimist in the family."

"No, because I know Caine would never let you down." Megan was getting tired of being the optimist in the family but it was hard to change her image after all this time. Sure, Faith had become a blonde with an edgy look but that wasn't Megan's style.

One former beau had described Megan as the girl-next-door type with her dark brown hair, blue eyes and freckles. Megan wasn't sure she liked being a "type." She knew one thing for sure—her fashion style was vintage. The classic 1950s dress she was wearing as the maid of honor was a perfect example. The pin-tucked black-taffeta-and-velvet dress had a scooped neck and full skirt, which made it both classic and elegant.

Faith looked beautiful in her wedding gown, a simple strapless design. She'd chosen a black-and-white theme with red rose accents for her evening ceremony.

Staring at their side-by-side reflection in the mirror, Faith said, "When we were growing up on the South Side of Chicago, did you ever think we'd end up here with me getting married at the Venetian in Las Vegas?"

Megan grinned. "Sure. Didn't you?"

"I knew we'd both be librarians when we grew up." Faith grabbed Megan's hand before turning to face her. "You know you're more like my sister than my cousin, right?"

Megan blinked away the tears. "Yeah, I know. Now don't make me cry." She waved her free hand in front of her face. "My mascara will run."

"Oh, no. What would Jane Austen say?" Faith teased her.

"Funny how you ended up going back to Jane Austen after trying to come up with some other incarnation," Megan said.

"Funny how you didn't have a similar identity crisis."

Megan had had her identity crisis at a much younger age and then moved past it. Faith had grown up with both parents. Megan hadn't. Sure, her dad had done his best to be there for her, but he couldn't replace a mother. Faith's mom had done her best too and Megan loved her to bits for trying. But it wasn't the same.

As if on cue, Faith's mom entered the room. "How are things going in here? Everything under control?"

"Absolutely." Today, Megan was all about control: the music, the flowers, the seating arrangement for the ceremony, the meal afterward. She'd checked and double-checked it all.

"You two." Faith's mom blinked back tears. Unable to continue, she instead simply cupped their cheeks.

Megan was well aware that the number two was a recurring theme in her life. She and Faith were born two days apart and lived two blocks apart. Megan's dad was two years younger than Faith's dad and two inches shorter. Her mom had died when she was two. Megan had only had sex with two men in her life.

Okay, she was *so* not going there today. This was all about Faith, not her. The only setback in the wedding plans had occurred when Caine's best man had to have emergency surgery two days earlier and hadn't been able to make the trip. Again with the number two. Megan and Faith's paternal grandmother was dating crusty private investigator–retired cop Buddy Doyle, who'd stepped in as a last-minute replacement. Otherwise everything was going smoothly.

Which was the way Megan liked it. Maybe it was

the librarian in her, wanting to keep things orderly. She didn't subscribe to the Chaos Theory in life. To her way of thinking, things were always better when they were organized and categorized. Like this wedding . . .

"Are you ready?" Megan asked.

Faith nodded.

"Okay then." Megan handed her the colorful Romanza bouquet of fresh red-tipped roses and greenery. "Let's go."

Faith's dad met them right outside the Venetian's wedding chapel. This was no Elvis impersonator drive-through wedding location. This was the elegant side of Las Vegas.

Megan walked toward the front of the room to the accompaniment of the Pachabel Canon. There were about two dozen guests present.

Megan's eyes teared up again when she saw the look of love on Caine's face as he got his first view of his bride-to-be. The two of them were meant for each other.

The ceremony was simple but moving. The minister said, "I now pronounce you—"

The doors at the back of the chapel flew open and a man ran into the room to bark out an order. "Stop the wedding!"

• • •

Logan Doyle hadn't slept in thirty-six hours. He'd just worked a double shift before hopping a plane to Vegas at his family's insistence. Did they care that he was sleep-deprived? No. He had a job to do and they expected him to do it.

Logan stared at the people gathered at the front of the room. Two women, two men and a minister. The brunette in a black dress was the first to react. She marched up to him while the others momentarily stood in stunned silence.

"I don't know who you are and I don't care. You are

not ruining my cousin's wedding. She's been through enough shinola. Leave right now."

Shinola? Logan frowned. Who said *shinola* anymore? No one outside of his grandfather's age group.

"Gramps, you can't do this," Logan called out.

"Who are you calling Gramps?" the groom growled.

"Him." Caine pointed to Buddy. "My grandfather Buddy Doyle. I'm Logan. Logan Doyle."

All eyes turned to Buddy, whose face was flushed. "You're ruining my surprise."

"What surprise?" Megan demanded. She was not having another wedding go down the drain. Her cousin deserved better.

"Ingrid has agreed to marry me," Buddy said defiantly. "And we thought since we're here in Las Vegas, we'd tie the knot."

"Wait your turn," Megan growled. "This is *Faith's* wedding. Faith and Caine's. No one else's." She turned to the bemused minister. "Finish what you started."

"I now pronounce you man and wife," he said hastily. "You may kiss the bride."

Everyone applauded while Caine took his time kissing his new bride.

"You two . . ." Megan grabbed Buddy's arm with one hand and Logan's with the other. "Come with me."

She marched them both outside onto the nearby terrace with its soothing fountain. "Talk about stealing the limelight, Buddy. What were you thinking?" She didn't give him a chance to answer before turning her wrath on Logan. "And you. What were you thinking barging in the middle of a wedding and trying to stop it? What have you got against your grandfather getting married?"

"Who are you?" Logan said.

"I'm the woman who is going to make your life miserable if you don't answer me."

Logan was impressed by her cleavage and her long legs but mostly by her moxie. She was tall but still a good five or six inches shorter than his six-foot-two frame, yet she stood toe-to-toe with him, refusing to back down despite his cop look, the one that got criminals to nervously back up.

"She's Ingrid's granddaughter, Megan," Buddy said.

Logan frowned. "I thought the bride was the grand-daughter."

"Ingrid has two beautiful granddaughters," Buddy said. "This is Megan. I've been trying to get you two to meet for months but you're both stubborn people."

"*He* may be stubborn," Megan said. "*I've* been busy." She pinned her disapproving gaze on Logan. "You're a cop so maybe you're used to intimidating people and ordering them around. But you have no authority here."

So the brunette with the great breasts had a thing against cops, Logan noted. Interesting. She was prac-tically bristling with indignation, which automatically made him get calmer. Appearing detached no matter the circumstances, no matter what he was feeling inside, was a critical requirement of a police officer and one that Logan had long ago perfected. "I have the authority of making sure Buddy doesn't make a big mistake."

"Marrying my grandmother is a not a mistake. If any-thing, she's too good for him. No disrespect, Buddy." She paused to give him a hug.

"None taken. I totally agree."

"Well, his family doesn't," Logan said.

"What possible reason could they have to disapprove?"

"The fact that he's still married."

"His first wife passed away. That's what you said. Right, Buddy?"

He nodded.

"I'm not talking about his first wife," Logan said. "I'm talking about his second wife."

Megan blinked. "Second wife?"

"That doesn't count," Buddy said. "It was a quickie Vegas wedding and only lasted forty-eight hours before I annulled it."

"See, here's the thing," Logan said. "She didn't annul it."

"She signed the papers."

"No, she didn't."

Buddy tugged on his tie. "I thought she did."

"You thought wrong."

"Are you sure?"

Logan nodded.

"Well, shit."

Megan stared at Buddy in stunned surprise. First off, why hadn't he ever mentioned being married a second time? And second, he'd made a big deal out of giving up cursing forever yet he'd just slipped up, for the first time since Megan had met him five months ago.

"You can't be engaged to one woman and still married to another," she said.

"I know that."

"And you certainly can't commit bigamy," Logan said.

"I know that too," Buddy growled.

Megan stared at Logan as if searching for answers. He didn't appear to have any, but he did have the kind of dark good looks that no doubt had women swarming over him at cop bars all over the city. Black Irish, some called it, black hair and moody blue eyes. It didn't matter. She was immune.

Megan was the first to admit that she had a chip on her shoulder where cops were concerned. She had good reason, not that it was any business of Logan's.

"How do you know the annulment papers weren't signed?" Megan said.

"Because my dad just ran across the unsigned papers on Buddy's desk at his home when he was there to give Mouse his shot."

"Who's Mouse?" Megan said.

"His diabetic cat," Logan said. "He needs an insulin shot every twelve hours. Gramps left the directions on his desk but the cat messed up the papers."

"Maybe there's another copy of the annulment papers that was signed?" Megan asked. Damn, but decades of being an optimist were hard to give up.

Buddy shook his head. "There was only one set of papers."

"If they were on your desk, you must have known that they weren't signed." She directed her comment to Buddy.

Logan answered. "You'd have to see Buddy's desk to understand. He's got piles of stuff dating back decades."

"Paperwork," Buddy muttered under his breath. "Damn paperwork will do you in every time."

"Everything okay out here?" Caine had his war face on as he stepped out onto the terrace.

"My grandson Logan is a Chicago police detective," Buddy said proudly.

"Caine is a former Force Recon Marine," Megan said. "He's not impressed that Logan is a cop."

"Yes, I am impressed," Caine said.

"Whose side are you on?" Megan said.

"Caine is a former Marine," Buddy said. "He's on the side of the United States of America."

"The U.S. has no stake in this matter," Megan said before telling Caine, "Go back to your bride, please, Caine. I've got this under control."

Caine raised an eyebrow at her confident claim but did leave after saying, "Just shout if you need any help."

She smiled and nodded before turning to glower at Buddy. "How could you make such a mess of things?"

"Hey, listen up, buttercup—" he protested.

She interrupted him. "No, you listen up!"

"Logan, are you going to stand there and let her talk to me like that?" Buddy demanded.

Logan just nodded.

"I had no idea you had such a temper," Buddy told Megan. "She must have Irish blood in her," he added for Logan's benefit.

"No doubt," Logan agreed.

"I don't believe you two. This is serious."

"What's serious?" Gram asked as she came onto the terrace. "Buddy, is there a problem?" She came to stand by his side, a concerned look on her face. Even though she was in her mid-seventies, Ingrid West was not your typical senior citizen. Her blue eyes and high cheekbones proclaimed her Scandinavian heritage while her gelled spiky haircut revealed her rebel nature. Today she was wearing one of her Chanel suits with a large red lapel flower and a Save the Polar Bears pin. "It's not the Swedish mob, is it?" she said in a semi-whisper. "Are they here in Las Vegas?"

"Gram, there's no such thing," Megan began when Buddy interrupted her.

"No, the Swedish mob has no foothold here."

"Swedish mob?" Logan frowned.

"That's right," Buddy sounded defensive. "Tell her they aren't here in Las Vegas."

"I have connections," Gram said.

"To the Swedish mob?" Logan said.

Gram nodded. "Why? Does Buddy have a problem? Do we need to call in the Swedish mob?"

"No, ma'am, I don't think that will be necessary," Logan said.

Gram gently socked his arm. "I've told you before to call me Gram, not ma'am. Were you feeling left out today, Logan? Is that why you stopped the wedding? You didn't want to miss anything? I'm sorry you weren't invited to the event." She patted his shoulder. "That was wrong of us." She turned to Megan. "Why wasn't Logan invited to the wedding? He's practically family."

"No, that's okay, really," Logan hurriedly said. "I wasn't feeling left out."

"He's a cop," Buddy said. "Third generation. Logan isn't all touchy-feely." Buddy shuddered at the thought. "Not at all."

"Then I don't understand why he wanted to stop Faith's wedding." Gram paused as a thought occurred to her. "Unless you thought it was Buddy's wedding to me. Is that what you thought?" Her expression reflected her hurt feelings. "I thought you liked me."

"It isn't about you. It's about Buddy." Logan said.

"What about Buddy?" Gram said.

"Are you going to tell her or should I?" Logan asked Buddy.

"I'll tell her. We could use a little privacy here."

Megan reluctantly stepped back inside but hovered near the doorway in case her grandmother needed her. Logan stood beside her. They were soon joined by Megan's uncle Jeff and her father. Jeff was the smooth, über-workaholic and Megan's dad, Dave, was the quiet, bookish accountant in the family. They both owned West Investigations, the largest private investigation firm in Chicago.

"Is somebody going to tell me what's going on here?" Jeff demanded. "Why wasn't I told that Buddy planned on proposing to my mother? I had no idea things had gotten that serious. They've only known each other a few months. I thought they were just . . . I don't know . . . playing bingo together."

"Strip bingo," Logan muttered under his breath.

Megan elbowed him in his side.

"What was that?" Jeff said. "I didn't hear you."

"Nothing."

"It was a mistake," Buddy said in a loud voice from the terrace. "I didn't know I was still married!"

"Still married?" Jeff's face turned red with fury. "Did Buddy just say he was still married? The bastard. How dare he . . ." he sputtered.

Megan's dad helped him out. "Tamper with our mother's affections?"

Jeff nodded. "Yeah, that. I've got a good mind to—"

"Beat up a seventy-something-year-old senior citizen?" Megan said, irritated by all the testosterone swirling around her. She hadn't missed the smack-down looks shooting between her uncle and Logan.

Her attention was diverted when Gram came into the room, tears running down her face. Megan's dad put his arm around her and guided her from the room.

"You." Jeff turned his wrath on Logan. "You couldn't have made this info public sooner? Dammit, I should have checked out the guy myself, but my mother made me swear I wouldn't. And Faith did a preliminary check on him. Clearly she didn't look deeply enough."

"My grandfather thought he was free to marry Ingrid," Logan said, sounding remarkably calm for a man who looked like he'd wanted to kill someone for a second there. Then he had his cop face back on. Megan recognized it because it was so similar to Caine's war face.

"Does he have dementia?" Jeff demanded. "Is that it? He forgets he still has a wife?"

"No, he doesn't have dementia." Logan's voice reflected his growing aggravation.

"So he's just an old geezer who likes conning rich old women?" Jeff said.

"You take that back!" Buddy growled as he joined them. "Ingrid is *not* old and neither am I. I'm for sure not so old a geezer that I can't take you, boy-o."

Megan put her hand on her uncle's chest, stopping him before he could do something stupid. "There will be no fighting here."

"Let's take it outside then," Buddy said.

"No fighting on the terrace either," Megan said. "No fighting anywhere, period."

"You stay away from my mother," Jeff told Buddy, pointing an angry finger at him. "If I catch you anywhere near her, you'll regret it."

Buddy pointed an angry finger right back, with one digit bent.

"Did you see that? He just gave me the finger," Jeff bellowed. "Get him out of here before I call security and have him tossed out."

"You and what army?" Buddy growled.

"Come on," Logan said, putting an arm around his grandfather's shoulders and guiding him toward the exit.

Megan's uncle followed them to make sure of their departure, leaving Megan alone in the room with the still-bemused minister.

"It was . . . uh . . . it was a lovely . . . uh . . . ceremony . . . for the most part," the minister said, trying to be cheerful.

"Yeah, it was just peachy." Megan said. The best-laid plans of mice and men and librarians sometimes went to hell very fast. Little did Megan know that things were about to get much, much worse.

Chapter Two

. . . .

"**Don't** say anything!" Megan was told as she was grabbed from behind the minute she entered the hotel's elegant ladies' room down the hall from the wedding chapel.

Megan turned to face her attacker. "Gram?"

"I don't want Faith upset," Gram continued.

"Neither do I."

"Then don't mention the situation with Buddy."

"What if she asks?"

"Lie. Say everything is fine. That it was all a big misunderstanding. She didn't see me crying, thank goodness." Gram released Megan to move closer to the large mirrors along one wall, and dabbed on more mascara.

"She's going to wonder why Buddy isn't here."

"I told her Buddy and Logan have gone to try the slots."

"Didn't she think it was strange that Buddy ditched the reception?"

"Strange or not, that's my story and we are both sticking to it. Understood?"

Megan nodded obediently. "Did you tell Dad and Uncle Jeff?"

"I already told Jeff to behave himself or else. I told your dad too."

Megan couldn't imagine her father not behaving. All her life, he'd been good. Absentminded, sometimes, often in his own world. But always good. Playing it safe. Just like her. If in doubt, don't do it. That was their motto. She'd been raised with the belief that taking chances was not a good thing.

"Come along." Gram hooked her arm through Megan's. "Showtime."

They entered the reception together. Barely a minute later, they were joined by Faith. "I know you said that Buddy and Logan were playing the slots, but they can do that later. Buddy is the best man. He needs to be here. He can gamble with his grandson later."

"Buddy is only a stand-in best man," Gram said.

"Is he upset about that?" Faith asked. "Is that why he's not here?"

"No, of course not," Gram said.

"Then what's going on?" Faith eyed them suspiciously. "I know something is going on, so don't bother denying it."

"It's your wedding reception," Gram began when Faith interrupted her.

"Yes, it is, and I want the best man here. Never mind, I'll go get him myself."

"Don't be silly," Gram said with a touch of desperation.

"I'll go," Megan volunteered.

"Thanks." Faith gave her a quick hug. "Come on,

Gram. Wait until you see the chocolate fountain they've got set up." Over her shoulder she added, "Megan, if you have trouble finding them, I'll go myself."

"Right." There went Megan's plan A—to say she'd looked but couldn't locate them. Still, maybe Buddy and Logan had taken off for parts unknown.

She didn't get to hold on to that hope for very long because she spotted the pair near the end of the very first casino aisle she walked down. There had to be a thousand or more slot machines here—all with bells, whistles and flashing lights.

Logan spotted her first. When he'd barged into Faith's wedding, Megan hadn't really paid a lot of attention to the details about him—like the fact that his light blue shirt encased his broad shoulders and his black pants hugged his lean waist. Had she noticed way his dark hair fell over his forehead or the intensity of his blue eyes? She wasn't sure, but she definitely knew that he did not look pleased to see her.

On the other hand, Buddy's face lit up when he registered her appearance. He immediately slid off the stool and stood. "Did Ingrid send you? Has she forgiven me?"

"Uh, no. Faith sent me. She wants you to attend the reception. She doesn't know what happened between you and Gram and we want to keep it that way. But Faith is getting suspicious that something is up because you're down here gambling with Logan."

"Tell her to mind her own business," Logan said.

"No way. Why don't you both just come with me . . ."

"Because we don't want to," Logan said.

"Sometimes we have to do things we don't want to because it's the right thing to do," Megan said

"And you always do the right thing?"

She nodded. "I would think a cop would be glad to hear that."

"I'm a detective," he said.

"One of Chicago's finest," Buddy said proudly. "He was recently promoted."

"I don't think she cares," Logan noted dryly.

Megan tried to be polite. "I'm happy for you."

"I'm so relieved to hear that." His smile was mocking. "Listen, I don't have time to stand around and make conversation with you two." The constant chirping and zealous beeping of the surrounding slot machines didn't make it a good spot for talking. "They are expecting me to bring you both back to the reception."

"And, again, you always do what's expected of you, right?" Logan said.

Yes, she did. But he made it sound like a crime, so she ignored his question. "If I don't bring you back upstairs, Faith threatened to come looking for you herself."

Logan refused to be ignored. "Is this bossiness a family trait of yours?"

"We are *not* bossy."

"You've been ordering me around since I arrived," he said. "Or *trying* to."

"That's not true. Tell him, Buddy."

"Well, you have been pretty bossy," Buddy said.

She glared at him.

"But Megan's not usually like that," Buddy hastily added.

"It must be the librarian in her, huh?" Logan said.

"Why does everything have to be an argument with you? It must be the cop in you, huh?" she retorted.

"Damn right," Logan readily agreed. "It's the cop and the detective in me."

She took a deep breath and held on to her patience as tightly as she was hanging on to her vintage clutch. "Are you both coming or not? No, forget I asked that. You *are* both coming."

"Not that you're bossy or anything," Logan said. "Do you plan on grabbing us by the arm and hauling us out of here?"

She refused to back away from his challenge. "I will if I have to."

"She won't have to," Buddy said. "We'll come along peacefully."

She heaved a sigh of relief.

"But if that uncle of yours insults me again . . ." Buddy said.

"He won't. Consider this a truce during the reception. We don't want anything ruining Faith and Caine's wedding day." A look in Logan's direction conveyed the rest of her thought: *Any more than it's already been ruined.*

"You're lucky you caught us before we got to the poker tables," Logan said.

"Are you a gambler?" she asked.

"He's a darn fine poker player," Buddy said. "I taught him everything I know. Well, not *everything* I know. A man has to keep some things private."

"That's what got you into this mess," Logan said before Megan could.

"It's more a misunderstanding than a mess," Buddy said before turning to Megan. "Back me up here, buttercup."

"How about an extremely messy misunderstanding?" she suggested.

"I'll go along with that," Buddy said. "You know, I'd hoped that you and Logan could meet under happier circumstances. You two have so much in common."

Megan hoped Logan's look of utter disbelief was reflected on her own face as well.

"You do," Buddy insisted.

"How do you figure that?" Logan said. "I'm a cop and she dislikes cops."

"I never said that."

"You didn't have to. Your attitude said it all."

"What attitude?" Her voice reflected her irritation.

"*That* attitude."

Megan tried staring him down before quickly discovering it was a lost cause. For one thing, his blue eyes were so deep you could fall into them and get lost forever. He had this rather uncanny ability to draw her in. She wasn't sure what it was about him exactly. Sure, he had great eyes and a hot body. And yes, his smile was endearing . . .

Wait, where had that come from? There was absolutely nothing endearing about Logan Doyle. He was totally aggravating. The man took great pleasure in pushing her buttons, waiting for her to explode. He was playing her as if she were a mega-jackpot slot machine.

There was no way she would pay out.

His mocking, non-endearing smile told her he thought otherwise.

Clearly, Logan was accustomed to getting his own way. He possessed an aura of power and control that went far beyond mere confidence. This was a man used to dealing with danger and winning. And he was smart enough to pick up on what he called her "attitude" regarding cops.

Not that she'd done much to hide her feelings. She had valid reasons for her them—and those reasons were none of his damn business. She squared her shoulders, lifted her chin and returned to her stare-off with Logan, deciding she'd given up too easily earlier.

"Yes, siree." Buddy was practically rubbing his hands with glee. "There's chemistry here. Definite chemistry."

"Between you and that slot machine maybe," Logan said. "Although it seems to have given you the cold shoulder tonight."

"Fight it all you want," Buddy told him. "I've been around long enough to know chemistry when I see it."

"You need new glasses," Logan said.

Buddy glared at him. "I don't need glasses at all."

"That's not what the eye doctor said."

"He just wants more business, that's all."

"And the fact that you can't read a menu?" Logan said, shifting his gaze to his grandfather.

"Means they make the print too small. I can read this." Buddy patted the slot machine.

"We need to get up to the reception before Faith comes looking for us," Megan reminded them, trying not to gloat that Logan had looked away first.

"I'm telling you, if that uncle of yours makes any fishy comments . . ." Buddy said again even as he followed her toward the bank of elevators.

"I told you, he won't."

"What about your dad?" Buddy said.

Megan kept her eyes on the elevators, willing the one in front of her to open immediately. "What about him?"

"He'd better not say anything either."

"My father is not into confrontations."

"Not even when it comes to protecting his own family?" Logan said.

She punched the up button several times.

"That doesn't make it come any faster," Logan said.

"Maybe not, but it makes me feel better."

"Feeling a little tense, are you?"

She hit the button more forcefully.

"They have classes for that, you know," he said.

"For what?"

"Anger management."

"I don't need any classes in anger management," she said.

His skeptical look fanned her aggravation, but she was determined not to let it show. She relaxed the death grip she had on her clutch and practiced deep-breathing techniques until she noticed the way Logan was staring at her cleavage appreciatively, following the rise and fall of her breasts.

Her body turned traitor on her. Instead of outrage, she felt something else. Her heart fluttered, skipped and then raced. Was she blushing? She hoped not.

Logan leaned closer and whispered, "Is there a problem?" His breath teased her ear.

She shook her head, bit her tongue and began mentally reciting the Dewey Decimal System *backward* beginning with 900—History.

Right, now she felt better. She hadn't completely lost her mind.

Logan reached around her to place his hand on the elevator opening to prevent it from closing and nudged her forward. She reacted as if he'd hit her with a cattle prod, jumping forward and heading straight for the farthest corner of the elevator.

Where had all that come from? Was her racing heart a result of the oxygen being piped into the casino? She liked that option better than thinking Logan could induce that kind of reaction without even trying. Imagine what would happen if he really tried to seduce her.

No, do not imagine that, she strictly ordered herself. *Do not go there. That's never going to happen.*

Faith greeted them as soon as they entered the reception room. "Finally. I'm sorry to tear you away from the slot machines, Buddy," she teased him, "but this wedding party isn't large enough that I can have anyone go missing."

"I was getting worried." Megan's dad stood beside her and gently squeezed her shoulder. "You were gone a long time."

"It's a large casino," she said, patting his arm reassuringly.

Dave nodded at Buddy and Logan before saying, "You

know, the odds of winning at a slot machine are approx-imately one in ten thousand. Your odds are better in blackjack."

"My dad is great at math. He's a mathlete," Megan said proudly.

"I like working with numbers," he said modestly.

"You'd be good at card counting," Buddy said.

Her dad frowned. "Isn't that illegal?"

"No. The casinos don't like it, and they can toss you out if they catch you doing it, but it's not illegal," Logan said.

"You say that with the confidence of a man who's been tossed out of a casino or two," Megan said.

Logan just gave her an enigmatic smile and shrugged.

"You're not banned from the Venetian, are you? Some security guard isn't going to haul you away, right?" Megan said.

"Will you be disappointed if I say no?" he said.

Faith laughed and answered on Megan's behalf, "No, of course not. Even though I'm not exactly sure why you wanted to stop my wedding, I don't hold it against you. It will make for a good story for my kids and grandkids. I still don't know exactly what that was all about, but Gram said you were just kidding around—that cops, doc-tors and Marines have an unusual sense of humor. She told me not to worry and just enjoy my wedding, so I'm going to do that. Especially since Aunt Lorraine isn't here this time."

Megan had to laugh. Aunt Lorraine, aka the Duchess of Grimness, was Faith's mother's older sister and hell on wheels. She'd refused to attend any wedding taking place in Las Vegas. Megan thought that had played a large part in Faith's selection of this location.

"But enough about all that. Now that everyone is here, Caine and I are ready for our first dance. Right, hus-band?" she called over to him.

"Affirmative, wife."

They took to the tiny dance floor to the sound of "Don't Stop Believin'" by Journey, a White Sox fan's favorite song. Not only was it played during their winning World Series season but it was what had been playing when Caine proposed to Faith at Comiskey Park, aka U.S. Cellular Field.

"I know the best man is supposed to dance with the maid of honor, but I don't dance," Buddy said apologetically.

"Me either," Logan said, just in case someone tried to press him into duty,

"Well, I do," Megan's dad said, holding his hand out to her as the next song, a slower ballad, came up.

"Gram talked to you about not making a scene, right?" she said. "Not that you would ever make a scene, but Uncle Jeff would."

"There won't be any trouble tonight."

"I sure hope not." She cast a worried look over her shoulder at Buddy before returning her attention to her dad. He looked rather dashing in his dark suit and crisp white shirt. His quirky math tie was filled with rows of gold and silver pi symbols on a red background. He had another tie with the same design on a blue background. They were the only two ties he owned. "Did you wear this tie to your own wedding?"

He shook his head. "I didn't have it back then."

Her parents' wedding picture sat in a place of honor back in Megan's Chicago condo. Her mother had worn a navy pantsuit as she stood beside Megan's dad—staring straight ahead at the camera with that awkwardness that comes from not liking to have your photo taken. "I know you and Mom were married at city hall, but what about your wedding reception?" She knew the story but not the reasons behind it. "Why didn't you have a wedding reception?"

"We went out and had a nice dinner. I'm not a party person, you know that. Neither was she."

"Did you ever dance with her?"

"No."

"That's so sad." Megan couldn't remember her mother, just the memory of her being gone. Growing up, she wasn't like the other kids who had moms. Instead, her dad had taken over all the parenting duties to the best of his ability. And she reciprocated by looking out for him. The older she got, the more responsibilities she took over: shopping for groceries, cooking dinner, taking care of the house.

"I know you still miss her," Megan said. "I mean, you never remarried after all these years. I'm sure she'd want you to be happy and find someone to spend your life with."

He shook his head. "We've had this conversation before. Many times. I'm a one-woman man."

"Soul mates, huh?"

"Something like that." He gazed over her head. "I, uh, couldn't help but notice the way Logan was looking at you."

"Hmm?"

"Logan. Looking at you."

"With aggravation."

"Not exactly."

"Irritation."

"No. More like attraction."

She stared at her dad in amazement. "No way. And since when have you ever noticed a guy looking at me? You're usually totally off in your own world. You'd forget to eat dinner if I didn't set up that automated program to call and remind you."

"I know, I know. But there's something different about Logan."

"He's a cop."

"That's not it. I've come in contact with plenty of police officers over the years in the course of the business. No, it's something else."

"If you tell me it's chemistry, I'm going to have to do something drastic to you. Buddy already tried that line and it didn't fly."

"So Buddy noticed it too. Interesting."

"There's nothing to notice," she said.

"You were certainly fast to confront him before any of us could."

"I'm the maid of honor. Part of my job is to prevent brash Chicago cops from messing things up."

"So you think he's brash?"

"That's just my opinion. And I've only just met him."

"But he's made an impression."

"That's an understatement."

"He's watching us now even though he's trying to hide it."

She glanced over her shoulder. "How can you tell?"

"I might be in charge of the numbers end of the business but I have picked up a thing or two about investigative and surveillance techniques."

Megan changed the subject because focusing on Logan was proving to be too distracting. "You don't think Faith suspects what's going on with Gram and Buddy, do you?"

"I think Caine can keep her distracted," her dad said.

He was right. Faith was glowing as the bridal party sat at the head table for dinner. Megan kept her toast sweet and short. Buddy did the same.

During the meal, Megan kept a close eye on Logan, who was seated beside Gram. There were only a little over two dozen people, including the wedding party, so it was impossible to completely avoid someone.

Had Gram shown any sign of stress, Megan would

have jumped out of her chair in a second. But instead Logan showed an empathetic side as he spoke to her, which Megan found surprising and completely endearing.

Oh no, there was that word again. *Endearing.* Pandas and kittens were endearing. Not men who wore power like a weapon.

He looked over and their gazes collided. Her body hummed like a tuning fork. She was about to start reciting the Dewey Decimal System backward again when he looked away. So did she.

When she caught Faith eyeing her speculatively after dinner, she read her cousin's mind. "Do not throw that bouquet of yours at me later," she quietly warned Faith. "You hang on to it. Remember, we talked about that."

"Fine. I can't believe you're such a sissy about it."

"I am not a sissy."

"You looked positively fierce when you dragged Logan out onto the terrace during the ceremony," Faith said.

"I'm not a fan of practical jokes, you know that."

"And you're not a fan of cops, either."

"You know why."

"Yes, I do."

"I don't want to talk about it."

"Then let's change the subject. How about sex?"

Megan grinned. "I'm sure your mother had that conversation with you. With *us*, actually. I was sitting right next to you as she told us about sperm eagerly swimming to the egg."

Faith laughed at the memory before saying, "No, I meant that I'm sensing some sexual stuff between you and Logan."

"Oh God, not you too."

"Not me too what?" Faith asked.

"Buddy and Dad already tried saying there's chemistry between Logan and me."

"Wow, it has to be pretty strong sexual mojo for those two to notice it."

"They're imagining things."

"And what is Logan imagining?"

"How to avoid me?"

"I doubt that."

"Forget about my sex life and focus on your own."

"Good advice," Caine said as he stepped behind Faith to nuzzle her neck. "When can we leave?"

"Not until we cut the cake."

He grabbed her hand. "Then let's do that ASAP."

Everyone gathered around to watch the couple complete the tradition, laughing as Caine smeared some icing on Faith's nose and she reciprocated. It was only afterward that Megan looked around and realized Logan had left.

"He flew right out here after working a double-shift back in Chicago," Buddy explained. "I sent the boy to my room to get some shut-eye. Do you think it's too early for me to leave too?"

"No. Thanks for coming back, Buddy." She hugged him.

"You can repay me by putting in a good word for me with your grandmother," he said. "I'd appreciate it, petunia."

She watched as Buddy made his farewells to the bride and groom.

"Good riddance," Jeff muttered beside Megan as he watched Buddy leave the room.

She socked her uncle's arm. "Be nice."

"That's my brother's job, not mine."

The wine flowed freely after that. Megan limited herself, but noticed that her uncle switched to Scotch.

"How are you holding up, Gram?" Megan slid onto the vacant chair beside her.

"Just peachy," Gram said tartly. Her voice softened as she added, "It was a lovely wedding. Faith and Caine look so happy. I remember the first time I saw them together. They were making out in a corner of a fancy restaurant."

"The first time I saw them together, Faith dumped a glass of water in Caine's lap."

"Trying to dampen his ardor, was she?"

Megan laughed. "Clearly it didn't work."

As the party wound down, people broke into even smaller groups. Faith's friends from her time working at the library in Las Vegas grouped together. Faith's family members gathered and talked about old times.

Faith held her bouquet over her head and teased Megan by pretending to toss it her way before Caine scooped her up in his arms and marched her out of the reception room. After that, people gradually said their good-byes and began filing out.

Megan, who'd been up since sunrise preparing for the wedding, was ready to call it a day. Kissing her dad's cheek, she wished him good night and headed out. She was in the elevator before she realized she needed to go back because she'd left her clutch behind. Being in the elevator reminded her of waiting for it earlier with Logan.

She still wasn't sure what had happened. What was it about Logan that got to her?

No, she told herself, she wasn't going to go down that path. Instead she remembered how thrilled she'd been to find the stunning vintage 1930s Art Deco–designed clutch on eBay. The black purse with the red faux-jeweled clasp was from Blum's-Vogue, a high-end Chicago store where the city's elite shopped before it had closed decades before Megan had even been born. There had been several other bidders, but Megan had won out in the end. She was still grinning about her retail victory when she reentered the reception room.

Her dad and Jeff were seated with their backs to her. Megan spied her clutch on the table by the door and quickly picked it up.

"I'm telling you, your past can come back and bite you big-time if you're not careful," Jeff was saying. "Trust me, you did the right thing letting Megan think her mother is dead."

Chapter Three

· · · · · · · · · · ·

Megan froze. She couldn't believe what she'd just heard. There had to be some mistake. She must have misunderstood what her uncle said. She moved closer, certain that it couldn't be true.

But one look at her father's panicked face when he turned and saw her told her that she hadn't misunderstood one word. She felt the blood drain from her face as her world as she knew it crashed around her.

"My mother . . . isn't . . . dead?" Megan could barely squeeze the words out past a throat tightened by emotions too numerous to label.

"Megan . . ." her dad pleaded as he stood to approach her.

She put out her hand to stop him in his tracks. "Just answer the question."

"He was doing you a favor," Jeff said.

"Shut up!" her dad growled at his brother.

"I don't understand. She's *alive*?" Megan's voice trembled with shock and anger.

"Yes," her dad said, "but let me explain . . ."

"No!" Megan had never moved so fast in her life. Pivoting, she ran out of the reception room and into a nearby elevator a second before it closed. The empty enclosed space felt like a coffin.

Her phone immediately started playing Mozart, her father's ringtone. He'd told her it was his favorite piece of music. But then, he'd also told her that her mother was dead.

She couldn't breathe. She felt as if all the air had been sucked from her surroundings, leaving her gasping like a fish out of water. She needed to get outside. She needed fresh air.

She frantically punched the next floor number, leaping off the elevator as if shot out of a cannon before ramming into someone.

"Sorry," she muttered and kept moving. She vaguely registered that she'd run into Logan, but she didn't care. Out. She needed to get out!

"Hold on a second," Logan said, gently holding on to her arm. "Are you okay?"

She shook her head.

"What's wrong?"

"I need to get out of here. My mother isn't dead."

"What?"

"I need to get out. I can't breathe in here!" Her voice rose.

"Okay, stay calm. Don't panic. You'll be okay. I know a shortcut to the lobby." He took her hand in his.

As promised, he got her outside in record time. Megan inhaled gulps of the cool night air.

"Better?" he asked.

She nodded.

"So your mother isn't dead. That's a good thing, right?"

"I have to find her."

"Okay." His voice was quietly confident. "Did she come to the wedding?"

"No. Since they told me she was dead, they didn't invite her to the wedding." Still freaked out by this revelation, Megan started walking away from the entrance.

"Hold on a second." He followed her. "Where are you going?"

"I don't know. Away from here."

"Talk to me."

She wrapped her arms around her middle as tremors started inside and spread throughout her body. If she didn't hold herself together, she'd crumble right there on the sidewalk in front of the entrance to the Venetian. "I have to find her."

"Okay. Well, luckily your family owns the largest PI firm in Chicago, so they can help you with that."

She shook her head vehemently. "They're the ones who hid her from me, who lied about her being dead. I can't trust anything they'd tell me about this."

Logan ran his hands up and down her upper arms as if to keep the chill and tremors from consuming her. She could tell by the look on his face that he was worried about her. She saw it in his blue eyes.

She realized that in his line of work he was accustomed to dealing with hysterical people and stopping them from going over the edge, whatever that edge might be. He projected a sense of commanding assurance, which helped keep her howling panic at bay.

"Come on," he said. "I know a place that serves the best pancakes you've ever tasted."

She blinked at the non-sequitur. "Pancakes?"

"Yes. Pancakes make everything seem better. You'll see. We'll go discuss the situation there. Calmly. Logically. I've got wireless Internet on my iPhone, so we'll do some research and see what happens."

"But it's after midnight."

"This is Vegas. Open 24/7."

She looked down at her black dress.

"They don't care what you wear. There is no dress code at Aunt Sally's Pancake House. Come on." He aimed her toward the curb.

She paused. "What's this?"

"A car. The car of all cars. A 1957 Chevy Bel Air." His voice was reverent. "The ultimate classic Chevy."

"Whose is it?"

"A good buddy of mine owns this baby." Logan patted the hood gently. "Harry lets me borrow it whenever I come to Vegas. He's a retired Chicago cop who's moved out here. He has several vintage cars in his collection. I helped him rehab this piece of automotive beauty when he found it back in Chicago. She was in really bad shape."

Megan could relate to that. She was in really bad shape herself at the moment.

"He calls her Lucille."

"Lucille?"

"I know. I'm not into naming cars, but my buddy won the coin toss and he wanted to name her. So hop in." Logan opened the door for Megan. She got in the car and fastened her seat belt.

Normally she would have appreciated the vintage car much more than she did, oohing and ahhing over every little thing. She was a big fan of the styles of the '50s—as her maid of honor's dress and antique clutch verified. And this car was definitely a representative of that time.

"It's aqua," she said, running her hand along the vinyl upholstery.

"It's blue," he corrected her as if she'd just insulted his mother or something.

"Sorry."

A pair of fuzzy dice hung from the rearview mirror, reminding her how life could change on the roll of the dice . . . or an overheard comment.

As they drove out onto the Strip, the brightly colored light extravaganza created a splashy circuslike show, but once they left the tourist area, things became darker and grittier. Her evening had turned out the same way—starting out with the extravaganza of the wedding before deteriorating into a mess. Not that the areas they passed were dangerously bad, but they weren't the finest part of the city by any stretch of the imagination. For the first time, she sensed the desperation and despair that was also a part of Las Vegas.

Then the streets became more commonplace to any franchise-ridden highway in America.

Aunt Sally's Pancake House was located near the outskirts of the city before the sprawl of the expressways leading to surrounding suburbs. The strip mall also included two pawnshops, a nail salon and an Asian market.

Once inside, Megan studied the plastic-laminated menu.

"Their oven-baked pancakes are really good," Logan said.

There were lots of choices: silver-dollar pancakes, buttermilk pancakes, Swedish pancakes . . . That last entry reminded her of Gram. Did Gram know that Megan's mom was still alive? Had she been part of the deception?

The thought made her stomach tie into even more elaborate knots.

"I'm not hungry." Her voice was flat as she slapped the menu onto the table.

"You will be when they put a plate of pancakes in front of you."

"No, I won't."

"Anyone ever tell you that you're stubborn?"

"No, but they've told me you're stubborn."

"And they're right," he cheerfully acknowledged. "I take after my granddad that way. He's the one who told you I was stubborn, right?"

"I'm not going to confirm or deny your statement."

"Did my granddad teach you that?"

She answered using one of Buddy's trademark sayings: "That's for dang sure." Her smile faded as her thoughts of Buddy reminded her of Gram, which took her right back to the appetite-killing possibility that her grandmother had been part of the family conspiracy to keep the truth from Megan.

Her mind was still spinning after everything that had happened. Part of her felt numb, unable to fully comprehend all the ramifications of what she'd overheard. The other part felt betrayed at such a deep level that she wasn't even able to comprehend it.

Had her grandmother been part of the conspiracy? What about her aunt, Faith's mother? Had she known the truth too?

And Faith. What about her? No, Megan refused to believe that Faith would keep anything like this from her. She was gut-certain of that.

But as for the others . . . Megan didn't know, didn't want to believe they were capable of deceiving her this way. But then she would have bet a million dollars that her own father would never have lied to her the way he had.

So what did she really know? That she felt awful, for one thing. That she'd apparently been living in a house of mirrors where nothing was what it seemed.

When a cheerful gum-smacking waitress who had to

be well past retirement age moseyed over to take their order, Logan said, "She'll have the chocolate chip pancakes and I'll have the oven-baked apple pancakes. And keep the black coffee coming for me."

"I told you I wasn't hungry," Megan said.

"You will be by the time the pancakes come. Thanks, Blanche," he told the waitress, reading the nametag on her uniform as she poured him his coffee.

Pulling out his iPhone, he focused his attention on Megan. "So tell me about your mother."

His tone was matter-of-fact. And that irritated her for some reason. Or maybe it was residual leftover aggravation about him disregarding her wishes and ordering her food anyway. She wanted to bang on the table and tell him he wasn't the boss of her but that would be childish.

Instead she gathered her composure and tried to answer his question as best she could in the circumstances. "She was a mathematician. I was told she died when I was two. I don't remember her. Tonight I went back to the reception room to get my purse and I overheard my uncle talking to my father. He said my father did the right thing letting me think my mother was dead." Just saying the words aloud made her feel like someone had smacked her across the face. "When I confronted my dad, he confirmed that she's really still alive and that he'd lied to me."

"Did he say why?"

"I don't care why."

"His reasons might be helpful in your investigation. You really should talk to him. He's probably worried about you and is looking for you at the hotel right now. You should call him."

She pulled out her phone, which she'd set to go directly to voice mail during the drive to the restaurant. There were ten calls from her father. She didn't bother listening to his voice messages, instead texting him a brief message. She used their secret code word, something the family had added after Faith had received a fake text from her father during an investigation into Caine's father's death.

"There." She set her BlackBerry on the table. "I let him know I'm okay." Which was a lie. She didn't feel okay at all.

"What about your mom? What else do you know about her? Do you have a photograph of her?"

"I thought she died more than twenty-five years ago. So, no, I don't travel with her photo. I have a framed picture of her at home."

"Are you sure you don't want to wait until you get home to investigate?"

"I can't."

"Why not? Like you said, you believed she's been dead for over twenty-five years. What difference will a few more days make?"

"What if she dies or something before I find her?"

"Why jump to a worst-case scenario?"

"My cousin does that." Megan's voice was unsteady. "She's the one who uses the worst-case scenario. Or she used to. I'm the optimist in the family. Or I used to be."

"Then use that optimism now. Your family owns the biggest investigative firm in Chicago. Get them to find her for you."

"Like I said, they're the ones who hid her from me and lied about her being dead. I can't trust anything they'd tell me about this. Faith would help me, but she'll be on her honeymoon." She looked at him with new eyes. "If you hadn't barged into Faith's wedding with the news about Buddy still being married, then my uncle wouldn't have gotten drunk and let slip the news about my mom."

He raised an eyebrow. "So now you're trying to blame me? That's not very logical."

"You wouldn't be logical either if the mom you thought had died when you were a child is really alive. My dead mother is alive. We're not doing logical. Logical isn't even on the menu!"

He gave her a minute to catch her breath after her outburst. "Feel better now?"

"Not really." At least she hadn't pounded her fist on the table.

Logan returned to his bossy cop ways as he said, "Give me your mother's name, date of birth and Social Security number."

She gave him a scathing look. "Do you know your mom's Social Security number?"

"Yes."

"You're weird."

"I don't need to help you, you know."

"Never mind. I'll have Buddy help me. He's a PI."

"A PI pushing eighty. You are *not* dragging my grandfather into this mess. He's got enough problems of his own to deal with right now. Come on, tell me what you know." His voice lost the cop edge and became more conciliatory. "Start with her name."

"Astrid West."

"That was her married name. What about her maiden name?"

"Astrid Meyer. She was born in Germany. She came to this country with her parents when she was ten. They were killed in a car crash when she was eighteen."

"What's her date of birth?"

"4-4-51."

"Okay, let's see what we can find." He got on the Internet and checked several databases. There were a couple of matches to Astrid Meyer with her date of birth, but he narrowed it down until he located her information. "I found her naturalization papers making her an

American citizen, her marriage license and the divorce decree."

Divorce? Megan's psyche took another blow. Only a few hours ago, she and her dad had been on the dance floor, talking about her parent's wedding and how he was a one-woman man. How Megan's mother had been his soul mate. Had it all been a lie? Had all the stories she'd been told about her parents' life together been totally fabricated? Had they really met in graduate school and fallen in love at first sight or was that another tall tale?

"She and my dad were divorced? When?"

"Right about the time they told you she died, I'm guessing," Logan said.

"Who filed the divorce?"

"She did, citing irreconcilable differences and granting your dad full custody of you."

Megan tried to absorb this new piece of the puzzle. "I don't understand. If they got divorced, why not just tell me that instead of lying about her dying?"

He pointed to her BlackBerry. "Call your dad and ask him."

"No." She felt as if the entire foundation of her life was suddenly on shifting sand, or quicksand that threatened to suck her in and completely submerge her. She had to stay focused here. She couldn't afford to lose it right now. "What else did you find?" Megan asked.

"Just this." He showed her the screen. "Someone named Fiona is guest blogging about how she and your mom went to Woodstock together decades ago when they were eighteen. According to the info Fiona has supplied about herself, she doesn't live too far from here."

"She lists her address online? That's a risky thing to do."

"Her brief bio at the end of her guest blog mentions a business she owns and its location, but she doesn't list a contact e-mail address. She hasn't posted anything new for a few weeks, so if you replied to the blog there's no telling when she'd read it."

"Then we have to go talk to her."

"Hold on," he said. "Let's see if there isn't more we can find."

Two hours, two platefuls of pancakes and countless cups of coffee later, they still had no additional leads. "I'm telling you that your best bet is having your dad track your mom down," Logan said. "He may already know where she is."

"If he knows I'm looking for her, he may try to hide her from me."

"Gee, paranoid much?"

"I never used to be." She had the feeling that very little about her life would be the same after tonight. "I'm tired of being reasonable and responsible all the time. I'm trusting my gut right now, and my gut says that I have a brief window of opportunity here to find her before they do. Or if they already know where she is, then I have a short period of time to reach her before they realize I'm looking for her. I don't care if that's logical or not. The bottom line is that I need to talk to Fiona. If you won't help me, I'll rent a car and go anyway. By myself."

"I didn't say I wouldn't take you."

"Then let's stop wasting time here and go find Fiona." She let her desperation show in her face and her unsteady voice. "Please."

Logan was silent for a minute before finally saying, "Okay." He signaled for the check.

"I'll pay for breakfast," Megan said. When he began to protest, she added, "To thank you for helping me out."

"I don't let women pay my way."

"Why not?"

"Because I wasn't raised that way."

"Well, I wasn't raised to dash off in the middle of the night with a strange man, but I'm doing it." Seeing his glare, she added, "Okay, so you're not strange. I take that back."

"Take it all back." He shoved her money across the table at her.

"Do you think I'm trying to bribe you or something?"

"Do you really want to fight about this or do you want to track down Woodstock lady?"

"Her name is Fiona."

"Whatever."

"I thought cops were supposed to notice details like that."

"Oh, I notice details when I need to. Like the fact that you're a five-foot-eight brunette with blue eyes and freckles who shoves her hair away from her face when she's stressed. You also have a habit of licking your lips when you're nervous . . . like now."

"Okay then," she said, determined to never again lick her lips in his presence. Hair shoving was okay, but she didn't want him focusing on her lips the way he was right now. "I'm glad we got that cleared up. We'll go Dutch." She slapped down enough money to cover her portion of the bill and tip. "Now, let's hit the road in your aqua Chevy."

"It's blue."

"Right." She held the door open for him. "Let's go."

• • •

As they headed out of Vegas, Logan wondered what it was about a damsel in distress that got him every time. He needed to get over that. It was not a good trait to have. That's how he'd met his ex-wife, Angie.

So what the hell was he doing getting messed up with Megan's drama? Her uncle played golf with the police superintendent and the mayor, for God's sake. He'd already pissed off her family by barging in on their wedding and then dropping the bombshell about his grandfather's marital status. He really didn't need to further alienate them by taking off with their precious librarian Megan.

She didn't really look like a librarian to him. She didn't wear those smart-girl glasses and didn't have her hair scraped back from her face. Instead, her hair blew in the wind coming through her open window. Strands flew across her face, but she didn't seem bothered. Angie would have had a fit. Angie would never be caught dead in a vintage car. Only top-of-the-line stuff for her.

Not that he could afford much top-of-the-line stuff on a cop's salary, but he'd tried his damndest to keep his wife happy because he'd been a stupid bastard. Those days were over.

Yet here he was, with another damsel in distress. But he didn't plan on having sex with this one. No way he was that stupid, no matter how awesome her cleavage was or how long her legs were.

His plan was simple: He couldn't let Megan pull his granddad, who had enough on his plate at the moment, into her web of a dysfunctional family problem. He'd keep her distracted long enough to keep her from involving Buddy and then he'd cut her loose.

It wasn't as if she was without resources of her own. She had a family. And once she calmed down, she'd realize the logical course of action was using their power to get the information she wanted.

He had to admit it was a little strange that there was so little information available in the databases about her mother. That wasn't normal. Not that he was a pro at normal. As a police officer, he'd seen more than his fair share of weird and nasty. He'd seen the dark side, lived it, been consumed by it and barely lived to crawl out of it . . . forever changed.

"It's really dark out here," Megan said.

Logan knew all about darkness. How it ate away at you from the inside out. How it messed with your mind and your decisions. How it screwed you.

Oh yeah. He was a pro at walking the line along that dark side. Most cops referred to the thin blue line as the line between police keeping order and protecting the public from complete chaos. But Logan had experienced another line, right at the edge of a different kind of chaos between sanity and despair.

Megan was one of those Suzie Sunshine types who believe that people were basically good and kind. Sure, she was feeling bitter at the moment about her family lying to her, but her optimism about the rest of the human race was still there.

As for him . . . well, he'd lost that positive outlook long ago. He knew better. Seeing small kids abandoned by their crackhead mother in a filthy vacant building with little food and no heat for days on end in the middle of winter did that to a man. Made him question things. So did finding a body tossed into a Dumpster, burned beyond recognition. He'd seen too much to be an optimist.

But he couldn't walk away. If he did, the darkness won.

So Logan kept his attention focused on the twin beams of light from the Chevy's headlights on the highway ahead and blocked out the memories of the life-altering mistake that haunted him in his nightmares. To do otherwise would destroy him.

Chapter Four

. . . .

Megan stared at Logan's face illuminated by the vintage dashboard lights. He'd barely spoken since they'd left Las Vegas. "If you're getting tired, I could drive," she said.

"No way."

She was insulted by his emphatic refusal. "I'm a good driver."

"No one drives this borrowed baby but me."

"It's just that Buddy said you flew directly to Vegas from work."

"I caught a few hours' sleep after leaving the reception."

"Oh. That's good. But the offer stands."

He waved her words away. "We're almost there."

"The Butterfly Ranch," Megan read the sign. "Do they raise butterflies? The Peggy Notebaert Nature Museum in Chicago has an incredible butterfly haven in a huge greenhouse."

A gate with an intercom blocked their entrance. Logan pressed the button and a male voice immediately answered, "Welcome to the Butterfly Ranch. We accept cash and most credit cards."

"Credit cards?" She looked around. Several extra-wide trailers were plunked amidst the sagebrush with bright lights illuminating the parking area. "They're open 24/7 and they charge to see the butterflies?"

"You could say that."

"They keep the displays in the trailers?"

He nodded as the gate went up. As soon as they pulled into the parking area, a huge guy who looked like a bouncer greeted them.

"Nice wheels," he said with an approving look at the car.

"Thanks."

"It's a pretty aqua," Megan noted as she got out.

The bouncer and Logan both looked at Megan with disapproval.

"It's blue," Logan said.

"Other women aren't allowed inside the ranch," the bouncer said.

"Right. We're here to talk to Fiona."

"She doesn't do tricks."

Megan's brain was slow, but things were starting to sink in. "This isn't a butterfly farm, is it?" she whispered to Logan.

"No, it's not."

"Right." She knew brothels were legal in several counties in Nevada, but she'd certainly never anticipated that she'd end up visiting one of them. "It just didn't occur to me. I'm not thinking clearly or I would have figured things out earlier. You could have warned me."

"Do you want to leave?" Logan asked her.

"No way," Megan said emphatically. Addressing her

next statement to the bouncer, she said, "We need to speak to Fiona about my mother."

"We don't talk about our employees."

"No, she didn't work here." At least Megan prayed she hadn't. "She and Fiona were best friends and went to Woodstock together. She wrote about my mother in a blog."

"Is something wrong?" A woman came from inside the trailer to ask. Her black capri pants and sequined turquoise tunic top accentuated her terrific figure. Her short hair, with its caramel and gold highlights, had obviously been styled by a pro. She had the husky voice of a smoker. She also fit the definition of a cougar, an older woman on the prowl.

She eyed Logan appreciatively. "The guy can come in, but not the female." She came closer to run her hand along Logan's muscular arm. "You don't need her, honey. We've got everything you could possibly want inside. You name it, we've got it. Beyond your wildest sexual fantasies. 24/7."

Megan quickly spoke up. "Are you Fiona?"

The woman nodded absently, her attention clearly remaining on Logan and his biceps.

"You knew my mother. Astrid Meyer. You went to Woodstock with her and talked about her on your guest blog. I'm her daughter, Megan."

Fiona reluctantly tore her gaze from Logan and switched it to Megan. "Oh, yeah? How's Astrid doing these days?"

"That's what I need to speak to you about."

Fiona gave her an appraising look before nodding at the bouncer. "It's okay. We'll talk in my office." She tilted her head toward a smaller trailer to their right. "This way."

Megan entered with some trepidation. She'd never

been in a brothel before. As it turned out, she still wasn't. This trailer was indeed a dedicated office, looking like it could have belonged to an accountant—an accountant who liked French country décor in sunny yellow. Two wing chairs upholstered in gold-and-red toile faced a large dark oak wooden desk. Framed oil paintings of Paris street scenes hung on walls not covered by built-in bookcases. A rustic wrought-iron chandelier with dark red lampshades hanging from the ceiling matched the wrought-iron desk lamp.

Megan was not about to comment on this version of a red-light district. Instead she kept her focus on Fiona's connection to her mother. "So you were her best friend in high school?" Megan asked.

Fiona gestured for them both to take a seat. "I wouldn't say *best* friend. I was a friend. Astrid didn't really have a best friend."

"Was she popular in school?"

"She was smart. Good at math. She loved the Band. That's why she wanted to go to Woodstock, to see them. I went for the vibe. So we packed a cooler and hopped into my VW, which came back after Woodstock with the grooviest psychedelic paint job. I wish I still had that car." She paused for a moment, clearly caught up in the fond memory, before continuing "Astrid's parents had died in a car accident a few months earlier. Astrid took it hard. Smoked some pot to help her get through. Hell, at Woodstock just about everyone was smoking something. Half a million people on a high."

Megan was having a hard time picturing her academically inclined mother at Woodstock.

"We kept in touch for a few years afterward. She sent me a wedding announcement. That's how I knew she'd married some guy named West from Chicago." Fiona paused to pop an Altoid in her mouth before continuing.

"I got married a couple of times myself. Divorced a few times too. My last husband died on me. Literally. I had a gambling problem at the time, so when I got his life insurance money I blew it in the casinos. This place was the only asset he had left. I got help for my gambling issues and started running the Butterfly Ranch, cleaning it up into a reputable establishment. It's not like Bertha's Brothel. I warned her that with a name like that she'd never make it and she didn't. But she was old school. Well, not really, *really* old like the heyday of the red-light ladies."

Fiona paused to point to a small antique black-and-white photograph in a dark frame on her desk. "Do you know who that is?"

Megan shook her head.

"That's Rosa May. She's something of a local legend in these parts. She was originally from back east, but she came to Nevada during the silver and gold rush days in the late 1800s. She was a big-hearted prostitute who died after taking care of sick miners during a pneumonia epidemic. Despite her act of generosity, the locals refused to bury her within the official cemetery grounds and she was put to rest outside the fence on her own. It's sad that she was ostracized even after death. You'd think that people would be a little more forgiving, but noooo." Seeing the expression on Megan's face, she added, "Don't look so surprised. Just because I run a brothel doesn't mean I'm stupid."

"No, it's not that. It's just that I'm a history buff."

Fiona's face lit up. "You are? Then you should visit the Comstock area around Virginia City and Gold Hill. The oldest hotel in the state is still operating in Gold Hill even if that's about all that's there anymore. But Virginia City still has a lot going on. That's where Mark Twain got his start writing as a newspaper reporter for the local paper there."

"I'm only visiting Las Vegas for my cousin Faith's wedding over the weekend, but she and I did visit Virginia City and Gold Hill a few years ago. We even stopped at the costume museum in Carson City . . . I forget what it's called."

"That's the Marjorie Russell Clothing and Textile Research Center. It's open by appointment only."

"Right. My cousin is a librarian and she set it up with the curator."

"A librarian, huh?"

Megan nodded. "I'm a librarian too."

"It figures that Astrid's daughter would do something brainy like become a librarian. I never had any kids myself."

Logan cleared his throat with male impatience. "So, Fiona, you've heard from Megan's mother over the years, right?"

Fiona nodded. "A Christmas card or two. Then nothing. I assumed she got busy raising a family. She's doing that, right?"

"I don't know," Megan said. "I haven't seen her since I was two."

"What do you mean?"

"I mean my father told me my mother died, but I've only recently discovered that she's alive after all. It's complicated."

"Sounds like it."

"Anyway, that's why I'm trying to track her down. So anything you could tell me about her would really be greatly appreciated."

"Well, like I said, we went to high school and then Woodstock together. After Woodstock, she went to some fancy college on a scholarship. Hold on, I think I have our high school yearbook." Fiona scanned her bookshelves, which held everything from the latest Susan

Elizabeth Phillips book to *Zen and the Art of Motorcycle Maintenance*. An entire shelf was dedicated to local history books like *Comstock Women* and *Mark Twain in Virginia City, Nevada*. "Yeah, here it is." She opened the book up and found the page she was looking for. "Here's what your mom looked like our senior year. That was before her parents died. She was an only child."

Megan's fingers trembled slightly as she took the yearbook Fiona offered her.

"She looks like you," Fiona added.

Megan had never seen her mother this young. The first photo she had was of her parents' wedding at city hall almost ten years later. She stared down at the school photo. Her mother's long dark hair was parted in the middle and she wasn't smiling. She looked very serious.

Fiona pulled out a box of photographs from a desk drawer. "I didn't post this photo on the blog about Woodstock because I thought I looked fat in it, but here's your mom." She pointed to the person in the center of a group all waving their hands in the air. There was Astrid, flashing the peace sign with two fingers and grinning as she stood in the mud.

Megan felt so strange. It was almost as if she'd stepped back in time. This photo showed an entirely different side of her mother. She looked so carefree and alive, despite the recent tragic deaths of her own parents. Had Woodstock given Astrid a chance to let go? Had the experience freed her to express her emotions, if only for that brief weekend, instead of being so serious? Had that been the only time her mother felt the joy and fun displayed in this photo?

"You know, despite moving all over the country, I've still got the pair of bell bottoms I wore, with the mud still on the hems. I've never had another experience quite like Woodstock," Fiona said. "And trust me, I've had a *lot* of experiences. I've done everything from working as a nanny to a stint as a grief counselor at a funeral parlor. Your mom swore she'd keep her Woodstock jeans too. I don't suppose you know if she did?"

Megan shook her head.

"Would you like that photo? This is a nice one too." She held up another shot, this one in color. Astrid stood in the foreground while the background had a dreamy, gauzy look. Even more than the previous Woodstock photo, in this one she was the center of the composition. Everything and everyone around her faded as the camera focused on her; she seemed to take pleasure in the attention. Her smile was heartfelt and her eyes sparkled with a mischievous expression that Megan had never seen displayed in other photos.

"Did my mom have a sense of humor?" Megan asked. "What was she like back then? Did she ever talk about having a family?"

"She did have a sense of humor even though not everyone understood it. I don't remember her talking about kids or a family. It was the sixties. We weren't thinking that far ahead. We were totally in the here and now."

"She looks like she's having a good time."

"She did," Fiona said. "I'd never seen her that way before."

Tears welled in Megan's eyes as Logan's earlier words came back to her. When he'd mentioned the divorce, he'd talked about custody. What had made her mother agree to give Megan's dad full custody? Why hadn't she asked for shared custody or visitation rights? Had Megan been such a bad child that her mother wanted nothing more to do with her? Or had Astrid been driven away?

Megan had so many questions. Each one made her heart painfully crumble a little more. She'd shoved those thoughts away when she'd first heard about the custody issue back at Aunt Sally's. But staring at the photos of her mother now, the doubts and fears all came back with a vengeance. People didn't just walk away for no reason. Especially mothers.

Megan couldn't imagine walking away from any child of her own she might have in the future. She'd always wanted kids. Now she just wanted answers.

"If you'd like, I can scan copies of those photos for you to take with you," Fiona said.

Megan got all choked up, barely able to say, "Thanks."

To Megan's surprise, Logan reached over and squeezed her shoulder. His offering of comfort both surprised and grounded her.

"How long has it been since you've heard from Astrid?" Logan asked Fiona.

"It was about ten years ago, before our thirtieth high school reunion. She e-mailed me out of the blue and asked if I was going to attend. I said no and asked how she was doing, but she never replied."

Ten years ago. Megan had been eighteen. The same age of her mother in those photos.

"Do you have her e-mail address?" Megan immediately asked.

Fiona shook her head. "I'm sorry, I don't. That computer crashed, taking my address book with it. But I remember it was from someplace in Europe, I think. Maybe she was just traveling there or something. I do know that she did not come to the reunion. I can check and see if anyone else from school has heard from her, but I wouldn't count on it. She wasn't really a people person."

"I'd appreciate you asking around, thanks. Here's my e-mail address." Megan wrote it down on a pad of paper that Fiona handed her. Fiona recited her own e-mail, which Megan immediately entered into her BlackBerry. "I appreciate you taking the time to talk with us."

"Sure, hon. No problem," Fiona said. "I just wish I could tell you more than I did."

Megan clutched the photos of her mom that Fiona had scanned. "You gave me more than I had when I arrived."

"I wonder why your dad would tell you she'd died."

"That's the first thing she's going to ask him when we get back to Vegas," Logan said. "We're heading back there right now."

Fiona shifted her attention to Logan. "Come back anytime." Fiona gave him a sultry look. "We'll give you a special rate."

"He's a cop," Megan said.

Fiona shrugged. "So? Prostitution is legal in this county."

"Thanks for the offer," Logan said.

"But you're not going to take me up on it." Fiona's sigh indicated her disappointment. "Because your heart belongs to Megan."

His jaw practically dropped. "No, it doesn't."

"Come on, now." Fiona patted his bare arm. "Don't be shy. It's obvious. Her heart clearly belongs to you as well. Tons of chemistry going on here." She pointed from Logan to Megan.

"Why does everyone keep saying that?" Megan demanded.

Fiona lifted an eyebrow. "So you two aren't having sex?"

"No!" Megan said, "We just met today. Yesterday, I mean."

"So?"

Megan realized that having this conversation with a madam was probably not a good idea. "Anyway . . . what I mean is . . . uh, thanks again for the photos and the info about my mom."

"Good luck with your search," Fiona said as she waved them out.

• • •

Trying to assimilate what she'd learned about her mom, Megan didn't say much after they left the ranch. Her brain felt all jumbled with images and information. Her mom flashing the peace sign at Woodstock, promising Fiona to keep the mud-spattered jeans as a memento of their time together that history-making weekend. Did her dad even know that Astrid had been at Woodstock? Had she ever told him about it? Did she still have the jeans?

Daylight had streaked its way across the broad sky, painting it bright hues of red and pink. Mother Nature's show rivaled any light display on the Strip. Granted, the surrounding landscape was barren, but there was beauty to be found if you looked close enough. Kind of like the picture she was trying to create of her mother's life.

Megan wasn't the only one keeping quiet. Logan also appeared lost in his own thoughts. A strange sound captured her attention.

"What was that noise?" Megan asked a short while later.

"Nothing good."

"Is it the car?"

"Yes." He swore under his breath.

"Are we out of gas?"

"No, of course we're not."

"It's just that cars this old don't get very good gas mileage."

"I'm aware of that." The noise—a cross between a clank and a rattle—got louder. "We're going to have to stop."

She looked out the window. They were surrounded by miles of sagebrush and little else. "But there's nothing here."

"I think there's a town nearby. Check the map on my phone."

It took her a few minutes to figure out how to use his iPhone, and he wasn't exactly patient about giving her instructions. "Yelling at me isn't going to make things easier," she said.

"I wasn't yelling."

"You may not have raised your voice, but it still sounded like you wanted to yell."

Seeing Logan grit his teeth, she was tempted to tell him that wasn't good for him, but decided that would just elicit more irritation on his part. So instead she focused on figuring out the map app on his phone. "According to this, the closest town is a place called Last Resort."

The grinding noise from the car got louder the farther they got from the main highway and the closer they got to the town. They passed a handmade sign hammered to a leaning fence post. The sign read WELCOME TO LAST RESORT. POPULATION: NOT MANY and had several gunshot holes in it. Next up were a few boarded-up cinder-block buildings that looked like they hadn't seen any action since the 1957 Chevy first hit showroom floors.

"This doesn't look real promising," Megan said.

"You think?" Logan said. He took the phone from her. "Great. We're in a dead zone now."

"You make it sound like zombies live here or something." She turned to face him, only then realizing he was referring to his phone.

"What about your phone?"

She checked it before shaking her head. She inadvertently hit the music play button and "Life Is a Highway" started playing. "Sorry," she muttered before fumbling to stop it.

Finally they came upon a small group of buildings huddled together like cold campers around a warm fire. A vintage sign with a martini at the top and a cup of coffee farther down welcomed them to JJ's Golden Lounge and Café, which didn't look like it had had any customers for several decades despite the OPEN sign on the dusty door.

Logan got out and came around to open the passenger door for her. Megan looked around cautiously. Another vintage sign next door proudly proclaimed that the Queen of Hearts Motel had color TV. The U-shaped building looked as if a stiff wind would send it tumbling into the surrounding sagebrush.

"Afraid to get out?" Logan said when she didn't move to leave the car,

"Of course not." She hopped out of the Bel Air. "I'm just sorry your aqua car is having trouble." Her eyes widened as she stared over Logan's shoulder. "Oh, look. We've got a welcoming committee."

Chapter Five

. . . .

Logan stared at the threesome, who looked older than dirt, walking toward them. His cop training kicked in as he sized them up: two male Caucasians in their late seventies, both just over six feet, wearing Western-style shirts and jeans, one with a head of white hair and the other with a hairpiece; one female Caucasian, probably late seventies, five-foot-five, one hundred twenty to one hundred thirty pounds, long platinum hair, piercing blue eyes, penciled eyebrows that were slightly crooked, huge dice drop earrings, colorful rings on eight of her ten fingers. Not exactly a threatening bunch of seniors.

They greeted him with huge smiles on their tanned faces.

He greeted them with a frown. "Is there a car mechanic in town?" His lack of sleep was catching up to him. His dark mood had gotten blacker when he'd reached for his iPhone and realized there was no service. Nothing he saw in front of him now improved his spirits any.

"What do you mean, exactly, by *mechanic*?" the woman said.

"Someone who works on cars."

"Well, Chuck here has changed the oil in my car," the woman said. "My name's Pepper Dior. Maybe you saw my act in Vegas?" She struck a pose. "I do celebrity impersonations."

"Show him your Marilyn Monroe," the man on her left said. "She does a slam-bang Marilyn Monroe."

Pepper socked the man's arm playfully. "You're just saying that. This here is Chuck Spicer. I'm sure you recognize him. Why, in the 1980s he was known as the Nevada King of the Infomercial."

"If Pepper and I ever married, she'd be known as Pepper Spicer." Chuck guffawed at his own observation.

"Nice car," the third man noted. "Had one of them myself. Chevy Bel Air, 1957, right?"

Logan nodded.

"I had the red convertible. Allow me to introduce myself. Rowdy Goldberg at your service. I'm the mayor of this fine town." He put his arm on Logan's shoulders. "Come on into the café and sit a spell. You look like you could use a cup of coffee."

"I could use a mechanic," Logan said. "Or a phone. Our cells don't work out here."

"Well, now, as it turns out we don't have landline phone service at this exact moment," Rowdy said cheerfully. "High winds over near Reno knocked down the lines. They should have it back up in no time. Meanwhile, come on in and take a load off. I don't believe I got your names."

"Logan Doyle and Megan West."

Rowdy held the café door open and ushered them in. "Well, Logan and Megan, welcome to the place time forgot."

He wasn't kidding. Booths with red vinyl seats lined one gilded wood-paneled wall. Framed photos of Frank Sinatra and Dean Martin hung on the wall along with lots of other faces he didn't recognize. Red bar stools stood in front of a luncheon counter with a fading gold-flecked Formica top. A large pass-through allowed a clear view of the kitchen. A vintage jukebox stood in the back corner behind the booths. This wasn't a rehabbed version, as was indicated by the duct tape holding it together.

"It still plays," Pepper said proudly. "You just need to know where to kick it. Just like a man." She paused before looking at Megan. "You are gorgeous, girl! I love your dress even if it is a bit fancy for Last Resort. I wore an outfit like that to a gala at the Flamingo Casino in 1955. Ah, those were the days, huh, Rowdy? The Rat Pack—Frank Sinatra, Dean Martin, Sammy Davis Jr."

Logan could tell by Megan's expression that her inner history buff was fascinated. He didn't share her enthusiasm. If he didn't get some sleep soon, he'd end up face-down on the counter no matter how many cups of coffee he drank. Rowdy motioned him to sit at one of the stools at the counter and quickly poured him some coffee in a chipped white mug.

He couldn't believe the way his trip to Las Vegas was turning out. Not that he'd had real high hopes given the fact that he was sent here to stop his grandfather from marrying and committing bigamy.

Sure, he'd expected a few speed bumps along the way. But he hadn't expected Megan. She was more than a mere speed bump. She was more like a force of nature.

When his grandfather had first told him about Megan the librarian, Logan had no burning desire to meet her as his matchmaking Gramps had wanted. Now that Logan *had* met Megan, there was a burning desire going on, all right. A desire for *her*.

He'd seen more beautiful women, although she was no slouch in the looks department. Great legs, great cleavage, sexy lips. Her body wasn't the only thing going for her. She had a one-track mind. So did he.

Watching her was like a drug. Maybe that was just exhaustion and too much caffeine talking.

Or maybe it was that "chemistry" everyone else kept going on and on about. Sure, he'd denied it aloud, but internally he recognized the claims were true.

Not that he could do anything about it. She had girl-next-door-white-picket-fence written all over her. She was no good-time badge bunny. You wouldn't find her warming a bar stool at a cop bar, waiting to pick up one of Chicago's finest for the night.

He couldn't help wondering why she had a chip on her shoulder about cops. He'd always been too damn curious for his own good. Were her reasons personal? Had some guy done her wrong? Cheated on her?

Or were her reasons philosophical? Was she one of those bleeding hearts who thought all cops were guilty of brutality? Logan always found it ironic that even those folks called 911 when they were in trouble.

Not that he condoned police misconduct. And Chicago had had more than its fair share lately—all making the local nightly news. But the stories of the majority of police officers who did their jobs and put their lives on the line every day went untold. If a cop saved someone's life or caught the bad guys . . . well, those stories rarely appeared in the media.

And that reality fostered the "us versus them" mentality in the force. Only another cop could understand what it was like.

"You're awfully quiet, Logan," Chuck said.

"Oh, leave him be. Maybe he's the strong, silent type," Pepper said. "Is that right, Megan?"

Megan, who was seated on the stool to his right, darted a glance in his direction. Not a nervous I'm-embarrassed-by-the-question glance, but more of an evaluating glance as if sizing him up. Whoa, that had unexpected connotations, he thought as he got hard. Apparently not all parts of his body were too tired to party.

"So, Megan, what do you say?" Logan raised an eyebrow. "Am I the strong, silent type?"

"I don't really know you well enough to say."

"How did you two meet?" Pepper asked.

"At my cousin's wedding," Megan said. "That's why I'm wearing this dress."

"You wore black to a wedding?"

"It was a black-and-white wedding with red roses."

"Sounds striking. So you ran off together. How romantic. Logan clearly had time to change out of his suit into jeans. But he couldn't wait for you to change your clothes before sweeping you off."

"To Last Resort? Who in their right mind would want to be swept off to this place?" Chuck said.

Pepper smacked Chuck's arm hard enough to make him wince. "Don't you go insulting our fine town."

"How many people actually live here?" Logan asked. There went his damn curiosity again.

"Not many," Chuck said vaguely.

"How about some breakfast to go with that coffee?" Rowdy suggested. "You're looking at one of the best short-order cooks in the West. One of the fastest too. How do you want your eggs?" Without waiting for an answer he said, "Over-easy sounds good. I can do that with one hand tied behind my back."

"Now, Rowdy, you know what happened the last time you tried that," Pepper said. "You made a mess. You need both hands."

"The magic is all in the fingers."

"Cappy isn't going to like you cooking in his kitchen."

"Cappy isn't here right now."

"Where is he?" Logan asked. He was starting to feel like he'd stepped into a *Twilight Zone* episode or something. Were these three seniors the only inhabitants of this ghost town?

"Sleeping off a hangover." Rowdy moved into the kitchen, though Logan still had a clear view from his seat at the counter. "Okay, people, stand back and observe the master at work."

To Logan's surprise, Rowdy was as good as his word. Using one hand, he cracked eggs and deftly dropped them on the grill before tossing the shells over his shoulder into the garbage with Michael Jordan precision.

"Show-off," Pepper said fondly.

Rowdy beamed. "I told you I hadn't lost my touch."

Something about the guy reminded Logan of his granddad. At least Logan had been able to briefly touch base with Buddy while Megan had used the rest room at the pancake house back in Las Vegas. The truth of the matter was Logan never thought he'd be gone this long.

Checking his watch, he realized it was almost nine in the morning. Okay, they hadn't been gone twelve hours yet. But it seemed like a lot longer than that.

He glanced over at Megan and wondered if she felt the same way. She'd been through a hell of a lot in a short period of time. Finding out your mom wasn't dead had to be rough. His own mom was very much alive and kicking, still furious with Logan's dad even though they'd been divorced for years now.

His mother lived in one of Chicago's famous brick bungalows on the South Side with his Polish grandmother, who made the best pierogies on the planet. Chicago had a huge Polish population—which his grandmother, who'd been born in Warsaw, took great pleasure in reminding him of every time he saw her for dinner on the first Sunday of every month.

He used to be joined at the family dinners by his two younger brothers, Aidan and Connor, but Aidan was now on the Seattle police force and Connor was a sheriff in a small town in Ohio.

Logan had added another brother his first day on the job when he'd met Will Riley. Logan rubbed a clenched fist across his forehead. No, he couldn't think of that now. He had to block out the grim memories.

"There you go," Rowdy said, sliding plates across the counter to him and Megan.

Logan started eating automatically.

"It's good," Megan said, daintily dabbing at her lips with a paper napkin, drawing his attention to her lush mouth.

Damn, his self-control was slipping badly. Not a good thing. He finished his food and stepped away from the counter and temptation.

"I need a little shut-eye. I'm going to stretch out in the backseat of the car."

"Don't be silly. You can stay in the motel," Rowdy said. "We've only renovated one room, but it looks really nice and has a very comfortable king-sized bed."

Logan shook his head. "No, really . . ."

"Nonsense. I insist," Rowdy said.

"What about the phones?"

"Nothing yet," Rowdy said cheerfully. "But if there's a change, I'll let you know. Megan, you're welcome to join him if you need to . . . uh, rest."

She blushed. "I'm okay. Thanks anyway."

"Would you like to see some of my costumes from the golden days of Las Vegas?" Pepper asked Megan.

Megan's eyes lit up. "That would be nice. I don't want to be a bother though."

"You're no bother, girl." Pepper linked her arm in Megan's and pulled her out of the café. "Let's go. My house is right behind the café."

Logan watched Megan walk away, noting the sway of her hips in the black dress she'd worn since the wedding. She should have looked rumpled after being up all night. Instead she looked . . . well, rumpled but sexy rumpled. Just-got-out-of-bed rumpled. Ready-for-sex rumpled.

Damn. He was getting hard again.

When would he learn that helping damsels in distress always landed him in deep shit?

• • •

"Ah, those were the days," Pepper said as she gazed at her closet with wistful pride. "Vegas in the fifties. This is the costume I wore for my Marilyn Monroe impersonations. It's a copy of the one she wore to sing 'Diamonds are a Girl's Best Friend' in the movie *How to Marry a Millionaire*. Nice, huh?"

Megan nodded. The bubble-gum-pink satin evening gown was tight and strapless. The big bow near the back and the slit up the side were edged with black lace.

"I even have the matching pink elbow-length gloves," Pepper said. "And, of course, the bling." She opened a heart-shaped box containing a jumble of costume jewelry. "Not the real stuff, but still nice." She held up a rhinestone bracelet to the ray of sunshine streaming in a side window before dropping it back into the box. "In the scene in the movie, all the other girls are wearing frothy full skirts with tons of tulle. Then there was Marilyn in this sheath gown. Such a stunning difference."

"I'll bet."

"I read someplace that the actual pink gown Marilyn wore was made from upholstery satin and lined with felt. I don't know if it's true or not. But mine isn't made that way. You can actually buy costumes of her dress online now. They aren't as nice as mine, of course."

"I'm sure they aren't," Megan said.

"What got you interested in vintage clothing?"

"My grandmother. She has several classic Chanel suits. They never went out of style. In fact, she wore one to the wedding."

"I could never afford designer stuff," Pepper said. "Too pricey. I'd rather have twelve dresses than one ritzy one. Not that I went for quantity rather than quality; I just picked stuff I liked. Same goes for men."

Afraid that Pepper was going to drill her about Logan, Megan quickly said, "Did you ever meet Frank Sinatra?"

"No, but I met Dean Martin once. I bumped into him backstage at the Sands. And I saw Elvis Presley several times. The city is very different these days."

"I imagine so."

"I started out as a dancer, but I wasn't very good at it. And those headpieces almost weighed more than I did. I kept losing my balance. But I was good at impersonations and singing."

"You were a showgirl?"

"In the beginning, yes." Pepper showed her a photo of a row of dancers who looked like the Rockettes. They wore skimpy red costumes and flashy feather-laden headpieces. "We showed a lot of leg for the 1950s, so our audience was mostly male. For the most part they weren't rowdy unless they had too much to drink. Then I could relate to what the saloon girls here in Last Resort or over in Virginia City must have put up with during the silver rush. Did you know there was something like a hundred saloons in Virginia City alone? We didn't have that many in Last Resort."

"Were you born here?"

"Yes. Same with Rowdy and Chuck. We're all Last

Resorters." She giggled. "That sounds funny when you say it that way. My family has been in Nevada for generations. My grandfather actually mined for gold and silver up in Virginia City. I remember the stories he told me when I was a little girl. Not that Virginia City was the only town with a colorful history. We have our own heritage here in Last Resort. A man named Fritz Holzenberger, who owned the Last Resort Silver Mine, founded the town in the 1880s. My granddad almost stayed in Virginia City. He tossed a coin my grandmother handed him and it came up heads, which meant moving to Last Resort, as my grandmother wanted. She was tired of Virginia City. Only later did my grandmother admit that the coin had heads on both sides. She was clever that way. Some might say I take after her. You know, our pasts have a huge influence on who we are today."

Megan couldn't argue with that. The problem was that the past she thought she had was disrupted by lies, leaving her off balance and searching for answers. She wasn't going to find them here in Last Resort, but this was a bit of a breather before she had to face her father back in Las Vegas.

"Did your grandparents tell you stories?" Pepper asked.

"Sometimes. But it turned out that my father told the wildest story of all." That Megan's mother was dead when she wasn't.

"Oh yeah? Is he a writer or something?"

"He's an accountant. A math whiz."

"And he told wild stories?"

Megan nodded.

"Wow. I love it. I would never have expected that from a math guy."

"He surprised me too." Megan knew her dad liked Thurber's short stories, but she never would have thought him capable of concocting the story about her mom that he apparently had.

"I never had kids," Pepper said before pulling a dress from the closet. "What do you think of this?"

Megan took a deep breath and shifted gears. She welcomed the distraction. "It's beautiful." The sundress had a full skirt and bold bunches of blue and purple flowers scattered across it.

"I'll bet you're what . . . a size ten?"

Megan nodded.

"Then this should fit you. Try it on. Go ahead. I'm glad you're not one of those super-skinny size-zero women. When I was young, there was no such thing. Women were proud of their curves. Look at Marilyn Monroe." Pepper pointed to a framed poster of her on the wall from the movie *Some Like It Hot*. "She had curves in all the right places, to quote Rowdy. A real hourglass figure. So did I, in my heyday."

"Did you ever meet her in Las Vegas?"

"Sadly, no. Here, take these two while you're trying that one on. And this one . . ."

Before Megan knew it, she had a pile of clothes that Pepper sent her into the large bathroom to try on.

"There's a full-length mirror in there so you can see yourself," Pepper said, "but do come out so I can see as well."

Pepper was right: The outfits all fit. From the beautiful sundress to the pastel baby blue sweater set and plaid skirt to the black pencil dress.

"I want you to have them. And this one." She held up a 1950s style blue floral print cocktail party dress. "These as well." She added a lavender lace hourglass cocktail dress and a pink taffeta full skirt shelf-bust cocktail party dress that swirled around her ankles.

Megan adored them all. But to be polite she said, "No, I couldn't . . ."

"You're right. You need more casual outfits too." Pepper added a plaid jumper and a black floral cotton full skirt to the pile. "And you must have this one, girl." She placed an ivory pleated skirt on top before returning to the closet. "This one is special. It's a landscape skirt. See?" She held out the full skirt, which had an amazing scenic print featuring rolling hills, a farmhouse, gorgeous vibrant flowers and bunches of wheat.

Megan couldn't resist touching the skirt. It was love at first sight. Ditto for the full-length party dress that Grace Kelly would have worn. Actually, she loved them all. "But I can't . . ." Her words sounded much weaker this time.

"It would save me having to sell them on eBay. I can't wear them anymore. They don't fit me."

"How about I pay you for them?" Megan said. "I mean, if you were going to sell them on eBay anyway. How much do you want for them?"

"I don't know. I'm not an expert at prices for vintage clothes these days."

"I'm no expert but I do have a good idea," Megan said. She did a quick mental tally of the items and offered Pepper a fair price.

"Let me throw in my old American Tourister purple hard shell suitcase to put it all in. I realize that nothing here is quite right for today's casual wear though, so we'll stop at the gift shop on the way down to the motel."

"The town has a gift shop?"

Pepper nodded. "It's not large but it's attached to the motel office. We have T-shirts and some other things."

Half an hour later, Megan tiptoed into the motel room where Logan was still sleeping. Pepper had given her a key. The drapes were drawn against the outside sunshine and she had to pause a moment to allow her eyes to adjust to the darkness.

Logan was sprawled out on the bed. He'd removed his T-shirt and loosened his jeans but hadn't removed them. He rolled away from her, leaving space on the king-size bed for her to sit down.

Megan cautiously moved forward. She didn't want to wake him, but she was so tired she was afraid she'd end up in a boneless puddle on the carpet, which was orange shag despite Pepper's assurances that this room had been rehabbed.

One step, two . . . She reached for the bed. She'd just rest for a few minutes . . .

She sank onto the soft mattress. She only had a second to enjoy the fact that the bed was so comfortable before she was grabbed and flattened by a half-naked Logan.

Chapter Six

· · · · · · · · · · ·

Megan looked up at Logan's face as he glared down at her, his arm across her upper chest. He blinked at her a few times before his expression changed and he quickly released her.

Scooting off the bed, she said, "Hey, if you didn't want to share the bed, you only had to tell me instead of grabbing me that way." She rubbed her shoulders.

"Did I hurt you?" His voice was husky and gruff.

She backed away. "You like your space. No problem."

"No, it's not that." He rubbed his hand over his face, drawing her attention to his shadowy stubble, which gave him a dangerously sexy look. "I'm sorry I grabbed you that way. I didn't mean to scare you."

"What did you mean to do?"

He shook his head and looked away. "I was having a nightmare," he muttered.

"About being attacked by a librarian?"

"No." His bark of laughter held no humor. "A lot worse than that."

She moved a little closer. "Something to do with your job?"

"Yeah. So now you're probably adding this incident to your list of reasons why you dislike cops."

"I realize your job is stressful."

"You don't have to make excuses for me."

"Trust me, I'm not."

"So why do you have this thing against cops? Did a former boyfriend cheat on you? Or is it a philosophical thing?"

"No, it's very personal."

"So you did date a cop."

Megan shook her head. "Not me. Wendy, my best friend in college. We were roommates and bonded the minute we met. We were both a little dorky, loved reading and were Nancy Drew fans as kids. Oh, and we both collected vintage Lilly Pulitzer. What are the odds of that?"

"Since I have no idea who or what Lilly Pulitzer is, I can't give you the odds."

"She's a designer. Wendy and I both loved her floral dresses from the sixties."

"Some fancy designer to go with your fancy Streeterville address?"

"Hey, I was not born with a silver spoon. Far from it. I grew up on the South Side. Two blocks from Faith's house. Both our houses were brick bungalows and had the same floor plan."

"Yeah, I know all about brick bungalows. I grew up in one too."

"My family's business didn't take off until I was a teenager. The dresses that Wendy and I collected in college were picked up at garage sales and thrift stores. It was the fun of the hunt. We'd hit church rummage sales searching for our next find. You wouldn't understand."

"Sounds like me and my brother looking for parts for the 1969 Mustang we restored together. We'd go to swap meets and car shows searching for parts. So, yeah, I know about the fun of the hunt."

She suspected looking for car parts wasn't Logan's only hunt. He went after what he wanted. Sometimes that was a good thing. Sometimes it wasn't.

"Anyway," she continued, "our friendship just got deeper after graduation. She got her teaching degree. I got my library degree. We started our first jobs in our new professions. There was this cop who used to stop by the library where I worked. He was funny and nice and we became friends. But there was no chemistry between us. So I recommended that he meet my best friend, Wendy. Sure enough, they hit it off and began dating. They got married a year later. They had a baby girl a year after that."

"So what's the problem?"

"The problem is that he abused her. Verbally at first. Then physically. He terrified her. Warned her that if she called the police, they wouldn't do anything. And he was right. They refused to help. They looked the other way. His buddies at the precinct were all on his side, blaming Wendy for being a bad wife, for not understanding the stresses he was under." Megan paused, trying to get her residual anger under control. Her emotions were so close to the surface right now, not just because of Wendy but also because of what Megan had been through in the past twenty-four hours and the fact that she hadn't gotten any sleep. "She was afraid to tell me. I couldn't understand why she'd cancel our get-togethers. I thought she was just busy with the baby and her new life. I had no idea what was going on until she showed up out of the blue on my doorstep with her daughter and nothing but her purse and the clothes on their backs. Wendy had a black eye and a loose front tooth."

Megan took a deep breath before admitting. "I felt so guilty."

"Why?"

"Because I was the one who introduced her to the bastard."

"Did he abuse her when they were dating?" Logan asked.

"No, not at all."

"Then how could you have known?"

"I should have picked up on something. He blamed Wendy for setting him off. Then afterward he'd be all apologetic and say it would never happen again. But it did. She was afraid to tell anyone. Afraid they wouldn't believe her because everyone said what a great guy he was. And she was also afraid for their safety, because he'd make threats about what he and his buddies on the force would do if she ever tried to leave him or tell anyone."

"He sounds like a real bastard. You should blame him, not the entire force."

"Come on. You know spousal abuse is a problem among law enforcement,"

"A few rotten apples . . ."

"It wasn't a few rotten apples. It's the mentality that cops are special. Special allowances are made for them. And alcohol didn't help matters any. I don't have to tell you about the us-versus-them mentality that is so pervasive. You're not denying that, are you?"

"You have to understand that it's hard to realize what the job is like unless you've done it yourself. That's why cops stick together."

"The only thing I understand is that there is an

underlying violence in them that can be unleashed on the people they claim to love."

"Look, I don't deny that cops are exposed to violence on a daily basis. That doesn't mean they're all abusers. Plenty of bankers, lawyers and doctors are guilty of domestic violence too."

"The difference is that cops are used to giving orders and having them obeyed. They are control freaks."

"There's too damn much we can't control," he said bitterly. "I only wish we could. Maybe then . . ."

She saw the darkness flickering in his eyes. She knew anguish when she saw it. Her voice softened. "Maybe then what?"

"Things might be different."

"Things? What kind of things?"

"All kinds of things."

"Care to be more specific than that?"

"Not really." He rubbed his hand over his face. "What happened to your friend?"

"She's safe now."

"And?"

"And that's all I'm saying."

"You don't trust me." It wasn't a question.

"Not with her information, no. I'd rather be safe than sorry."

"That seems to be a personality trait of yours. Yet you took a risk and left the Venetian with me."

"Yeah, and look how well that turned out."

"What, you don't like our plush accommodations?" He swept his hand around the room. "You don't think they're quite as grand as your room back at the Venetian?"

She looked around. The drapes had large hearts on them and the painting over the bed was of dogs playing poker. "Not even close."

"You don't like the way they've 'rehabbed' the place?"

"I had no idea orange shag carpet was coming back," she said.

"This carpet looks like it never left."

"At least there are no stains on it."

"That you can see."

"I prefer to be an optimist," Megan said.

"How's that working for you?"

"It's gotten me this far, but I am starting to rethink that approach. It's true that I've always been the optimist in the family, but . . ."

"But?"

"I don't know." She shrugged. "I'm tired of always being the one to find the silver lining."

"Hey, it's a tough job . . ."

"But someone has to do it. Yes, I know."

"Finding the good in a bad situation is a special talent," Logan said. "I wouldn't knock it if I were you."

"I'm guessing you're not an optimist yourself."

"You've got that right," Logan said. "I come from a long line of pessimists. If you think your family is strange, you should see mine."

"I *have* seen yours. Your grandfather Buddy."

"He's only the tip of the Irish iceberg. And then there's the Polish side. Between the two branches, I have enough cousins and other relatives to fill a couple tour buses. I'm not kidding."

"What's strange about coming from a large family? Growing up, I thought it would be nice to have a lot of relatives. Do you have a lot of brothers and sisters?"

"No sisters. All brothers."

"How many?"

"Two brothers and two much younger half brothers still in middle school. My dad married three times and got divorced three times."

"Wow."

"He's a cop. As you said, the profession is tough on a personal life."

"What about you? How many times have you been married?"

"Just once," he said.

Megan's heart stopped. Had she been lusting after a married man? Had he been flirting with her? He didn't wear a wedding ring, but that didn't mean anything.

"I've only been divorced once too," Logan said. "And before you ask, no, it wasn't because of any abuse. I came home from work one night and found her in bed with another man."

"I'm sorry."

"Yeah, well, shit happens."

"Yes, it does. But I wish it didn't."

"That's what makes you an optimist."

Her eyes met his and the visual connection was incredibly intense, making her quickly look away. Or maybe it was the fact that he looked incredibly hot sitting in the bed, shirtless.

What had they been talking about? Wishes. Right. The thought flashed in her mind that she wished she was in bed with him, nestled against that bare chest, running her fingers over the impressive definition of his muscles . . .

Okay, she needed to stop that train of thought before it turned into a train wreck. She had to stop drooling and say something sensible. They'd been talking about his siblings.

"I wish I'd had siblings," she said, rather proud of how calm she sounded.

"Be careful what you wish for. My sibs are hell on wheels. But they've got my back."

"My dad had my back. At least, I always thought so. Now I don't know what to think. Why would he tell me my mother is dead when she wasn't?"

Logan shrugged. "You're asking the wrong guy. You need to ask him."

"I will. As soon as I get my head together."

"And we get out of here. *If* we ever get out of here."

"What makes you say that?"

"They don't seem real eager for us to leave, have you noticed that?" he said.

"They're just lonely. They don't get many visitors."

"That's an understatement."

"But they seem like nice people. Pepper showed me some wonderful vintage clothes. She offered to give them to me, but I insisted on paying for them."

"Of course you did."

"What's that supposed to mean?"

"I don't trust them," he said.

"They're a bunch of senior citizens who have led really amazing lives, if you take the time to listen."

"I heard about Pepper's Marilyn Monroe impersonation,"

"She never met Marilyn, but she did meet Dean Martin. She has some incredible stories."

"Incredible being the operative word. As in fiction."

"You think she's making everything up?" Megan asked.

"I think she's making a lot of stuff up. And she's not the only one. I think her two male sidekicks are guilty of the same fabrications."

"So maybe they elaborate their stories a little. That's not a crime."

Logan made a noncommittal sound.

"What? You think these people are criminals? What? They cheated at bingo? Stole some extra sugar packets from an all-you-can-eat buffet?"

"I don't know what they're up to, but they're up to something," he said.

"I'll bet you think everyone is up to something, right?"

"And I'd be right."

"Were you this suspicious before you became a cop?"

"I come from a long line of law enforcement officers."

"So the answer is yes."

"You've met Buddy. He isn't exactly trusting."

"Granted. But my grandmother has helped him see the silver lining in life."

Logan didn't look convinced.

"You don't think that's possible?" she said.

"To turn my grandfather into an optimist? Maybe where a slot machine is concerned."

"I can't believe he had a quickie marriage in Las Vegas and never had it annulled."

"He meant to. He's the first to admit he's not good with paperwork."

"Yes, but this was important."

"Cut the guy a break, would you?" Logan said. "Nobody is perfect. Not even you."

"What are you insinuating?"

"That you think you're smarter, better than . . ."

"Than Pepper? Than Rowdy or Chuck? *You're* the one who's been putting them down."

"You like them because they have good stories," he said. "You're a librarian. You like stories. Fiction is your thing."

"And distrusting people is your thing?"

His expression darkened. "If you'd seen the things I've seen . . . Never mind."

"I'm sorry. I didn't mean to imply that you haven't been exposed to some awful things."

"Forget it."

"Can you? Can you forget it?"

Logan didn't answer her question. "So you and Pepper bonded over a bunch of dresses, huh?"

"I guess you could say that. Anyway, I think I'll take a shower and change."

"I thought you were going to take a nap. I thought that's why you sat on the bed before. I didn't mean to spook you. Here, you can have it all to yourself." He climbed out of bed. "I can go sit in the chair."

"No, that's okay. I really need to get out of this dress." Right. That got her thinking of him helping her disrobe. Thankfully he didn't offer his help. "I got an oversized T-shirt and some other stuff from the gift shop." She picked up a plastic bag from near the door.

"They have a gift shop?"

She nodded. "There's not a lot of selection." She pulled the T-shirt from the bag and held it up.

"I Had Fun in Last Resort," he read. "I don't suppose the phones are in working order yet?"

"Not yet. Pepper said sometimes they go out for twenty-four hours at a time."

"Did she tell you how many people supposedly live in this place?"

"No. The subject didn't come up."

"Too busy talking about clothes, huh?"

"And local history."

"Wow, edge-of-your-seat stuff," he drawled.

"I thought it was. You probably wouldn't agree."

"Try me."

"Well, Fritz Holzenberger founded the town in the 1880s."

"And he named it Last Resort because Holzenberger was too long for a town's name?"

"No. He named it after a silver mine he owned: the Last Resort Silver Mine."

"It's a weird name."

"This area is full of strange names. Things could have been worse. The town could have been called Pickhandle Gulch. That town went belly-up."

"What a shame."

She giggled. "Yeah, I thought so." Her smile faded. "I don't even know if my mother has a sense of humor."

"Are mathematicians known for their sense of humor?"

"My dad has one. It's sort of a Thurber sense of humor. That's one of his favorite short-story writers."

"You really do need to sit down with your dad when you get back to Las Vegas and get the whole story." He held up his hand to quiet her protest. "I know, I know, you don't think he'll tell you the truth. But he might. And you won't know that until you confront him."

She pulled the photos of her mother out of her clutch bag and studied the young woman in them. "She looks so young. I can't believe she was at Woodstock. My mom, the hippie." She shook her head. "The question is, where is she now? Any why is she so hard to track down? Do you think my dad did that? Covered her tracks so she couldn't be found?"

"West Investigations is a big fish in Chicago, but there's no way they have the kind of power to erase data on the Internet."

"What if she's in the Witness Protection Program or something?"

He shook his head. "Jeez, you do have an active imagination. First you worry that she's going to somehow die before you find her and now you think she's in the Witness Protection Program. What's next, that she's been abducted by aliens?"

"How far *are* we from Roswell?"

"That's in New Mexico and we're far enough away."

"Don't worry," she said. "I'm not that hysterical. I'm not hysterical at all. I think I've been very calm, considering the things I've been through in the past twenty-four hours. A wedding, a crazy man trying to break up the wedding—"

"Hey, I'm not crazy—"

"I didn't know that at the time," she said before continuing to list her experiences. "The discovery that my grandmother's fiancé already has a wife, the discovery that my dead mother is alive after all, my first visit to a Nevada brothel, and now I'm marooned in a semi-ghost town and a motel with only one bed."

"I can sleep in the car."

"Are you protecting my honor or your car?" she asked.

"It's not my car. It's my buddy's car. He trusted me to take care of it.'

"Are you afraid someone is going to vandalize it or steal it? Last Resort doesn't seem like a high-crime area."

"Looks can be deceiving."

His ominous words stayed with her as she showered in the tiny bathroom. The pink tile around the tub was vintage but the toilet and sink were new. The towels were surprisingly soft and thick. The T-shirt went down to her knees and a pair of shorts took the place of her lacy black underwear, which she'd washed and left hanging to dry on the shower rod.

When she'd put them on yesterday afternoon, she'd never dreamed that she'd end up taking them off in the Queen of Hearts Motel in Last Resort with a sexy half-naked man of the other side of the bathroom door.

There was no way she could have anticipated the things that had happened to her in such a short time. Wiping the steam from the mirror, she stared at her reflection. Her wet hair curled damply around her shoulders, and her freckles stood out on her flushed cheeks. She looked like what she was . . . the girl next door. She tugged the baggy T-shirt off one shoulder and tried to strike a pose like Pepper had. The result made her crack up. No, she was definitely not sex kitten material.

Logan knocked on the door. "You okay in there?"

"Yeah." She turned the lock and stepped out. Her floral flip-flops were from the gift shop and went with her present outfit better than her other shoes.

"I heard you laughing in there. What was so funny?"

"Me." She pointed to herself.

Logan eyed her from head to toe. She didn't see a smidge of humor in his gaze. Instead, there was plenty of heat and sexual tension. He'd told her that looks could be deceiving, but he hadn't warned her that *his* looks at *her* could be downright heart-stopping.

That's when Megan realized she was in danger of having her heart stolen, and that was a felony she simply couldn't risk.

Chapter Seven

. . . .

A three-hour nap had Megan feeling a little rested but still somewhat on the groggy side. Before she'd fallen asleep, Logan had muttered something about a recon mission to check out their surroundings and left her on her own.

She sat up as he returned to the room.

"I didn't mean to wake you," he said.

"You didn't. What did you find out?"

"That we are definitely in the twilight zone."

"What's that supposed to mean?"

"I didn't see anyone but Rowdy, Chuck and Pepper."

"Maybe it's siesta time. People were in their houses taking naps like I was."

"I didn't go around knocking on doors," he admitted. "But the place looks deserted."

"Ah, but as you recently pointed out to me, looks can be deceiving."

"Rowdy wants us to join them in the café for dinner."

"Okay." She tossed back the covers. "I hope it's okay that I put a suitcase in the car earlier. It's filled with the clothes I bought from Pepper." She'd kept one outfit aside to wear this evening. She hurried into the bathroom to change, aware of Logan's watchful gaze as she paused to grab the clothes on her way. Her fast-drying underwear, which she'd left hanging in the bathroom, were ready to put on again. The jumper and a white shirt Pepper had tossed in at the last minute showed less skin than most of the outfits.

Yet the minute she stepped out of the bathroom, Logan eyed her and murmured, "Very sexy."

"You're kidding, right?"

He raised an eyebrow with pseudo-innocence. "You could always put the T-shirt and boxer shorts back on again. I was a fan of that look too."

"I'm starting to think you're a fan of women, period."

"Something wrong with that?"

"With the fact that you're a player?"

"I never said I was a player. A player would try to seduce you . . . like this." Bracing his hands against the wall on either side of her, Logan effectively boxed her in and caged her in his arms. "And then I'd try to make a move on you . . . like this." He leaned closer until his lips almost touched hers. "But I'm not doing that." His warm breath bounced off her mouth.

"You're not?"

He shook his head and back away. "No."

"Why not?" Wait, that hadn't come out right. She shook her head to clear it. She'd heard of the good cop/ bad cop routine, but hadn't heard about the seductive cop routine. And, wow, was Logan good at it. Clearly he was able to switch it on and off at will. The way he was wickedly grinning at her was proof of that. "I mean . . . never mind what I meant. Let's go eat."

Logan started his interrogation of Last Resort's trio of residents the minute he entered the café. Seductive cop had been replaced with inquisition cop. "Any luck with the phones yet?" Logan asked Pepper.

"Not yet."

"You know, you never actually said how many people reside in Last Resort now."

Pepper just shrugged and said, "I'm not good with numbers."

Logan turned his attention to Rowdy, who grinned and slapped him on the back. "Just relax and enjoy a good burger. How do you like yours?"

"Why is it so hard to get a straight answer out of you?" Logan said.

"Why are you so curious?" Rowdy retorted.

Logan narrowed his eyes at him. "Because something's not right."

"I'll tell you what's not right," Pepper said. "That some towns have actually had to disappear entirely because everyone left. Why, they've even had to sell some small towns. Coaldale was for sale—lock, stock and barrel."

"Of course, it was in a movie in the early '90s and it had an airstrip, so that made it more appealing," Rowdy added.

"We haven't put Last Resort up on the auction block. We're working hard to keep this town alive. We don't give up easily here in Nevada. We persist through drought and indifference." Pepper paused to grin. "Don't you love the way those two words sound together? I read that someplace and always remembered it. Well, not where I read it, but the two words. We're a tough bunch in these parts."

"And creative," Rowdy added. "Chuck is going to update our website."

"I have a grandson who's great with computers and Photoshop," Chuck said.

"He's phenomenal!" Pepper's voice rose several decibel levels.

"Can you tell Pepper is a big fan of Mary Murphy, aka the Queen of Screams, the judge from that TV show *So You Think You Can Dance*?" Chuck said. "Pepper can mimic her voice perfectly."

"Getting back to the website. We should play up the fact that the Last Resort Silver Mine is rumored to be haunted," Rowdy said.

"And have a treasure hidden in it," Chuck added.

Rowdy nodded. "Yeah, those would both be great hooks. We could get the ghost crowd as well as the treasure hunters."

"Tell me about the ghost and the treasure," Megan said.

"See? It's working already," Chuck said. "Our first interested customer."

"Your first *stranded* customer," Logan said. He eyed them suspiciously. "Unless this has happened before?"

"Unless what has happened before?" Rowdy said. "That someone drove into town in a 1957 Chevy that needs work? Not lately, no."

"Who do you know at the Butterfly Ranch?" Logan said abruptly.

Pepper blinked, then whispered, "Do you mean the brothel?"

Rowdy glared at Logan. "What kind of question is that to ask in front of a lady? Two ladies," he amended. "I don't know what they do in Chicago, but out here, we treat our women with more respect. I think you owe them both an apology."

Logan didn't back down. "And you owe me an explanation."

"Of manners?"

"No, of how we ended up stuck here."

Rowdy shrugged. "I can't explain fate."

"Was it fate?" Logan said. "Or was it sabotage?"

Now Rowdy was the one narrowing his eyes. "What are you talking about?"

"It wouldn't take much for a buddy of yours working as a bouncer at the ranch to tamper with the car so it would break down and force us to stop here. There was nothing wrong with the car until now. I can't help be suspicious as to why we'd suddenly run into trouble right outside your town. Maybe that's how you get people to stop here. Maybe you're running a con."

"Why would we want someone who visits brothels with his girlfriend to visit our fair town?" Rowdy folded his arms across his broad chest. "Doesn't sound to me like you're exactly a good example of an upright citizen."

"I'm not his girlfriend," Megan said.

"That's all you've got to say?" Logan stared at her. "How about coming to my defense?"

"I just wanted to clarify the girlfriend thing first," Megan explained. "We were only visiting the ranch to speak to the owner. We never actually entered the brothel part of the establishment. The owner knew my mom when they were both teenagers."

"Does your mom run a brothel too?" Pepper asked.

Megan quickly shook her head. "No, she's a mathematician."

"I believe you still owe these two ladies an apology," Rowdy reminded Logan.

"I'm sorry if I said anything to offend you," Logan said stiffly before glaring at Rowdy. "It's just frustrating when I can't get a straight answer."

Rowdy glared right back at him. "Are you accusing us of tossing cow paddies in your direction?"

"We've tried to be as truthful as we can," Pepper said.

Logan immediately latched on that. "As truthful as you *can*?"

"Right. I don't know when the phone service will be working again, so I can't give you the answer you want."

"I just want a straight answer."

"She just gave you one." Rowdy's expression changed to that of genial host . . . or circus ringmaster. "Now, let's get back to that burger. How do you want yours? Our credit card machine is out what with the phone lines being down, so you'll have to pay in cash. We don't take checks." He pointed to the sign next to the cash register. It was right next to the one that read NO SHOES, NO SHIRT, NO SERVICE.

"Things could be worse," Pepper said. "The electricity could be out as well." She turned to Rowdy and Chuck. "Remember that time a rattlesnake got into one of the transformers and the lights went out? In that case, we'd be eating fried rattlesnake by candlelight. And that's not as romantic as it sounds."

Megan didn't think it sounded romantic at all.

"Rattlesnake isn't on the menu tonight," Rowdy said. "So just tell me how you want your burger, Logan."

Logan sighed, apparently realizing this was one battle he wasn't going to be winning for now. "Medium-rare."

"How about you?" Rowdy asked Megan.

"Do you have any salad?" she said.

He looked at her as if she'd just asked him if he'd seen aliens. "Never mind," she quickly said. "I'll have my burger medium."

She'd never eaten in a place where the cook and others stood around and watched every bite you took. "How is it?" Rowdy asked.

"No one makes better burgers," Chuck said.

"Even Sinatra would love them. Dean Martin too," Pepper added.

"Aren't you guys going to eat?" Logan asked them suspiciously.

"Sure. We didn't know if you wanted us to join you. We didn't want to crowd you or anything," Pepper said.

Chuck pulled over another table, and a few minutes later they were all munching on burgers.

Out of the blue, the jukebox started playing all on its own, startling Megan. The song was Elvis's "You Ain't Nothin' but a Hound Dog." The song played through the "you ain't no friend of mine" verse before stopping as abruptly as it started.

"It does that sometimes," Pepper said. "Nobody knows why."

"Maybe it's that ghost from the Last Resort mine," Logan drawled.

"I'm just guessing that you don't believe in ghosts," Pepper said.

"You've got that right."

"You don't believe in much, do you?"

"Right again."

"It must be difficult being such a pessimist," Pepper said.

"Nah, it's easy," Logan said.

"Because you see the dark side of life in your line of work."

He nodded. "That would be an accurate observation."

"That's such a shame."

His expression hardened. "No need to feel sorry for me."

"Sure, there is. Right, Megan?"

Megan pointed to her mouth, which was full of a bite of burger she'd just taken.

"You can just nod," Pepper told her.

Megan shrugged instead.

Everyone stared at her, waiting for a longer response. She hurriedly swallowed, grabbing for her root beer when she almost choked. Logan patted her on the back.

His touch was beginning to feel right and natural and welcome. Very, very welcome. A dangerous sign.

They were in a place that time and everyone else had forgotten, creating a cocoon that wasn't real. She couldn't afford to forget that. Besides, she wasn't exactly in the most stable emotional state to begin with, given her recent discovery about her mother.

Earlier in their motel room, he'd demonstrated how vulnerable she was to the physical attraction broiling right beneath the surface between them. Leaning in to kiss her that way . . . teasing her.

"You okay?" Logan asked.

She nodded. She had to be okay. She had to stay strong and stay focused.

"So, do you feel sorry for me?" he asked Megan.

"No."

"I didn't think so." He tucked a strand of her hair behind her ear.

The rest of the meal was uneventful, perhaps because Megan remained silent, focused on her reaction to his simple touch. She really should be concentrating on ways to find her mother. Taking notes of things she recalled about her. Or had been told about her was more accurate since she didn't really have any memories of her. She'd been too young when she'd died . . . *disappeared*, she corrected herself.

Pepper picked up the conversational slack by telling colorful stories about the history of Last Resort told to her by her grandfather. "He made a fortune and then lost it on the turn of a card. I tell you, it just brings the hair up on my arm. Not that I have hairy arms, because I don't. Feel."

Megan and Logan quickly refused her offer and instead made their excuses to return to their motel room. Once inside, Megan opened the drawer in the bedside stand.

"What are you looking for?" Logan asked.

"Paper and a pen. A-ha." She triumphantly held up a small pad. "I wanted to make some notes."

"About your mother?"

"Of course. What else?"

"Maybe Pepper's stories."

"That was a nice distraction, but I haven't forgotten my mission." She perched on the edge of the bed. "I didn't bring my BlackBerry charger with me, so I didn't want to use up my battery by putting my notes there." She paused as a new thought occurred to her. "Won't Buddy be worried about you disappearing? I sent a text to my father saying I was okay. But Buddy doesn't have a cell phone."

"I was able to reach him before we left Las Vegas. He was in his room for a change."

"Why couldn't you have called him from Chicago to tell him about the annulment papers?"

"Because he was never in his room. I left voice mails but he didn't acknowledge them. He was probably staying in Ingrid's room."

Megan's eyes widened.

"What, that never occurred to you?" Logan said.

She waved her hands. "TMI. Too much information."

"Maybe they were platonically sharing a room like we are."

"You are such a liar."

"I'm a damn good liar," he said.

"Their situation is different than ours. Buddy and Ingrid were engaged. You and I are strangers."

"We're not strangers any longer," he said.

"Sure we are."

He shook his head. "I know you like chocolate chip pancakes and your burgers medium. You have 'Life Is a Highway' on your BlackBerry playlist. You like vintage clothes and Lilly Pulitzer designs."

She was surprised he'd remembered that much about her. Maybe being stuck with her, marooned here in Last Resort, meant that there was nothing else to think about. They were basically out of contact with the outside world.

"And you read Nancy Drew books as a kid. I also know you're tougher than you think you are," he added.

"How do you know that?"

"I'm a detective. It's my job to know these things."

"Your job?"

"Right."

"Your job really defines you, doesn't it?"

"It seems to—in your eyes."

"And in yours. I know you're a Chicago cop who likes his coffee black and his burgers medium-rare. But that's about it."

"That's not true. I told you about my family. About my marriage. It's more than you've told me about your personal life, aside from your mother."

His words made her realize he was absolutely right.

"Or did you block all that from your memory bank because knowing it would make me more human?" he said.

"I don't know what you mean."

"Yes, you do. And it scares you."

"I don't scare easily."

"No?"

"Okay, sometimes I do get scared, but not all that often."

"There's a definitive answer."

"Hey, I can be as definitive as the next person. I was definitive when you crashed the wedding."

"Yes, you were. You were damn definitive."

"Damn right I was. And don't you forget it."

"I'm not likely to. You're pretty unforgettable."

She smiled ruefully. "Not many women hijack you into tracking down their mother, huh?"

"No, not many." He looked around the room. "And not many end up with me in a cross between the movies *Deliverance* and *Viva Las Vegas*."

She laughed. "That's an unusual combination."

"Everything about the past twenty-four hours has been unusual," he said.

"Yeah, I know what you mean. It has been pretty strange."

"Law enforcement officers are accustomed to strange."

"I'm sure you are."

"You're not going to start feeling sorry for me like Pepper was at dinner, are you?"

"No way."

"I'm glad to hear that."

"I think you're trying to distract me from brooding about my mother. It worked for a while, but now . . ." Megan refocused her attention on the notepad in front of her. "Why would she walk away from her own child like that?"

"Maybe she thought she didn't have a choice."

"You mean my father threatened her?"

"No. I mean she could have had her own reasons for leaving that had nothing to do with you."

"But to leave your two-year-old daughter behind . . ." Megan shook her head. "I need to know why."

"Then you need to ask your father. Even if he doesn't tell you the truth, you have to ask."

"How can I know if he's telling me the truth or not?

That's the problem. I don't trust him anymore. He's broken that trust."

"Don't be so quick to dump on your dad. You don't have enough information to make any decisions. And you're exhausted. I got some rest this afternoon, but you didn't get much."

"I had a three-hour nap."

"So you're not tired?"

Her yawn gave her away.

"Why don't you go to bed?" he said. "I'll sleep in the car."

"But it's cold out there."

"It's balmy compared to Chicago in January."

"Balmy, huh?"

"Yeah. One of Buddy's contributions to my vocabulary."

"He does have an interesting way of verbally expressing himself. Faith told me he'd given up cursing, but she didn't know why."

"That's his story to tell."

"Right. I wasn't trying to be nosy or anything. So, uh, I guess this is good night then."

Logan nodded.

"Okay, then. Well, good night."

He headed for the door.

"Wait."

He turned to face her.

"You'll need a pillow and a blanket." She gathered both from the closet and handed them to him.

"See you in the morning, when we'll be leaving this twilight zone no matter what," he said.

"Sounds like a plan."

She shivered as the night air hit her. Logan waved her back into the room, his gesture assuring her he was fine. He had his tough cop expression going on, along with a sexy stubble thing that was altogether seductive. He was a man accustomed to having his orders obeyed, and she was a woman . . . but what kind of a woman was she?

Right before the wedding, she'd decided to move away from her girl-next-door image. She supposed visiting that brothel yesterday had been a step away from the good girl behavior. To be fair, she'd only been there because of Fiona's ties to Megan's mother. And Megan had been totally clueless about the ranch being a brothel.

So she wasn't a wild rowdy girl . . . woman. She changed back into the oversized Last Resort T-shirt and boxer shorts she'd bought at the gift shop. Staring at her reflection in the medicine cabinet mirror, Megan wondered what her real persona was. Was she like her mother? Would she have gone to Woodstock had she been a teenager at that time?

Not very likely. Megan had always played it safe. Until now. And look where her spontaneous actions had gotten her: washing her face with a guest-sized bar of Ivory soap in a pink-tiled bathroom. She brushed her teeth before switching off the light and opening the door.

She yelped when she saw Logan standing near the bed.

"Sorry," he muttered. "I left my iPhone." He held it up as if to prove he wasn't lying. His smile slowly grew until it became a grin as he eyed her with definite male interest.

"I didn't mean to startle you," he said.

Okay, then. What *did* he mean? She recalled all too well how she'd reacted to him staring at her cleavage back at the Venetian's elevator bank. She had gone all weak-kneed and fluttery inside several times since then. Right now being one of those times.

"Uh, I should be going," he said.

"Right."

"Lock the door after me," he ordered.

She did. And then she climbed into bed and tried to

sleep. She really did. But to no avail. She kept worrying about him out there in the cold. That blanket she'd given him was too thin to provide much warmth. She turned on the light and rummaged through the closet to find another thicker blanket. She took it out to him. Logan's body, sprawled out along the backseat, had replaced the suitcase she'd placed on the backseat earlier.

She knocked on the car window—gently because she knew how he felt about the borrowed Chevy.

He immediately hopped out of the car. "What's wrong?"

"Nothing. I just thought you might need a thicker blanket, that's all." She started to take it from around her shoulders when he stopped her.

"You need that."

"No, there's another one just like it inside." She happened to look up while looking over her shoulder and was stunned by the number of stars. "Wow. Is that the Milky Way?"

"Yeah." He moved closer and guided her a little to the right. "And that's the Big Dipper."

"You don't get night skies like this in the city," she said, trying to sound calm and nonchalant, while her hormones were shooting stars.

"No, you don't."

Right. She should move away. She really should. She kept her eyes on the stars. Then her sense of fair play took over. "It's really freezing out here," she said. "You should come inside. It's a king-sized bed. It's big enough for both of us."

"I'm tough."

"I can't sleep if you're out here."

"Afraid of the dark?"

"No."

"Then what's the problem?"

"My sense of fair play." Her teeth started chattering. "Come inside. It's too cold to sleep in the car."

He hustled her inside, thicker blanket and all, pausing only long enough to grab the extra blanket and pillow from the backseat. "I put your suitcase in the trunk, in case you were wondering."

"Okay."

She scurried into bed and pulled the covers up to her chin. Logan paused in front of the thermostat to turn up the heat. "Let's hope that works."

"It's a big bed," she said. "There's enough room for both of us."

Instead of commenting, he merely nodded, kicked off his shoes and climbed under the covers fully dressed.

"Good night, then." She turned so that her back was to him. She thought it would take her hours to fall asleep but she quickly drifted off.

She woke with her cheek on something warm. Blinking in confusion, it took her a moment or two to realize she was resting on Logan's bare chest. He must have discarded his T-shirt during the night. The room had gotten quite warm and they'd both kicked the heavier covers out of their way. She tried to shift away before he woke up and caught her cuddling against him. But when she moved, he tightened his hold on her.

She froze. Great. Now what should she do? She waited a minute or two and tried again. This time she got a little farther away before he hauled her back. Muttering something, he nuzzled her neck before sliding his lips across her jaw to her mouth. He was kissing her. In his sleep. And he was doing a damn good job of it.

His hands were on the move now, sliding beneath her oversized T-shirt to cup her breasts. She really should protest. Had that moan come from her or from him?

She was playing with fire here, a dangerous pastime and one she'd never indulged in before. Her body's instant response bypassed her brain. She wanted him. He wanted her. He kissed her again. He wasn't aggressive, he was damn tempting.

One of his hands shifted from her breast lower, to the waistband of her boxer shorts. His fingers had barely slipped beneath before she came to her senses. She had to stop this . . . now!

She shoved him away and rolled out of the bed. She stood there a moment, trembling, her fingers pressed against her lips still throbbing from his kiss.

Unable to speak coherently, she escaped to the bathroom. Fifteen minutes later, she finally found the courage to come out. She was wearing the jumper and white shirt again from the night before.

Looking out the open motel room door, she could see that Logan was once again wearing his T-shirt and was out by the car. As she packed up her few belongings, he came back inside and went into the bathroom without saying a word. When he came out, his dark hair was damp, as if he'd splashed cold water on his face.

"Let's get out of here. I don't care if the car is still busted, we aren't staying."

"We can't leave without saying good-bye. And what about paying for the room?"

"Fine," he growled. "But we are not lingering. Got that?"

"Got it." Neither one of them referred to what had happened in the bed they both avoided looking at.

Rowdy greeted them as they walked into the café. He was sitting on a chair near the door. "Morning, folks. Sleep well?"

"Not really." Logan cautiously eyed the shotgun Rowdy had setting across his lap.

"Here's the deal," Rowdy said in a no-nonsense voice of authority. "The two of you spent the night together in the same motel room without benefit of marriage. And that's illegal here. Looks like you two are going to have to tie the knot or face the consequences."

Chapter Eight

. . . .

"Tie the knot?" Megan repeated in disbelief.

"Back up a minute. What do you mean, it's illegal here?" Logan demanded. "You mean here? In Nevada?"

"No. Here in Last Resort. It's also illegal to spit on the sidewalk."

"You don't have any sidewalks."

"If we did, it would be illegal to spit on them." Rowdy shifted his hand on the shotgun. "Lucky for you, I'm a justice of the peace, as well as mayor and town sheriff. You have a choice—jail or a wedding. And the costs for a marriage license and ceremony come to a thousand dollars."

"This is ridiculous."

"It's a fair price," Rowdy said defensively.

"I'm not talking about the money," Logan said. "I'm talking about this con."

"I agree," Megan said. It wouldn't be the first time someone had underestimated her, thinking she was a mild-mannered librarian only to find she was more than capable of looking out for herself. "You are the one who put us in that room, Rowdy. You said you only had the one room available."

"It *was* the only room we had available."

"Then why didn't you mention this little law of yours when you offered us the room?"

Rowdy shrugged. "You didn't ask."

"How could I ask about a law I never heard of?"

"Not being aware of the law doesn't give you the right to break it," Rowdy said.

Megan gritted her teeth and counted to five before saying, "Logan slept in the car."

"Only for an hour."

"How do you know that? Were you watching us? Did you have some kind of hidden camera on us? That is soooo illegal. And sleazy!" Her stomach turned at the thought of him watching her and Logan in bed this morning.

"Calm down. There were no cameras involved."

"Then how do you know Logan didn't sleep in the car?"

Rowdy pointed out the window. "I sat here and watched you. I saw him go in the room with you and he didn't come out until this morning."

"Maybe he did in the middle of the night. Maybe you fell asleep and missed that part."

"I didn't miss any part."

"I think you did," she said. "I think you fell asleep and missed the part where Logan slept in the car."

"Nice try, but no cigar."

Which was something Buddy would say, but that

didn't endear Rowdy any to her. "This would never stand up in a court of law."

He shrugged.

"Where's Pepper?" Megan demanded. "I can't believe she'd approve of this."

"I've heard of speed traps in small towns, but nothing this asinine," Logan said as Pepper came out of the café kitchen.

"Hey, we are not a small town," Pepper said. "We are an itty-bitty-teeny-weeny town with revenue issues."

"So you try to make money by forcing people to get married?" Megan shook her head in disbelief. "How crazy is that?"

"No crazier than you going to a brothel to find out about your mother."

Logan held Megan back, as if afraid of what she might do to Pepper. Instead he gave Pepper an icy stare and said, "That was a cheap shot."

Pepper looked embarrassed. "Yes, it was. I'm sorry. I shouldn't have said that about your mother, Megan. You can't help the fact that her high school friend is a madam."

"Hey, people in glass houses shouldn't throw stones," Megan said. "It's not like you all are taking the high ground here by threatening us with a shotgun wedding."

"What's the problem? You know you like Logan," Pepper said. "We're just speeding along the inevitable. You two were meant for each other."

Logan released Megan to turn her to face him. "What did you tell them?" he said suspiciously.

"About what?"

"About us. Did you and Pepper have a little heart-to-heart over those vintage dresses? Did the two of you come up with this plan?"

"What?" Megan blinked at him in amazement. "What are you talking about?"

"You're not denying it."

Furious at his accusation, Megan turned to Rowdy. "I'll pay a thousand dollars *not* to marry him."

"No can do. And I'll have to tack on another five-hundred-dollar fine for trying to bribe a city official."

"Nice going," Logan told Megan thirty minutes later as they both stood in Last Resort's version of a jail cell.

"Me?" she said. "What about you?"

"What about me?"

"You should have done something."

"Like what?"

"You're a cop. I thought you were supposed to be trained to handle situations like this. Instead you did nothing. Which makes me think maybe you're the one who planned this."

"How do you figure that?"

"Like I said, you were passive. That's not like you."

"The guy had a shotgun."

"So?" she said. "I'm sure you've faced armed situations before, right? You could have taken him. Heck, *I* probably could have taken him."

"Don't even think about it. I've seen too many cases where things went bad fast because someone got cocky where a gun was involved." He took her by the shoulders and gave her a stare meant to make her obey. "Promise me you will not do anything stupid."

"Define stupid."

"Trying to grab anyone's weapon."

"Okay."

"Or disobey my orders."

"Whoa, I have a problem with that one," she immediately said.

"Why?"

"Because you're too bossy."

"*I'm* too bossy? What about you? You're the one who got the additional charges against us. I could have talked us out of it," he said. "That's what I'm trained to do. Instead you flew off the handle and made things worse. And now we're locked in some stupid storage room."

"I did *not* fly off the handle."

He rolled his eyes.

"And the only talking you did was to accuse me of plotting the shotgun wedding with Pepper," she said. "That did not help the situation."

"I'll tell you what didn't help the situation. You offering to pay a thousand dollars not to marry me."

"I can't stay here forever. I've got a flight to catch."

"Like I don't?" he said.

"We wouldn't be in this mess if your car hadn't broken down."

"Excuse me?"

"You heard me."

"You are unbelievable. The truth is we wouldn't be in this mess if you hadn't insisted on leaving Las Vegas in the first place," he said.

"I didn't know we were heading for a brothel."

"Would that info have made any difference?"

"No, probably not," she said. "I can't believe they locked us up in here!" She kicked the door in frustration.

"That's a good way to break a toe," he said, unimpressed with her temper tantrum.

"They didn't even let us eat breakfast before they arrested us. My stomach is growling."

"Get over it."

"Get over it? That's your way of being supportive?"

"Yeah."

"Well, it stinks," she said. "That is not supportive."

"We could make out."

Her eyes widened and her mouth dropped open. "What?"

He shrugged. "Hey, you wanted supportive."

"Sex isn't supportive."

"It is if you do it right."

Megan was momentarily distracted by the image of having sex with him before she recovered enough to make a response. "I'm not speaking to you and I'm not making out with you."

"You made out with me this morning."

"I was asleep."

"Not so asleep that you didn't respond to me."

"You grabbed me."

"You didn't protest."

"I was asleep."

"So you already said."

She narrowed her eyes at him. "Are you accusing me of lying?"

"I'm accusing you of bending the truth. But I'm not really telling you anything you don't already know. I can tell by that blush on your face that you know damn well you responded and you were awake. Very awake."

Megan silently cursed her pale complexion. "That's not a blush. I'm flushed because it's hot in here." She banged on the door. "Let us out!"

"I don't think that's going to help."

"Well, I'm not going to just stand here and wait for help." She looked around the room, searching for something to aid with their escape. The storage room held an odd assortment of things—from ceramic flowerpots to velvet paintings to stacks of quilts . . . and teacups. They had teacups! Or one special teacup. She was a "cupa-holic." She collected both orphaned teacups and saucers as well as just orphaned teacups without their matching saucers.

She couldn't believe her eyes as she gazed upon the Wedgwood teacup and saucer she'd been searching for since her college days. Her breath caught and her heart beat faster. It couldn't be.

She stood on tiptoe trying to reach the top shelf, where the teacup and saucer forlornly sat amid miscellaneous broken crockery. Her fingers were still a few inches away. She looked around trying to find something to stand on.

"What are you doing?" Logan said.

"I'm trying to reach that cup."

"Why? Do you think it will unlock some secret passageway out of here?"

She refused to answer him. Instead she tugged a rickety chair from the other side of the room.

"Please tell me you're not dumb enough to try and stand on that," Logan said.

She lifted one foot, ready to step up when he swooped in from behind her to stop her. She wiggled against him. A bad move, because her bottom was pressed against the placket of his jeans and she could feel his arousal. She froze.

"I'll get the damn cup for you," he growled in her ear.

She shivered at the brush of his mouth against her skin.

He abruptly let her go and reached around her to retrieve the teacup from the shelf.

"Careful," she said as she saw the dainty china in his large hands.

"If I was careful, I'd have stayed in Las Vegas," he muttered. "Hell, if I was careful I would have stayed in Chicago."

"No, you wouldn't have. You had to help Buddy."

"And I've never been accused of being careful. Here." He shoved the cup and saucer at her.

She cradled them in her hands and stared down at them in awe. "I can't believe my luck."

"Yeah, I can't believe my luck either. It's gone down the toilet since I met you."

"That's not fair," she said. "None of this is my fault."

"Well, it sure as hell isn't mine."

Distracted as they were glaring at each other, they didn't realize the door had been opened. Rowdy stood there behind the screen door with its safety bars.

Rowdy shook his head at them. "Well, you two have certainly caused a major kafuffle. I'm not sure what to do with you."

"Let us go right now and we won't press charges against you," Logan said.

"Against me?" Rowdy's eyes widened.

"For unlawful detention. Extortion. Entrapment. Assault with a deadly weapon. Unlawful use of a firearm."

"I didn't assault you," Rowdy protested.

"You threatened to do so," Logan said.

"I did no such thing."

"Like I said, release us, let me call a tow truck and we'll be out of your hair."

"The wedding thing seemed like such a good idea when Pepper, Chuck and I talked about it," Rowdy said morosely.

"Has it worked before?" Megan had to ask.

"You were our first attempt. Maybe if we'd fixed some of the bugs . . ."

Megan shook her head. "I'd stick with that haunted mine thing instead. A much better bet."

"Possibly." Rowdy sighed. "What do you two have against marriage, anyway?"

"A shotgun wedding isn't exactly the beginning of a dream marriage," Megan said.

"So if we toned down the shotgun part . . ."

"It would still be a bad idea," she assured him.

"Why do you have a teacup clutched against your chest?" Rowdy asked.

"It called to me," she said.

Rowdy looked at her as if she were a few pancakes short of a stack.

"Being locked in that room nearly drove her over the edge," Logan said. "You could be looking at a civil lawsuit on your hands here. Do the smart thing and call a tow truck to come get us. I know the entire landline phone thing was a con."

Rowdy sighed. "You don't need a tow truck. Chuck was a top mechanic before he went into infomercials."

"Forgive me if I don't trust him or you," Logan said sarcastically.

Chuck joined the group, wiping his greasy hands on a paper towel. "The Chevy's ready to go."

"How do I know you haven't sabotaged the car to die a few miles from here?"

"You've got my word on it. Come on, I'll show you what the problem was."

"He has to release us first," Logan said.

"Just lift up on the left bar. The door pops open." Rowdy stepped aside and regretfully watched Megan and Logan walk past him.

Megan gathered her teacup and saucer close and hurried after Logan. She found him bent at the waist, leaning over the side of the Chevy, with the hood popped open. He and Chuck were examining the fine points of the engine and other stuff she couldn't follow.

"You can keep the teacup," Rowdy told her. "And the shotgun wasn't loaded."

"That doesn't excuse your behavior," she said.

"That law really does exist. It's still on the books here."

"Then you better repeal it."

"It seemed like a good idea when Pepper found a book about strange laws around the country," Rowdy said. "We decided to take a look at our town's laws and . . ."

The sight of Logan's denim-clad butt as he leaned over the car distracted her from the rest of Rowdy's apologetic explanation. She remembered seeing a T-shirt at the airport when she'd first arrived proclaiming that Girls Go Nuts for Cowboy Butts. Logan might not be a cowboy, but he definitely had a very fine butt.

She didn't know whether to be relieved or sad when Logan straightened and got in the car to turn the ignition. The car purred like a cat. Or so Chuck proclaimed proudly.

Logan returned to the motel room to grab her stuff and toss it into the car before telling her, "Let's go."

Looking at Pepper and Rowdy's woebegone faces, Megan couldn't help feeling sorry for them. "What about the hotel bill?"

Rolling his eyes, Logan shoved his credit card at Pepper, who raced inside to run it before returning with the slip for him to sign.

"Wait, I should pay for that," Megan said. "As you pointed out, we wouldn't be here if it weren't for me."

"And as you pointed out, we wouldn't have stopped here if it weren't for the car. So we'll split the bill. You can pay me back later."

"Why are you holding that ugly teacup?" Pepper asked as she joined them beside the car. Her long platinum hair blew in the breeze, as did the neon–lime green hair bow that matched her neon-lime jacket and capri pants.

"She wants to take the cup with her," Rowdy said.

"You're welcome to it, girl. I meant to toss it in the trash years ago. Hey, I'm sorry things didn't work out with the marriage thing. I hope ya'all come back and visit us again sometime."

"I'd rather poke a stick in my eye," Logan muttered under his breath.

"You drive careful now, you hear?" Pepper added.

Megan briefly wondered why Pepper seemed to be channeling Granny from *The Beverly Hillbillies*, before deciding she really didn't care to know the answer.

"Be sure to tell your friends about us as a tourist destination," Pepper shouted out.

Logan rolled his eyes. "Right. Like that's going to happen."

Megan elbowed him from the passenger seat. "Be polite."

"They're lucky I'm not pressing charges against them."

"We didn't sabotage your car so you'd stop here," Chuck said. "I hope you believe me."

"I believe you," Megan said.

"We're leaving now," Logan stated.

"I hope you enjoyed your stay at the Queen of Hearts Motel," Pepper said.

"Yeah, it ranks right up there with the Bates Motel," Logan said.

"Good luck," Rowdy said, waving them off.

The elderly trio stood there and watched them leave. Megan knew because she couldn't resist turning around and looking. "I hope they'll be all right."

"Stop waving at them. You're just encouraging their bad behavior."

"Rowdy told me the shotgun wasn't loaded."

"So that makes it all okay?" Logan said.

"No, I told him it didn't."

"Well, then that's peachy," he said sarcastically. "As long as you and Rowdy made up. Your stay worked out fine. You left the place loaded with old clothes and an ugly teacup."

"It's not ugly. And you should be counting your blessings instead of complaining."

"How do you figure?"

"We could be returning to Las Vegas as a married couple."

"Now there's a scary thought," he said.

"Not that it would have been legal anyway."

"Yeah, but who needs the hassle."

"Right." Nice to know that he considered her a hassle. But then, could she really blame him? After all, she was the one who'd talked him into helping her, who'd insisted on tracking down Fiona. And if they hadn't been out at the Butterfly Ranch, the Chevy wouldn't have broken down and left them stranded in Last Resort.

"It is now Monday morning," Logan said, "and we've been gone since Saturday night."

"Technically, it was early Sunday morning. It was past midnight when I got into your aqua car."

"It's blue, not aqua. And it's not just a car."

"It's a classic Chevy 1957 Bel Air."

"That's right. You need to show proper respect."

"It's a nice car."

"Nice? Nice is for wimps. Not for a baby like this."

"Will your friend be upset that we put so much mileage on it?"

"It's not like we drove all the way to Reno and back. And he trusts me to take good care of her."

There was that word again. *Trust.* Hard to earn, and even harder to restore.

Megan also noted the way Logan's voice softened when he talked about the car, as if it were a living being.

Take good care of her. Logan had actually taken pretty good care of Megan during their time together, starting curbside back at the Venetian when he'd rubbed her arms against the chill of the night air. And then there were the more sensual touches—sliding a strand of hair behind her ear, almost kissing her last night, and totally making out with her this morning . . .

Being held at gunpoint and then tossed into the storage room "jail" had distracted her from thinking about that kiss and those caresses. But now that she was in the car with him, there was no escaping the memories. Megan hoped she wasn't blushing.

Sure, they'd talked about it in the storage room. But Logan clearly hadn't bought her excuse that she'd still been asleep when she'd let him kiss her. As excuses went, even she had to admit that one was pretty lame. But what was she supposed to say? That she'd been so incredibly turned on that she couldn't think straight?

Like she'd ever admit to that. It did occur to her that her actions spoke louder than her words, and her actions had clearly indicated that she hadn't been thinking clearly. But since then, Logan had gone out of his way to let her know that he thought she'd brought him bad luck and that she was a nuisance.

There had been that comment about having sex while they were in the storage room, but he'd just been teasing her. She certainly wasn't going to bring up the subject again anytime soon.

"How long until we're back at the Venetian?" she asked.

"Less than an hour now." He reached for his iPhone and made a call. "Hey, Gramps, I'm on my way back and I need a favor. Can you pack up for me and bring my bag to the front of the Venetian so I can make my flight? Thanks. Yeah, we're fine. See you soon."

Megan's stomach flip-flopped. She wasn't ready to face the music yet. Sure, the road trip had been a way to get information about her mom, but it had also allowed her to avoid confrontation with her dad.

She still didn't know what she was going to say when she saw him. And she saw him sooner than she expected, as he was waiting along with Buddy at the entrance of the Venetian.

Her dad's brown hair was rumpled and his face was lined with worry.

"How did you know I'd be here?" she said as she got out of the car, still clutching the teacup and saucer. Logan had also gotten out of the car and come around to join his grandfather.

"Buddy told me," her dad said.

"He's been acting pretty crazy," Buddy explained. "They all have. Except for Ingrid, of course, although she's still mad and not speaking to me unless it's about you and Logan. So when Logan called me, I passed the info along. Nice car, by the way."

"It's blue," Megan and Logan said in unison.

Her gaze got caught up in his for a moment before he broke the eye contact.

"I've got a plane to catch and a vintage car to return," Logan said impatiently.

"Can I hitch a ride with you to the airport?" Buddy asked. "I've got all my stuff." He pointed to a suitcase beside him.

"Sure." Logan picked up the suitcase and put it in the car. The bellman at the Venetian had already removed Megan's vintage suitcase and bags from the trunk.

"Right. Well, thanks again for your help," Megan told Logan as he slid into the driver's seat.

Instead of answering, Logan simply drove off. No good-bye, no wave, no hug.

And just like that, Megan's road trip was over, and it was back to reality . . . a reality she still felt unprepared to face.

Chapter Nine

. . . .

Megan reluctantly turned to face her father.

"Where have you been?" he demanded. "I've been worried sick about you."

Megan had had the entire drive back to think about what she was going to say to her dad, but instead she'd been distracted by that wildly intense kiss she'd shared with Logan. She could no longer deny that there was tons of chemistry between them.

Yet he couldn't dump her fast enough and head off into the sunset, leaving her alone to face the music.

Fine. She could cope on her own. No problem. She didn't need Logan.

Sure, she *wanted* him, but she'd get over that.

Thank heavens she hadn't been coerced into marrying him in Last Resort. It wasn't as if she'd been the one trying to trap him in a shotgun wedding. She'd even offered to pay a thousand dollars *not* to marry him.

Was that why he'd taken off so fast? Because she'd insulted his male ego? Why was she even worrying about this now when she had this huge family crisis to deal with?

"Are you okay?" her dad repeated. "Where have you been?"

"We went to a brothel. But I didn't marry him." Okay, so Megan must be more out of it than she realized for those words to have come tumbling out of her mouth uncensored. She clasped her hand over her mouth to prevent any more verbal mishaps.

"Logan wanted to marry you in a brothel?"

She paused to try to mentally collect herself before replying. "No, nothing like that. He didn't want to marry me."

This news did not improve the disapproving look on her father's face. "He took you to a brothel and refused to marry you?"

"It was only because we spent the night together," she said.

"What?"

"The shotgun wedding. Not that they went through with it."

"Who?"

She waved his question away. She wished she could wave all his questions away. "It's not important."

"Logan takes you to a brothel, spends the night with you and then involves you in a shotgun wedding scenario, and it's not important?"

"He was probably trying to marry her to get his hands on her money," Jeff said, having joined them in time to hear Megan's rambling explanation. "He can't be making much on a cop's salary."

"He's a police detective," she said.

"I'll have his badge for this," Jeff growled.

"No, you won't." Megan glared at her uncle. "You won't do a thing to Logan. Leave him alone."

"How can you defend him?" Jeff demanded.

"Because he was helping me."

"By taking you to a brothel? How could that help you?"

Megan wasn't ready to admit she was looking for her mom. Not yet. So she had to come up with some other reason no matter how lame. "The history of prostitution. You know how I've always been interested in history."

"So he took you there as a history lesson?" her dad said.

"Yes." She nodded emphatically.

"Bull," her uncle said. "I'm not buying that story for one minute."

"Enough," Gram said, coming forward for the first time to put her arm around Megan's shoulders. "Can't you see how tired the poor girl is? Let her be now. She's returned and she's okay. That's all that counts. So you boys just back off. Megan and I are going to go have some alone time." She indicated to the bellman to follow with Megan's vintage suitcase and her bag. "What a lovely teacup," she said as she guided Megan through the lobby to the elevators leading up to their floor.

"I've been looking for it for ages."

Gram frowned. "Did you lose it somewhere?"

"No."

"I don't understand."

"I know."

"Your room or mine?" Gram asked.

"Mine."

"Where did you get the suitcase? I had one of those back in the sixties."

"It's a long story."

"We've got some time."

Megan tipped the bellman and closed the door after him. Looking around, she was astonished to realize how much had changed in her life since the last time she'd been here. She'd been preparing for Faith's wedding, so happy for her cousin. Never suspecting that her own life was about to change dramatically. Megan decided to get right to the point. "Did you know that my mother is alive?"

"No. Neither one of my sons told me their hare-brained idea or I would have set them straight. I only found out yesterday."

Megan wearily sank onto the bed. "Why couldn't my father just tell me that he and my mother got divorced? And why did she leave and not want to see me again? Was she driven away? Threatened?"

Gram sat beside her. "I can't see your dad threatening anyone."

"But I can see Uncle Jeff doing that," Megan said.

"Possibly. Your mother wasn't the easiest person to get to know."

"I already heard she wasn't a people person."

"Who told you that?"

Megan paused, wanting to confide in Gram but unsure if she could trust her.

"What are you up to? And don't try saying nothing. I can read that face of yours like a map. I know every freckle, every expression . . ." Gram's eyes reflected her love as she cupped Megan's cheek with her hand.

"You have to swear not to tell anyone else," Megan said.

"More lies? More secrets? Don't you think it would be best to just come clean?"

"No. Not yet."

"Why not?"

"Because they'd prevent me from doing what I need to do."

"They?"

"Dad and Uncle Jeff."

"And what is it exactly that you need to do?"

"Find my mother."

* * *

"Flight 1231 to Chicago Midway has been delayed because of bad weather in Chicago." The announcement was made with blasé indifference. "We'll update you when we have more information. Please remain here in the gate area for further announcement."

"Great." Logan swore.

So did Buddy.

Logan raised an eyebrow. "I thought you gave up cursing."

"I did."

"So what changed?"

"Everything, boy-o," Buddy said morosely. "Everything."

"Care to be a little more specific than that?"

"I will if you will."

"Meaning?"

"Why did you take off with Megan like that?"

"It's complicated."

"I wrote the book on complicated."

"You sure did. Which is why you need to concentrate on clearing up your own affairs and not worrying about other people's problems."

"Problems?" Buddy instantly latched onto that. "You have problems?"

Logan shrugged. "Everyone has problems."

"Work-related problems?"

Logan just gave him a look.

"Fine." Buddy shrugged. "Don't confide in me. Are you the only one with problems or does Megan have problems too?"

"Like I said, everyone has problems."

"I knew it." Buddy slapped his hand on his thigh. "I knew something was up. You wouldn't just take off with her like that."

"You make it sound like I kidnapped her or something."

"That's what Megan's dad and uncle thought."

"That's ridiculous. Why would I want to kidnap her?"

"Money. They always think about money. I mean, that dad of hers is a numbers guy, after all. So you and Megan just took off for some alone time? Time to explore the chemistry you claimed didn't exist?"

Logan gave him another look.

"What?" Buddy said. "You don't think I can put two and two together?"

"You can put two and two together, all right. And come up with five."

"If that's not the reason, then what else is going on?"

Logan wasn't about to tell him. The whole point of this exercise was to keep his grandfather out of Megan's drama. But he knew Buddy well enough to know that if he didn't say something, his grandfather would just start digging on his own. So he chose the lesser of two evils. "Fine. It was the chemistry."

Buddy slapped his knee. "I *knew* it! I told you the two of you would be a good match."

"Yeah, well, we'll see about that."

Now it was Buddy's turn to give Logan a look. "Don't you go breaking her heart now. I've got enough trouble with Ingrid without having you alienating her by hurting her beloved granddaughter."

"Which is why we shouldn't get involved any further."

"Balderdash."

Logan wasn't sure if it was a good sign or not that Buddy had reverted to his customary selection of arcane expressions instead of cursing. Hopefully it meant that things were returning to normal. Which would be a good thing. The past weekend hadn't been normal. But then, he hadn't seen normal in some time.

"Don't let the fact that your dad has been unlucky in love turn you off a good relationship," Buddy said.

"I'd call three divorces more than just unlucky."

"So he's made mistakes. We all have. Like your marriage to Angie. I don't know what you were thinking. Well, I do know. You were listening to the wrong part of your anatomy. I know that situation was tough on you, her cheating on you that way. And with an EMT, of all people."

Logan held up his hand. "Don't start."

"From your own district. Is that why you transferred? You shouldn't let a woman get to you that way."

"Like Ingrid hasn't gotten to you."

"She'd never cheat on me. And besides, she's my soul mate, not a badge bunny."

"I didn't know Angie was a badge bunny when I married her."

"I know Megan doesn't have a thing for men in uniform," Buddy said. "You wouldn't have to worry about anything like that happening with her. She wouldn't cheat on you. She's as honest as the day is long. I mean, look at that face." He pointed over Logan's shoulder.

Logan glanced over his shoulder. Megan was walking from the gate agent's desk toward them.

"I thought you'd be on your way back to Chicago by now," she said when she was standing in front of Logan and Buddy.

"I thought so too," Logan said.

"Our earlier flight had mechanical trouble so we were transferred to this one and now it's delayed," Buddy said before glancing behind her. "Where's Ingrid?"

"She's in the ladies' room."

"And the rest of your family?"

"They're around."

"We were just talking about you," Buddy said.

"You were?"

"Yes. Logan told me why you two hooked up this weekend."

Megan prayed that Buddy didn't know the current connotation of "hooked up," as in, "had sex."

"Logan finally admitted it was the chemistry between you two that did it."

She exchanged a look with Logan. Even though it had only been a few hours since she'd seen him, she'd missed him. She was only now realizing that. She shared a connection with him, a bond that showed no signs of abating, despite him dumping her at the Venetian like unwanted baggage. That really should have cured her of whatever it was she had going with him. "What exactly did you tell Buddy?"

"To mind his own business."

"He didn't say those words exactly, just gave me one of those looks. You know."

Megan nodded. She knew. She'd been on the receiving end of a number of looks from Logan. From that intensely sexual stare while waiting for the elevator shortly after they'd first met to his look of impatience when she and Fiona talked about local history, to his visual seduction when she put on that jumper and white shirt. "Would you mind if I talked to Logan privately for a second, Buddy?"

"Not at all. You two lovebirds go right ahead."

Once she and Logan were a safe distance away, she said, "What did you tell him?"

"I didn't say anything about you looking for your mother, if that's what you're afraid of."

"I'm not afraid of that. I could use his help."

"Hey, the agreement was that I help you and you don't drag my grandfather into your mess."

His words stung. Here he was again, making her feel like a nuisance. "Then what did you tell him?"

"I let him think . . . you know . . . that there was something going on between us."

"You did what?"

"It seemed better than the alternative."

"To you, maybe. Not to me."

"News flash: The world doesn't revolve around you."

"It doesn't revolve around you either," she retorted.

"What's that supposed to mean?"

"You're a detective. Figure it out for yourself."

"Are you upset that Buddy thinks we have a thing going on?"

"A thing? Is that what you called it?"

"I didn't label it exactly. What's the problem? We can use that as a smoke screen for a few days."

So he thought he'd only have a "thing" with her for a *few days*? Sounded more like a fling to her. She supposed she should warn him about her earlier verbal flubs. "My relatives think we're doing more than just dating."

"Why?" he said suspiciously. "What did you say?"

"I let a few things slip."

"What kind of things?"

"Um, I may have mentioned visiting the brothel and . . . um . . . sharing a bed."

"You *what*?"

"And I let slip about the shotgun wedding, but pointed out that we didn't get married."

"So you told your relatives that I took you to a brothel, bedded you and then refused to marry you. Great. I'll bet that went over well."

"My uncle was pretty upset," she said. "I had to make up a reason for visiting the brothel."

"I'm afraid to ask."

"I said you were helping me."

"Right. Helping you. By taking you to a brothel."

Megan nodded. "Because I was interested in the history of prostitution in Nevada."

Logan rolled his eyes. It was an expression she was coming to know quite well.

"That's the best you could come up with?" he said.

"I didn't have a lot of time to think about it."

"I can't believe they bought that."

"They didn't really, but I've been avoiding them since then. Except for Gram."

"Talking about me?" Gram said as she joined them. Turning to face Logan, she added, "Megan told me how you helped her in her mission to track down her mother," she said. "I appreciate you looking out for her."

"Gram is sworn to silence," Megan added.

"And I know that I can count on you to continue looking after her once we're back in Chicago," Gram said to Logan.

"I don't need 'looking after,'" Megan said.

"That's a matter of opinion," Logan said.

"Hey, I'm not the one whose car broke down in the middle of the dessert, stranding us in Last Resort. That was not my fault."

"It wasn't my fault either," he said. "It's not like I wanted to be marooned there any more than you did."

"Right. You never want to see me again. I get that."

"I never said that."

"You didn't have to. The way you dumped me on the doorstep at the Venetian said it all."

"I didn't dump you."

"You sort of did," Gram said.

"Thank you." Megan's look told Logan, *See? I was right.*

Logan defended himself. "I had a flight to catch, which was canceled when I got here. I've got a job waiting for me back in Chicago."

"So do I," Megan said.

"Children, children." Gram shook her head. "Try to be nice."

"Is there a problem over here?" Buddy asked almost hopefully. "Anything I can do to help?"

"Yes. Don't propose to a woman if you're still married to someone else," Gram said tartly.

"I told you, I didn't know I was still married. I thought it was annulled. It only lasted two days."

"A lot can happen in two days." Gram gave Megan a meaningful look.

"Children, try to be nice," Logan said, repeating Gram's earlier words.

"Can I get you girls anything while we wait?" Buddy asked. "A drink or something to eat? I saw a couple of places along the concourse."

"We're fine," Gram said. "We don't need your help."

"Now Ingrid, don't be like that. How long are you going to stay mad at me?"

"As long as it takes."

"What are you two doing here harassing my family?" Megan's uncle demanded as he joined them. "Don't make me call security. Beat it."

"You beat it," Buddy said, sticking his chest out like a riled-up rooster. "We were here first."

"And they weren't harassing me," Megan said. "We were having a pleasant conversation, which you interrupted."

"They're seeing each other," Buddy said. "You better get used to it."

"What do you mean, 'seeing each other'?" Uncle Jeff demanded.

"What do you think I mean?"

"All I know is that your no-good grandson took my niece to a brothel. Did he tell you that?"

Buddy looked at Logan, who remained silent.

"And then he took her to bed," her uncle added for good measure.

Buddy's bushy eyebrows rose to his hairline. "You bedded her at a brothel? Megan, I thought you were a librarian."

"I am a librarian," she said. "What does that have to do with anything?"

"Librarians shouldn't be doing such things." Buddy shook his head.

"I didn't bed her in a brothel," Logan growled. "I didn't bed her at all."

"There was only one room available at the Queen of Hearts Motel and we had to share the bed, but it was a huge king-sized bed," Megan explained.

"So there was no hanky-panky going on, then?" Buddy said.

Megan cursed her blushing cheeks. "That's none of your beeswax," she shot back, using one of his favorite phrases.

"Look, the car broke down, we were stuck in this rinky-dink town in the middle of nowhere for the night." Logan's voice was matter-of-fact. "That's it."

"What about the shotgun wedding?" The question came from her father, who'd just joined them.

"It was the mayor's idea of a joke," Logan said.

Wow, Logan was a much better liar than she was. Megan decided to keep quiet and let him do the talking for a while.

"Sounds like a strange joke to me," her uncle said.

"The mayor was a strange kind of guy. Right, Megan?" She nodded. She could do that without messing up.

"We got things straightened up and got the car repaired and headed straight back to Vegas," Logan said.

"Why didn't you call from . . . where did you say you

were?" Her uncle eyed Logan as if administering a visual lie detector test.

"Last Resort. And their landlines were out," Logan said. "We couldn't get any cell service. Right, Megan?"

Another nod. She was getting good at this. Not that she was a yes-girl. She had her own mind.

But she needed a break from the inquisition. And she had yet to sit down and talk to her father about the lies he'd told her most of her life. She just wasn't ready to go there yet.

"It all sounds suspicious to me," her uncle maintained.

"Everything sounds suspicious to you," Gram said, rejoining them with a giant smoothie from the health food stand a short distance away.

"You could benefit from being more suspicious," Megan's uncle told Gram. "You too," he told Megan.

"Come along, Megan." Gram hooked her arm in hers. "We don't have to put up with this."

"Wait." Megan was afraid to leave Logan and Buddy with her male relatives. Not that her dad would do anything, but her uncle was another matter.

As if reading her mind, Buddy said, "There now, don't you be worrying about us. We'll be just fine." His glare at Megan's uncle belied his statement.

She looked at Logan, seeking reassurance. Instead she got another eye roll.

"Maybe I should stay . . ." she said uncertainly.

To her astonishment, Logan slung an arm around her shoulders and tugged her closer. Since her other arm was still hooked with Gram's, her grandmother came along with her, bumping into Megan, which forced her even closer to Logan's body.

Leaning down, he whispered in her ear, "Beat it." Then he kissed her on the forehead and set her free.

Chapter Ten

. . . .

"**I'm** so glad to be home. You have no idea what I've been through," Megan told her black cat, Smudge, who greeted her at the door. Megan dumped her suitcases and sank onto the nearest chair. Smudge immediately jumped onto her lap and commiserated by butting the top of her head against Megan's chin. "I'm a different person than when I left. I have a mother now. A mother who is alive."

Funny how she could talk to her cat about it, but not her father. She'd managed to avoid him for the most part in their hurry to make it to the airport in time for their flight. And then she'd bumped into Logan. She was sure he'd have already left.

He'd ended up being seated across the aisle from her. Her dad and uncle watched him like hawks from their seats in the row directly behind. He responded to their surveillance by putting his seat back and sleeping for the duration of the flight. Buddy had gotten stuck in a seat way in the back of the plane.

Her cell phone rang and the ringtone of "Memories" from *Cats* told her that it was Gram calling. "Hi, Gram."

"I just wanted to make sure you got home okay."

"I got home just fine. Smudge was here to greet me. How about you?"

"I think I might have a nap. It was a very busy and eventful weekend."

"That's an understatement."

"Yes, it is. Anyway, check your e-mail because Faith sent us some pictures from New Zealand. She and Caine seem to be having a great time."

"I'm glad someone is."

"Me too."

"I don't want Faith to know about this situation with my mother," Megan said. "I'll tell her myself when she gets back from her honeymoon. Unless she already knows?"

"No, she is as clueless as I was."

"So only my dad, Uncle Jeff and Aunt Sara were in on the deception?"

"That's what your dad told me. You can't avoid talking to him forever, you know."

"I know. I just need to get my head straight first. Remember, you promised not to say anything about me trying to find my mother."

"I know."

Smudge bumped her nose against Megan's chin and gave her yodeling meow that said, "Feed me."

"I've got to give Smudge her dinner."

After disconnecting her phone, Megan just sat for a moment, petting her purring cat and enjoying the sensation of being home. She'd decorated her condo to be a comfortable space. It started in the living room with one wall covered in built-in bookcases. Another wall was taken up with floor-to-ceiling windows with a view of Lake Michigan. She'd stuck to a palette of just three colors in her decorating—blue, pink and green. A mix of painted wood and rustic pine furniture combined with a soft, light blue slipcover on her comfy couch gave the room a cozy feel. The framed set of Carl Larsson prints on the wall had been a gift from Gram.

Smudge meowed again, reminding Megan to feed her. "Come on, you."

Smudge's purr increased several decibel levels as Megan picked her up and carried her to the kitchen. The white cabinets with their glass fronts in the upper cabinets contrasted nicely with the honed black granite countertops and old-fashioned black hardware. The mahogany-stained oak floors throughout the condo provided a warm base.

After giving Smudge some gourmet cat food as a reward, Megan started unpacking. She started with the Wedgwood teacup she'd found in the storage room in Last Resort. Opening one of her upper kitchen cabinets, she carefully placed it beside her small but special collection of other orphan teacup-and-saucer sets. They all displayed similar vivid reds that had turned to pale pink and blues. Most had a floral motif. About half had matching saucers, while the others she'd matched herself, introducing a solo teacup to a new saucer companion.

She had a story for each of her dozen or so collectibles. She'd found the Royal Staffordshire "Devonshire" teacup and saucer when she and Faith had stopped at a garage sale on the way back from the Kane County Flea Market. The Royal Doulton "Spring Meadows" teacup beside it was from the flea market. And the 1930s Polka Rose cup and saucer were a find from a Stillwater, Minnesota, antique shop she'd visited while in Minneapolis for the Public Library Association convention a few years back.

Staring at the Wedgwood addition reminded her of Logan's suggestion that they have sex in the storage room. On the plane, she'd been amazed to discover that he was just as sexy asleep with his head tilted at an awkward angle. He hadn't appeared to have any nightmares during the flight.

They'd shared a lot during their weekend together. Not the least of which was that embrace in bed. No, embrace didn't begin to cover what they'd done. "Making out" wasn't sufficient either. It was so much more than that. His hands on her bare breasts, his mouth consuming hers.

Megan shook her head and firmly closed the cabinet door. She could still see the Wedgwood through the glass. Just as she could still feel his hands on her body.

The last words he'd said to her were, "Beat it." Sure he'd kissed her forehead after that, but . . . what did it all mean? She didn't have a clue.

Megan focused on finishing her unpacking. But the memories continued unabated as she unpacked the new clothes she'd bought from Pepper in Last Resort. She laundered some and set aside those that needed dry cleaning, all the while remembering her time in the semi-ghost town. Especially her time in bed with Logan.

She rushed around, determined to get everything back in order. The clean clothes went in her closet and drawers, the suitcases in the back of her coat closet.

She shouldn't be thinking about Logan. She needed to focus on her mother. She had so many questions that they were all starting to jumble together, so she got her BlackBerry and started making a list of questions to ask her dad. She'd never really been a huge list-maker in the past, but helping Faith with wedding planning had convinced her otherwise.

QUESTIONS TO ASK DAD.

Why did he say my mother was dead?

Why did they get divorced?

Why didn't they share custody of me?

Had he been in touch with my mother since she'd left?

Had she ever tried to get in touch with me?

Did he know she'd gone to Woodstock?

No, she couldn't let him know that she knew that or he'd want to know how she'd found out. She quickly deleted that last question off her list. Surely she had more questions than, what . . . she counted them . . . just five. But these were a good start. And maybe his answers would instigate more questions.

At this point her thoughts were just so confused that she needed some kind of guideline to keep her focused. Because the feeling of having the rug yanked out from under her hadn't gone away.

•   •   •

Logan headed straight from the airport to start his shift at the police station. The building was old and smelled of industrial cleaner and old coffee. He was greeted at his desk by Ria, aka Detective Maria Delgado, his partner.

"Must be nice to take off for Vegas on a minute's notice," Ria said.

"I have a cousin who works for the airlines." It was the only reason he'd been able to get a seat on the next flight out, even if it meant sitting across from Megan. If her family had had its way, he and Buddy would still be sitting in the Las Vegas airport a week from now. "Besides, I told you it was a family emergency."

"Yeah, right. As in you had to play some serious poker or you'd go crazy. Was that your emergency?"

"There was a situation with my grandfather."

"Who is an even more serious poker player than you are. Did the old guy get into trouble?"

"Yes, but not at the poker table."

"Really?" Ria prodded him with her elbow. "Come on, share the juicy details."

"Get a life."

"I have a life."

"Then focus on that."

She stared him down. As the daughter of a Marine drill instructor, Ria was damn good at stare downs. Then she slowly smiled. "You met a girl."

"I meet a lot of girls."

"No, you met a *girl*. A woman. In Las Vegas. Is she a stripper?"

"Hell, no."

"A showgirl?" Ria asked.

"I was there to help out my grandfather."

"Was *he* in trouble with a stripper or a showgirl?"

"You have a one-track mind. Get it out of the gutter."

"It's the company I keep. It's hard to be all girly-girl hanging around you morons." She swept her arm in a semi-circle to include the rest of the police officers in the vicinity.

"Hey, don't blame us. You were that way before you became a cop. I think you were born with that don't-mess-with-me attitude," Logan said.

"I'm just trying to make my pop proud," she said. "How about your dad? Is he doing better about you transferring here?"

"Define better."

"That bad, huh?"

Logan shrugged. "Families are a pain in the ass."

"Yeah, but they've always got your back."

Logan remembered telling Megan that and her confessing that she'd wished she'd had some siblings.

"A-ha!" Ria pointed at his face. "I knew it! You're thinking about that girl you met in Vegas."

"You're delusional."

"Don't bother putting your cop face on now. It's too late. I saw the look in your eyes."

"When was your last vision test, Delgado?"

"A month ago, and I have 20/20 vision," she instantly replied.

"Been sniffing any glue? Smoking any weed from the evidence room? Stealing any vodka from the flask in Schmidt's bottom desk drawer?"

"None of the above. I'm just naturally observant."

"Yeah, right."

"Don't try changing the subject. There's no wiggling out of this. You met a girl and you're afraid to talk about her. And you got defensive when I thought she might be a stripper." Ria paused and narrowed her dark eyes at him. "*Ay dios mio,* tell me she's not another damsel in distress."

His stony face gave nothing away, but Ria knew him well.

"She is!" Ria socked his arm. "Will you never learn? You didn't marry her in Vegas, did you?"

"Of course not. Marriage made me what I am today— happily divorced from my ex-wife."

"Which was the right move for you. I have to admit that marriage doesn't always suck," Ria said. "Sometimes it works out okay. I had my doubts and it took my guy two years to convince me to say yes to his proposal. But I'm glad I did. And he's lucky to have me."

"You really have to deal with this low self-esteem problem you have, Delgado."

Ria grinned. "Hey, if you want something in this life, you've got to ask for it and go after it. My guy did that. Nobody is going to hand it to you on a silver platter. At least not in our families. Now, the West family is another matter."

"The West family?"

"Yeah, the owners of West Investigations, the biggest investigation firm in the city."

"What about them?"

"Their head honcho was in talking to the chief a while ago. You wouldn't happen to know anything about that, would you?"

"No. Why should I?"

"Because his parting words, which we all heard, were 'Tell Doyle to stay away from my niece.' So the girl in Vegas was Megan West, huh? I Googled the family and found the info. I knew all this when I started interrogating you. I gave you the chance to confess on your own . . . which you didn't do."

"I'm not confessing diddlysquat."

"Diddlysquat? Is that another one of your grandfather's sayings? I love those. I should keep a list of them."

"I didn't do anything wrong."

Ria sighed. "If I only had a dollar for every time a guy said that to me."

"Tell me again why I agreed to partner with you?" he growled.

"Because you like me. Adore me, actually. Would be totally lost without me."

Logan rolled his eyes.

"I realize you can't admit it out loud," Ria said, "but we both know it's true."

"I'll tell you what's true. And I'll even take a polygraph test to prove it." He motioned her closer and pointed to the pile of papers on his desk. "I didn't join the police force because I like paperwork."

"I'd really like to help you out, but I picked up the slack while you were off wooing Megan in Vegas. I figure this is payback time."

"Come on, Delgado. I'll order Chinese from your favorite place."

"I have a husband at home waiting for me. He already ordered Chinese from my favorite place. But nice try."

Logan sighed.

"And good luck with Megan," Ria added with a grin. "It sounds like you're gonna need it. Or you could be smart and stay *far* away from damsels in distress like her."

• • •

Megan was ready to return to work Tuesday morning. It was downright cold, in the low 40s, as she stepped outside, but then this was Chicago in November, not Las Vegas. A few yellow leaves stubbornly clung to the trees lining her street. They matched the yellow sweater she wore along with brown pants and a faux sheepskin coat. Her Ugg boots kept her feet warm during her commute to work at the North Shore branch of the Chicago Public Library.

In really bad weather, she took the bus. But since the CTA had raised fares yet again, she walked whenever she could. She didn't have a gym membership and didn't need one with the eight-block hike.

She stopped midway though her walk to drop a few dollar bills in the open guitar case of a street musician, a regular on her route. Nodding his appreciation, he kept playing despite the cold weather. He'd once told her that he grew up in Anchorage so Chicago's weather didn't faze him.

A gust of wind threatened to lift her cloche off her head so she tugged it down even farther. Nothing like fresh air in the Windy City to really wake you up. Most of her fellow commuters making their way to work on foot had their iPods playing, as did she, although she'd paused it when approaching the street musician even if he didn't know she had done so. It seemed the polite thing to do. She resumed play as she crossed the street and moved on.

Instead of listening to some of her favorite tunes, she was playing a podcast from the American Library Association conference that had taken place way back in July. So she was a little behind schedule. She'd been busy helping her cousin plan her wedding.

Megan had saved some of the photos that Faith had e-mailed from New Zealand. She and Caine looked divinely happy.

"How was the wedding?" Tori Holt asked the second Megan stepped foot in the library staff room. Tori was part Southern belle and mostly punk rocker, an unusual combination that made her one of Megan's favorite friends at work. Tori's short hair was dyed neon pink, and not only were her ears pierced multiple times, but so was her nose. Her musical tastes ran from Muse to Mozart and her literary faves included Shakespeare and too many graphic novels for her to choose a favorite. Born and raised in Alabama, she'd gone up north for college and stayed.

Megan removed her hat and hung up her coat before answering Tori's question. "The wedding was fine."

"Uh-oh. Something in your voice makes me think there was trouble during the trip. Did you lose money at the slot machines or something?"

"Or something."

"My cousin lost over five hundred dollars gambling in Vegas."

Megan had lost more than that. She couldn't put a price tag on losing the trust she'd had in her father because of his lie. No amount of money could replace that. She planned on speaking with her father after work today . . . unless she chickened out, which was a definite possibility.

"I'll bet your cat missed you." Tori was a big animal lover who frequently volunteered at the Anti-Cruelty Society.

"I was only gone four days, but Smudge acted like it was four weeks."

"I remember when you first got her from the shelter. A skinny little black kitten. Black kittens and cats are often the last ones adopted, but you went right for her. Remember how you had us trying to come up with a name for her?"

Megan nodded and smiled at the memory. "You came up with some innovative ones."

"Some of my faves were Elsie—or LC for Library of Congress. Dewey had already been used too much and is a male name. But Izzbin would have been good for ISBN."

"She responded to Smudge."

"How progressive of you to let your cat choose her name. Just one of the many things I like about you. I also like the fact that you don't nag me about the fact that I haven't submitted the rest of my paperwork for the workshop at PLA."

"Your first workshop at the Public Library Association is a big deal. What are you waiting for?"

Tori grinned. "For you to nag me."

Megan complied. "Get a move on, girl."

"That should light a fire under my heinie," Tori said.

Megan laughed. "I haven't heard it put quite that way before. Is that wording a Southern thing?"

"It's a Holt family thing. One of my uncle Bo's favorite sayings. He's a real character. Every family has one, not just Southern families. Actually, some of my family members think I'm the character in the family tree." She tugged on her pink hair. "Not that I agree with them. What about you? Who's a character in your family? Is it your dad? I love the way you call him a 'mathlete' when you talk about him. I think that's so cute. So is he the character in your family?"

A week ago Megan would have denied that. Her dad was the quiet, reliable one. Now he defied labeling.

"What are the requirements for 'being a character'? If it's unusual sayings, then the award would have to go to my grandmother's fiancé, Buddy." Megan hoped that Buddy would once again become Gram's fiancé after they got over this bumpy patch. "He says stuff like *balderdash*. Or *none of your beeswax*." Megan wanted the spotlight shifted from herself to someone else. Shanti Gupta, the branch's children's librarian, arrived just in time. "What about your family, Shanti? Is anyone strange?"

Shanti's long, silky black hair was gathered back with a colorful hair clip. She favored wearing dark colors with splashes of color, which today were provided by a silk scarf in shades of red and purple to accentuate a black top and pants. "Everyone in my family is strange," Shanti said.

Aisha Davis, the branch library's circulation manager, who'd heard Shanti's reply, joined the discussion while stashing her packed lunch in the staff fridge. "Hey, if you really want strange, then you should've seen the family that came in here yesterday. They were all dressed like vampires. The mom and the two tween girls."

"Obviously big *Twilight* fans," Megan said.

"Yes, but do you really have to dress the part?"

"Apparently they thought they did."

"The thing is, they didn't want a recommendation on vampire books. They were looking for a cookbook of Siberian pastries. I sent them over to the reference desk."

"Because if it was an easy reference question, they'd just ask Google," Tori said. "We get the tougher ones."

"Yes, but we are librarians," Megan said. "We can handle it. We can handle anything."

"Except more budget cuts from the city," Shanti said. "We're already badly understaffed as it is."

"Which reminds me," Megan said, "I've got circ desk duty tomorrow, right, Aisha?"

Aisha nodded

Megan said, "But first I've got to get through today, including finishing last month's report. And getting ready for the Adult Book Club meeting here tomorrow night."

"Good luck getting all that done while working the reference desk all afternoon," Tori said.

Megan grinned. "I'm good at multitasking. It's a requirement here in libraryland." She felt better being on her home turf. Here she was sure of her identity. She was confident of her place in the world.

Time went by quickly as the reference desk was busy with one patron after another. One was a fan of narrative nonfiction like *Devil in the White City* set in Chicago; another had just finished *Seabiscuit* and wanted recommendations on what to read next. Megan had to gently ask what appealed to the reader of each book in order to hook her up with something she'd like. Next came a complicated question about genealogy, and then a very pregnant mom-to-be wanted baby name books.

The rest of the day was a blur as Megan completed the October monthly report and made notes about discussion questions for the book club meeting the following evening, as well as going through several issues of *Booklist*, *Publishers Weekly* and *Library Journal* for book purchases. Then there was the pile of paperwork on her desk, which had somehow grown to twice the size it had been before she'd left for Las Vegas. She also had to create two book displays and refill the one for Thanksgiving cookbooks.

Life was hectic here in libraryland. But it sure beat having to deal with her family situation. Megan knew she couldn't keep hiding forever, though. So after work, she headed to West Investigations where she knew her father was working late.

She walked into his office, took a deep breath and said, "We need to talk."

Chapter Eleven

· · · · · · · · · · ·

Her dad's face paled. Megan's heart ached at his nervous reaction to her words. They'd always been so close. She would have bet a million dollars that he'd never lie to her, certainly not about anything big.

Sure, he might fib and tell her she was the smartest girl in the world when she was growing up. Or that freckles were God's way of saying you're special. But to tell her that her mother was dead when she wasn't . . .

"Why don't you sit down?"

Megan shook her head. She was too wound up to sit. "Why?"

He sighed. "I never meant for you to find out the way you did."

"You never meant for me to find out, period."

"I thought maybe when you were older . . ."

"I'm almost thirty, Dad. Were you waiting for me to

collect Social Security before telling me? Or were you waiting for my mother to really die?"

"No. It's complicated." He nervously tugged on his trademark quirky math tie. "I never wanted to hurt you. That was the last thing I wanted. I was trying to protect you."

"From what? My own mother?"

"I just thought it was simpler to tell you that she'd died."

She couldn't believe what she was hearing. "Simpler? How can you say that?"

"Divorce is a complicated subject for a small child to comprehend."

"Other parents manage. They don't lie and say that someone has died when they haven't. What did you do to drive her away?"

"Me?"

"Or was it Uncle Jeff? Whose idea was it to lie about my mother's death? Gram says she didn't know anything about it."

"She didn't. We figured the fewer people who knew the truth, the better."

"Who is *we*? You and Uncle Jeff?"

He nodded.

"Yet Aunt Sara knew."

He made no reply.

"What were you thinking?" Megan demanded. "I don't get it. Did you pay my mother off to stay away from me?"

He still didn't comment.

She immediately pounced on his silence. "You did, didn't you? I knew it!"

"She received a generous divorce settlement."

"And in exchange, you got complete custody of me."

"Your mother loved you, but she wasn't able to cope with parenthood."

"What do you mean? Did she have postpartum depression or something?"

"Something like that."

"Then why didn't you get her help? Take her to a doctor or something."

"I tried. She wasn't real cooperative."

"Is that why you got divorced? Because she went into depression?"

"No." He looked hurt by her accusation. "I'd never abandon her in her time of need like that."

"Then what happened?"

He rubbed his forehead. "It's hard to explain."

"What aren't you telling me?"

"Relationships are complicated."

"Was she cheating on you?"

"No."

"Were you cheating on her?"

"No!"

"Then what?"

"We grew apart."

"Have you been in touch with her since she left? Has she been in touch with you?"

More silence.

"You're still not telling me the truth. I should have known that after lying all these years, you wouldn't be willing to tell me everything."

"I've made a mess of things."

Tears prickled the back of her eyes. "Yeah, you have."

"I don't know how to make it right."

"By telling me the truth."

"I can't. Why can't you just believe that I did what I did because I thought it was in your best interests? You know I'd do anything for you."

"Anything but tell me what really happened." She wiped her tears away. "I have a right to know."

"I know you do. I just don't know how to tell you."

"Is she in some kind of Witness Protection Program or something?"

His startled look told her that hypothesis wasn't accurate. "No. What makes you think that?"

"The secrecy. Was *everything* you told me about her a lie? Did you really meet her when you both reached for the same book at the library when you were in graduate school?"

"That's the truth."

"Is she really a mathematician?"

"Yes."

"I don't know what to believe anymore."

"Believe that I love you and that I always will."

"That might have been enough when I was a small child, but it's not enough now. You've broken the trust. You were the one who did that, not me. And telling me that you did it to protect me without saying anything more than that . . . Is it your way of trying to turn me against my mother? By making her into this scary figure that I needed protecting from? Is she an evil person?"

"No."

"If you had problems, the two of you, that's okay. I get that. Marriages break up all the time. So do families. But what would make my mother walk away from me? It had to be a very large sum of money. And how could you do that to me? Deprive me of knowing my own mother by telling me she was dead? We even spread her ashes over Lake Michigan when I was eight years old. You said she loved to sail on the lake."

"She did. And you seemed to need some kind of closure. We never had a memorial service or anything at the time. You wanted a funeral like you'd had for your goldfish. Those were your exact words. 'Goldie had a funeral and so should Mommy.' "

Megan couldn't believe what she was hearing. "So because my goldfish had a funeral you made up one for my mother?"

He nodded.

"The difference is that my goldfish really was dead and my mother wasn't! What was in that urn? What did we spread over the lake?"

"Ashes from the fireplace," he admitted.

"That's sick!"

"I was desperate."

"And I was just a kid. A kid without a mother."

"I tried to make that up to you."

"Instead of telling me the truth. That's all you had to do."

"It's not that black-and-white."

"Yeah it is, Dad. It really is. Until you're ready to tell me the truth, all of it, I don't think we have anything further to say. Call me when you're ready to tell me everything. Until then, I'd rather be left alone."

She left his office but her little-girl heart remained behind—bruised and battered. Her entire childhood had been based on a series of lies. She needed to go home, hug her cat and eat some pizza. A *lot* of pizza.

• • •

Later that evening, Megan was curled up on her couch wearing her favorite comfort lounging outfit—a red waffle-knit henley teamed with red-and-black flannel pants—while waiting for the pizza delivery guy to arrive. Smudge was waiting with her, doing her purring lap cat thing.

"Miss Megan, this is Danny Boone, your doorman, calling."

Hearing her doorman's gentle Southern voice on the phone always made Megan smile. Born and raised in

Dolly Parton's hometown of Pigeon Forge, Tennessee, Danny retained his country drawl despite having lived in Chicago for three years. Obsessively polite and fiendishly organized, Danny did his job with Swiss-timepiece efficiency. Or Swedish efficiency, as Gram would say. Tall and lanky with warm brown eyes, Danny sounded more timid than he actually was.

"Yes, Danny?"

She expected him to tell her that the pizza guy was here and ask for permission to send him up. Instead Danny said, "There's a police officer here to see you. He says his name is Detective Logan Doyle with the Chicago Police Department. His badge and ID confirms that. I wanted to alert you to his presence before I allowed him farther. He doesn't have a warrant or anything like that, or I would have had to let him in without telling you."

No wonder poor Danny sounded more timid and concerned than usual.

"Send him up, Danny. And send up the pizza guy when he comes, please."

"Sure enough, Miss Megan."

Danny only used "sure enough" when he was really flustered.

Megan could relate. She felt pretty flustered herself. What did Logan want?

She soon found out.

Logan did not look like a happy camper. But he did look like a sexy unhappy one. Grumpy looked good on him. "Did you know that your uncle showed up at headquarters and spoke to my boss about me not seeing you again?" he said.

"Oh, no! I told him not to do that."

"For all the good it did."

"I'm so sorry. I'll speak to him again."

He gave her a mocking look. "Yeah, that'll work."

She gave him a librarian look, the one full of power and reprimand. "You didn't have to come all the way over here to tell me this. You could have just called me."

"I wanted to see your face when I asked you about it. To see if you were lying or not."

"I'm not lying!"

He made some noncommittal noise. Wait a second, was that his stomach growling? She gazed down at his washboard tummy covered with a chambray blue shirt tucked into dark pants. "When was the last time you ate?"

"I had something from the vending machines at the station."

As if on cue, the pizza delivery guy stepped out of the elevator. She handed the box of Giordano's deep-dish to Logan while she signed for the pizza, and tip, to be charged to her credit card.

"You might as well come in while you're here," she told Logan.

He gave the box he was holding a yearning look before shaking his head. "I've got to go. I just wanted to see if you were behind your uncle's visit."

"I wasn't. How could you even think that?" She paused after catching sight of a neighbor walking down the hallway. A very nosy neighbor. Grabbing a handful of his shirt, she tugged Logan and her pizza into her apartment before quickly shutting the door.

"I'm guessing you're not used to men turning down your invitations to come in?" he noted dryly.

"I don't issue that many invitations."

Smudge meowed as if confirming that statement.

"Nice cat." He set the pizza box onto her rustic dining table in order to lean down and pet Smudge. "I had a black cat named Trouble. He died a few years ago of old age."

"I'm sorry."

"Why? Trouble had a good life." He straightened. "I should be going," he said abruptly, as if regretting sharing that piece of personal information with her.

"Come on. Stay. I can't eat all this pizza by myself."

"Then why did you order it?"

"I was depressed at the time."

"Why? What happened?"

"I talked to my dad."

"I'm guessing from the look on your face and the size of that pizza that it didn't go well."

"He didn't really give me any straight answers. Just said he was trying to protect me."

"From what?"

"He wouldn't say." She stepped into the kitchen to gather plates, cutlery and napkins before returning and setting everything on the table. "I asked, but he wouldn't be specific. He did confess that he'd paid off my mother to stay away. Here, eat." She handed him a plate with a two-inch-high piece of deep-dish pizza on it.

"Bossy much?"

She took the plate back. "If you don't want it . . ."

He grabbed the plate and gave her a hot look. "Oh, I want it, all right."

She nearly dumped the piece she was trying to serve onto the table, so distracted was she by his husky voice and bad-boy look.

"I haven't had any luck finding out anything more about my mom," she said.

"I still think it's strange that there is so little information about her. She's not listed on any wanted lists, no-fly lists or terrorist watch groups," he said.

Her eyes widened as she looked at him.

"What? I'm a detective. Being suspicious is part of my job. Surely I've mentioned that before."

"Yes. I never thought she might be a criminal or

something. I asked my dad if she was an evil person and he said no."

"Do you believe him?"

"I don't know." She ate a bite of pizza before elaborating. "I think I believe his answer, but lately I'm suspicious of everything he says." She shot him a teasing look. "Maybe that's from hanging around with you."

"Hey, don't blame me. You were suspicious before I met you. At least, you were suspicious the second I walked in on your cousin's wedding."

"You didn't just walk in, you tried to stop it. Faith had already had one wedding go bad. I wasn't about to let another one go down the drain."

"You're protective of the people you love. That's a good thing."

"Thanks." Feeling a blush coming on, she said, "Do you want something to drink? I've got a nice Merlot from Argentina."

"Do you have any beer?"

"Yes." She escaped to the kitchen and cooled her hot cheeks with the air from the fridge. There was absolutely no reason for her face to be turning red. It's not like he'd said anything suggestive or anything.

We're just sharing a pizza, that's it. No big deal. So get back out there and act normal.

She brought two beer glasses to the table along with two bottles. "I realize that Southsiders drink their beer straight from the can and Northsiders drink it from the bottle, but here we drink it from a glass. Deal with it."

He tilted the bottle to read the label. "Goose Island."

"I suppose you have something against microbreweries as well?"

"You suppose wrong. And what do you mean by 'as well?' What else am I supposed to have something against?"

"Me."

"If I had something against you, I wouldn't be sitting here eating with you."

She gave him an unconvinced look. "Come on. It's free pizza."

"I can pay for it." He put his fork down and went to reach in his back pocket.

She put a hand on his arm. His skin was warm to the touch. "Put your wallet away. You're an invited guest. *My* invited guest. So eat. Would you like another piece?" Without waiting for an answer, she served him another large slice of the pizza so thick no one would eat it without a fork and knife.

"You're nervous," he noted. "Why?"

"I told you. I talked to my dad and it didn't go very well."

"He admitted that he paid off your mother to stay away? What else did he say? Did he give you any idea where she was?"

"No. He wants me to just trust that he did what he did to protect me and to leave it at that."

"But you can't do that."

Megan shook her head.

"So you need my help locating your mother."

"It would be appreciated."

"And you'll reward me with . . . pizza?"

"If that's what you want."

"What if I want something else?" he said.

"Like what?"

"Like . . . you."

"Me?" she squeaked.

He nodded and grinned at her expression. Gazing deep into her eyes, he said, "You making me . . . a home-cooked meal."

"How do you know I'm a good cook?"

"Are you?"

"Yes."

"I knew it."

She wondered what else he knew about her, but was afraid to ask. He'd already told her back in Last Resort the details he remembered about their time together. But now they were back in Chicago, back to reality. Yet the chemistry between them was as strong as ever.

"So is it a deal?" he said.

She wanted to kiss him so badly, she couldn't speak.

He misunderstood her silence for reluctance. "Forget it. You don't really have to cook for me."

"I want to," she said huskily.

"You do?"

She nodded. He was staring at her mouth as intently as she was staring at his.

He reached out to touch her lower lip with his thumb. "You had some tomato sauce there . . ."

Instead of sitting across from him, she'd made the unknowing decision to sit beside him. She thought it was so they could both face the view out her living room windows. Now she knew that wasn't the real reason. The reason was so she could be closer to him. So that he could reach her and she could reach him.

She licked her lips.

He groaned and moved in to kiss her. He paused millimeters from her mouth. "Stop me if you don't want this."

"I want," she murmured.

"Me too."

He started out kissing her gently, as if to reward her for her positive reply. He tasted as good as the pizza. Better.

One kiss turned into ten. Somehow his tie and his shirt were undone and she ended up on his lap as he turned in his chair to face her. Her knees bracketed his hips and his fingers slid through her hair as he tugged her closer to intensify their kiss. His tongue play was unbelievably seductive.

He slid both hands into her hair to brace her as the kiss intensified. She looped her arms around his neck. He nipped her bottom lip. His hunger for her was mirrored by hers for him. She lowered her hand to his bare chest beneath his open shirt and ended up banging her elbow on the edge of the dining table.

Logan responded by standing up with her in his arms. She wrapped her legs around his hips as he carried her the short distance to the couch where they tumbled down and sank into its deep softness. He shifted so that he was above her.

"Better?" he said.

"Mmm." His body was pressed against hers from her shoulders to her now bare feet. "Much."

"Now where were we? I think I was here." He kissed the right corner of her mouth. "Or was I here?" He kissed the left corner of her mouth. "Maybe it was here?" A nip to her bottom lip.

"Let me refresh your memory," she murmured, parting her lips and meeting his kiss halfway.

His groan of pleasure emboldened her to increase her exploration of his body as she slid her hands beneath his open shirt to his back. She trailed her fingertips down his spine.

He vibrated against her.

It took Megan a moment or two to realize that the vibrating was coming from his beeper.

Swearing under his breath, Logan broke off their kiss and sat up. Yanking the beeper from his belt, he looked at it and then at her, still prone on the couch, breathless.

"It's work," he said curtly. "I've got to go."

He stood and headed for the door. He was gone before

she had time to form a reply or regain her senses. The same senses she'd lost the second his lips touched her.

Great. Her determination not to get involved with a cop had toppled like a row of dominoes. Which left the score at Chicago cop: 1, Megan: 0.

Chapter Twelve

. . . .

A week later, Faith was back from her honeymoon, but Megan was no closer to finding her mother. She didn't want to burden her cousin with her problems, but Faith immediately knew something was up. She appeared on Megan's doorstep Tuesday evening with food from their favorite Chinese take-out and strong-armed Megan into telling her everything.

Megan ended by saying, "All of a sudden, my life is falling apart."

"Well, not completely," Faith said. "You've still got your home, your job and your family . . . certain members of your family. I can't believe they did this to you. Lying about your mom that way. That's just so wrong."

"I shouldn't have dumped this on you the minute you're back in the country."

"You didn't. I've been back twenty-four hours."

Megan proficiently used her chopsticks to add more walnut shrimp and scallops to her plate. "We should be talking about you and your honeymoon."

Faith used her chopsticks to wave Megan's words away. "And we will. Later. But getting back to your mother, I get how you'd feel totally betrayed."

"I knew you'd understand." Faith's former fiancé had left her at the altar on their wedding day. But while Faith's humiliation was more public, the betrayal was by a man she'd only known a year or two. Megan's betrayal was by the man she'd known her entire life and had trusted more than anyone aside from Faith.

"I didn't know the truth about your mom until now," Faith quickly told her.

"I didn't think you did."

"I can't believe my parents were involved in the cover-up for decades. What about your dad? What did he say?"

"That it was complicated. It was hard to get a clear answer from him."

"So what's your plan now?"

"First you have to swear you won't tell anyone. Pinkie swear."

"Done. So what's your next step?"

"I'm trying to find my mom," Megan admitted. "But I'm not having any luck."

"I can help you with that. I'm the best researcher West Investigations ever had."

"You can't let anyone know you're investigating her."

"No worries. No one knew I was investigating Caine's father's case. Believe me, I know how to do this and keep it quiet."

"I sure hope so. Logan and I didn't have much luck."

"Gram said something about you and Logan disappearing for a lost weekend right after the reception. What was that about?"

"Did she tell you about her situation with Buddy?"

"Yes, but let's get back to your situation first. What's the deal with Logan?"

"There is no deal."

"OMG, that is such a lie."

"You're doing your *Gossip Girl* thing."

"Sorry. But everyone saw the chemistry between you two from the second you met."

"He was crashing your wedding."

"He was trying to save his grandfather from committing bigamy. You can't blame the guy for that."

"Did you know that your father went to Logan's boss and told him to make sure Logan stays away from me?"

"Damn. My dad can be such a pain in the butt sometimes. I love him but . . . I thought he knew better."

"Apparently not."

"What was Logan's reaction?"

"He was not a happy camper."

"I'll bet. So you've never even kissed him, huh?" At Megan's startled blush, Faith laughed triumphantly. "A-ha, I knew it! Caught ya. So, is he a good kisser?"

"Did I interrogate you about Caine this way?"

"Absolutely. Turnabout is fair play."

"I apologize. I should have minded my own business. But you're a better woman than I am and don't need to make the same mistakes I did by butting into someone else's private life to this extreme."

"To quote Buddy, toughen up buttercup. Now tell me all the juicy details."

Knowing Faith wouldn't give up until she got an answer, Megan gave in. "Yes, he's a good kisser. But he's a cop. A divorced cop."

"Buddy told me once that Logan's wife cheated on him."

"That's right."

"So the divorce wasn't his fault. Which means the problem isn't that he's divorced. It's the fact that he's a cop, right?"

Megan nodded. "You know why I feel that way."

"What happened with Wendy wasn't your fault."

"That's what Logan said."

Faith's expression reflected her surprise. "You told him about Wendy?"

"I had to. We were stuck together in a motel room."

"Whoa, stop right there." Faith put her hands out. "You and Logan shared a motel room? That must have involved more than just kissing. Am I right? I am! I'm right. I can tell by looking at your face. I can't believe you were going to leave that part out." She tossed a crumpled paper napkin at Megan. "What else did you leave out?"

"The shotgun wedding part."

"OMG, you and Logan are *married*?!"

"Stop squealing. We are not married. We refused to be participate in the extortion plan."

"Extortion? This is getting juicy. I think you better start at the beginning. How did you and Logan hook up in the first place?"

"At the reception I overheard Dad talking to Uncle Jeff, who said my mother was still alive. I was so freaked I confronted my dad, who said it was true. I ran out of the room and bumped into Logan a few minutes later. I couldn't breathe. There was no air . . ." She shook off the upsetting memory. "To calm me down, he took me to get pancakes in Lucille."

Faith's face reflected her confusion. "Lucille?"

"A blue 1957 Chevy Bel Air that's really aqua."

"Right."

"A friend loaned it to him."

"And the pancakes?"

"Logan thought they'd make me feel better."

"That was sweet of him."

"So he did a database search on his iPhone and didn't get much aside from the fact that my mother was at Woodstock."

"Really? How cool is that!"

"Yeah. Someone blogged about going with my mom to Woodstock. And it turned out, this person didn't live that far away, so we went to go speak to her. We couldn't call or e-mail. The only contact was her address."

"What about the blog?"

"She hadn't posted for weeks. So we went to the brothel."

"Whoa! The brothel?"

"She owns a brothel. The Butterfly Ranch. But she's smart and nice."

"Hey, I don't judge. But a brothel?"

"I know, it was a little strange at first. Not that we really went inside. Just to Fiona's office in a trailer by itself. She had the neatest French country furnishings. Anyway, she gave me two photos of my mom. Well, they're copies, but still I thought that was nice of her." She took them from a nearby table and showed them to Faith.

"Fiona and my mom went to high school together," Megan continued. "After Woodstock, they both promised to keep their mud-spattered bell-bottom jeans. Fiona kept hers. I don't know if my mom did."

"Did you ask your dad?"

Megan shook her head. "I couldn't. If I said I knew about her being at Woodstock, then he'd know that I'd been investigating her myself. And I don't want him to know that in case he or your dad try to sabotage my search."

"Right."

"So after we left Butterfly Ranch, we headed back to Vegas but had car trouble. So we stopped in this teeny-tiny town of Last Resort. That's where the Queen of

Hearts Motel was. And Pepper Dior. She did Marilyn Monroe impersonations and was a Vegas showgirl. And she had the neatest vintage clothes. I bought a bunch of them from her. Not her Marilyn costumes, of course."

"Why not?"

"You're the mad bad blonde. I'm not."

"You're the big bad brunette."

"No, I'm not. I'm the optimist in the family. The girl next door. But I'm getting tired of that."

"Trust me, the girl next door would not be shacking up with a guy at the Queen of Hearts Motel. Why didn't you take separate rooms?"

"They only had one room. There was a king-sized bed. Can we please get back to the subject of my mother?"

"If you insist."

"I do."

They spent the next hour going over the information Megan did have on her mom.

"We'll find her," Faith said. "But are you prepared for what might happen when we do? You might not like what we discover."

"I realize that," Megan said. "But I have to know. I have to find her."

• • •

Logan sat across the table from his grandfather in one of Chicago's many South Side Irish bars. This one happened to be Buddy's favorite. Something to do with the way they pulled the Guinness on tap.

Logan was wiping the froth from his upper lip from his first sip of Guinness when out of the blue Buddy said, "How are the nightmares going?"

"Who said anything about nightmares? Have you been talking to Megan about me?"

"Whoa there, boy-o. Paranoid much?"

"You didn't answer the question. Who told you about the nightmares?"

"You did, by your reaction. And you need to see someone about that. What made you think Megan had spilled the beans?"

"She was present when I had one of my nightmares," Logan said gruffly.

"Present, huh?"

"That's right."

"So you two are . . . ?"

"No, we're not," Logan said.

"Why not?"

"Because she has a thing against cops."

"What kind of a thing?"

"You should ask her."

"Believe me, I will."

"No, on second thought, don't do that," Logan said.

"Why not?"

"Because talking about it upsets her."

Buddy's face darkened. "Was she attacked by a cop or something?"

"No."

"Was her heart broken by a two-timing cop?"

"No."

"Well, whatever it was, she shouldn't hold it against you. You didn't have anything to do with it, did you?"

"No."

"Are you buddies with any of the perpetrators?"

"No."

"Then tell her that."

"She knows. Besides, she's got enough on her plate right now."

"What's that supposed to mean?" Buddy demanded.

"Nothing."

"Is this bad cop causing her trouble?"

Logan shook his head.

"Then what's her problem?"

"It's personal."

"Is it about her grandmother? Is something wrong with Ingrid?"

"No. Paranoid much?" he asked, repeating Buddy's earlier comment.

Buddy heaved a sigh of relief before taking a sip of his beer. "Did I tell you the one time I spoke to Ingrid, she had the nerve to accuse me of deliberately trying to delay our nuptials by not getting the annulment?"

"Is she right?"

"What do you mean, is she right? Of course not."

Logan raised an eyebrow. "Do you regret asking Ingrid to marry you?"

"No," Buddy said emphatically.

"Then what's the problem?"

"Danged if I know. I can't believe this woman is so hard to track down."

"The one you married in Vegas?"

"Right. I'm a seasoned pro at finding people. It's what I do, which is why Ingrid is finding it hard to believe I'm having trouble."

"I can see her point."

"You're a lot of help."

"I'm just saying . . ."

Buddy held up his hand. "Don't be saying."

"Okay."

"So when are you going to talk to Megan about my situation?"

"Uh, never," Logan said.

"Come on. I need some help here. Ingrid loves Megan and would take whatever she says seriously. I need you to tell Megan that I am doing everything I can to clear up this situation so I can be with Ingrid. Will you talk to her?" Buddy paused before adding, "Please. I don't ask you for much."

Logan gave in. His grandfather's hangdog expression was too pitiful to resist, which is why Buddy used it in the first place. "Fine. I'll talk to her. But don't expect miracles."

"Thanks." Buddy whacked him on the back with enough force to make Logan wince.

"You still pack quite a punch there," Logan said.

"I'm glad something still works the way it should."

Logan wasn't sure he wanted to hear his granddad's shortcomings or, God forbid, a Viagra confession but wasn't sure how to stop him without being rude.

"I just don't seem to have the energy I used to have," Buddy said. "And don't you be telling me to go to the doctor."

"Why not? You just told me to see someone for my nightmares."

"That's different."

"Is it now?" Logan mocked Buddy's brogue.

"Don't you be making fun of my accent. I'm Irish born and bred."

"Until you came to this country with your parents when you were five."

"Speaking of parents, how's that dad of yours doing?" Buddy asked.

"He's dating a girl younger than me."

"He's afraid of growing old."

Logan shrugged. He'd never been able to figure out his dad and he doubted that would ever change.

"Have you told him about the nightmares?" Buddy asked.

"Are we back to that again?"

"Yes, we are. You haven't told him."

"He's the last person I'd tell."

"You should tell someone before they eat you up inside."

Logan shrugged. "I'm fine."

"Sure you are. Come on, boy-o. You haven't been fine since your partner died in the line of duty."

"Will was more than a partner. He was like a brother to me."

"Which made losing him all the harder."

What made it harder was that Will's death had been Logan's fault. Not that he could say that to anyone, even his granddad. Buddy was right about one thing: Keeping quiet was eating him up inside. But that was pittance compared to what Will had gone through.

"You wouldn't be feeling guilty now, would you?" Buddy asked.

Logan made no reply.

"Because that would be a silly thing to do and nothing that Will would be approving of." Buddy's Irish brogue got a little thicker when he was emotional.

Logan didn't say a word.

"So that's what the nightmares are about." Buddy nodded as if proud he'd solved some complicated mystery.

There was no mystery as far as Logan was concerned. Sure, he'd been cleared of any wrongdoing, but that didn't erase the guilt in his heart. He should have done more—been more aware, been faster.

"You're replaying that scene again in your head, like some video that won't turn off."

Logan remained silent.

"Fine. Don't say anything. It's better if I do all the talking anyway. Not that you'll listen. I can see you're not there yet. Not ready. But you will be. And it had better be soon, boy-o, because you don't want those nightmares to win. You don't want them taking over, spilling into your waking hours. You think I don't know what you're going through? I lost friends in the course of my thirty years with the police department."

"It's not the same," Logan muttered.

"How do you know?"

"Because . . ."

"Can't come up with a reason, can you?"

"I know it's hard for anyone to lose someone. But . . ." Logan shook his head, unable to continue.

"After all this time, you still can't deal with it. It's been a year. That's not a good sign."

"You think I don't know that?"

"So what are you going to do about it?"

"What do you propose I do? See some shrink and get tied to desk duty for the rest of my life?"

"Nothing that dramatic. Talk to me, just me—your granddad who knows you like I know my own self. If you don't want to talk here, we can go to my place or yours. But we need to talk. *You* need to talk. So what's it going to be? Your place or mine?"

"I'm not ready."

"Then get ready. Because time is running out. Don't wait until it completely eats you up inside and something bad happens."

Logan didn't have the heart to tell him that something bad had already happened. Not only was he lusting after Megan, he was finding it harder and harder to resist her.

• • •

"Thanks for meeting me," Logan told Megan the next evening. She'd suggested the Comfort Café and he'd agreed. It was near her condo and one of her favorite places to eat. They served comfort food with a twist, like the mac and cheese with shallots, Gruyere and mascarpone cheese she ordered. Logan ordered the pot roast.

"You said it was important."

"It is. It's about my granddad."

"Is he okay?"

"No. He's pining for your grandmother. And he needs your help."

"What does he expect me to do?"

"To talk to her," Logan said. "Help her forgive him."

"He would have done better to just tell the truth in the beginning. He could have avoided all this."

"He didn't realize the papers weren't signed," Logan said.

"It's just hard when that trust has been broken . . ."

"Are we still talking about my granddad or about your situation with your dad?"

"It's hard not to find similarities."

"You mean your dad didn't realize your mom was still alive?"

"No."

"Then I'm sorry, but I don't see the similarities."

"Because you're a guy."

He frowned at her. "What does that have to do with anything?"

"You're not as in touch with your emotional side."

"Talk about a sexist comment."

"But true. Some guys are in touch with their . . ."

"Feminine side," he mocked.

"Yes."

"That's not me," Logan said.

"That's what I'm saying."

"So are you going to help or not?"

She sighed. "What exactly can I do?"

"Talk to her. You're good at that."

"What's that supposed to mean?"

"What I said. You're good at talking to people."

"So are you."

"What?" He pressed his hand to his heart in mocking disbelief. "Did you just give me a compliment?"

"Come on. That is not the first time I've complimented you."

"Really? Name one other time."

She paused to think about it.

"See?" he said. "This is the first time."

"It is not. Give me a minute to think."

"Take all the time you want. You're not gonna come up with anything."

She decided it was time to change the subject. Opening her large tote bag, she handed him a check.

"What's this?" he said.

"It's my portion of the hotel fee. In Last Resort."

"It was a motel, not a hotel. A motel with a dogs-playing-poker painting over the bed."

Logan talking about the bed got her hot and bothered. This was the first time she'd seen him since he'd dropped by her apartment and they'd ended up on her couch and almost made love. That had been a week ago, and she hadn't heard a word from him until today. She should be totally aggravated with him. The truth was, she'd welcomed that week to try and figure out what was going on. Would they have had sex had he not been called into work? Did she have that little self-control where he was concerned?

Megan didn't know the answer to those questions. The bottom line was that Logan had called and she dropped everything to meet him. Not that she had plans for tonight, but still . . .

"Talk to your grandmother," Logan said. "She listens to you."

"She's one of the few people who does," Megan muttered.

"Hey, I listen to you."

"And ignore half of what I say."

"I act on the important stuff."

"Like what?"

"Like you saying, 'I need immediate help finding my mom.' You would never have known that your mom was at Woodstock if it wasn't for me."

"I would never have gone to the Butterfly Ranch either."

He grinned at her. "Another plus."

"Or stopped in Last Resort."

"Did you have to bring that place up?"

"I checked their website, did I tell you? Chuck's nephew has done a pretty impressive job with it," she said.

"To this day, I don't know if Cappy really exists or how many people actually live in Last Resort."

"The population is listed as . . ."

"Not many. Yes, I know. I saw the sign."

"They've started a blog about turning obstacles into opportunities."

"Bully for them."

"You're still holding that shotgun thing against them, aren't you?"

"Damn right I am," he said.

"It must have been a blow to your ego."

"Leave my ego out of it. I wasn't the one who offered to pay a thousand dollars not to get married."

"Another blow to your ego, no doubt."

"My ego is doing just fine, thank you. What are you smiling about?"

"It's nice to push your buttons for a change," she said. "I mean, you're so good at pushing mine."

"Really? And is that all I'm good at?"

"No," she admitted softly. She leaned closer. "You're also good at rehabbing cars. Or so I hear."

"And you're surprisingly good at flirting."

She sat up straight. "You didn't expect me to be a good flirt because I'm a librarian?"

"A hot librarian I want to kiss again. Does that surprises you?"

"I . . . uh . . . uhm."

"Apparently it does. It shouldn't."

She reached for her water, but instead of reaching her glass, her fingers encountered his. He traced the top of her hand with his index finger. "I know I didn't call you," he said. He looked her in the eye and she couldn't speak.

Damn, you'd think she'd be used to his brooding dark blue eyes, but no. They still had the power to get to her.

She licked her lips.

"You're nervous," he said. He lifted his finger to trace her lips. "You lick them when you're nervous."

They were interrupted by the arrival of their food, for which Megan was infinitely grateful. It gave her a chance to recover.

"This is really good," Logan said after his first taste of his pot roast. "Just about as good as my mom makes."

"If your mom is such a great cook, why do you need me to cook for you?"

He gave her a heated look. "Because you're not my mom."

Okay then. She took a quick bite of her mac and cheese.

"Speaking of family, I haven't come up with anything new regarding your mother," he said.

"Faith is going to help me with the search."

"Does that mean you don't need me anymore?"

"I didn't say that."

His beeper went off before she could elaborate. "It's work. I've got to go."

It was only after he was gone that she realized he'd hidden the check she'd given him beneath the money he'd left for his portion of the meal. Yet another example of how stubborn the man could be. She felt awkward being so indebted to him. Paying her portion of the motel bill from Last Resort was her way of maintaining her independence.

He'd said at the time that she could pay him back later. But when she tried to do so, he ignored her wishes. Cops were used to being in control, being the boss and being obeyed. All those traits made her leery about getting involved with Logan.

He hadn't really displayed those more than any other guy, a little voice inside her said. Maybe his pride prevented him from accepting money from her.

Even so, she'd be wise not to forget that Logan was a cop first and foremost. Everything else came in second. It took a special kind of woman to deal with that kind of relationship. And Megan wasn't at all sure she was that kind.

Chapter Thirteen

. . . .

After careful consideration, Megan decided it was better to confront Gram about Buddy face-to-face rather than over the phone. With that approach in mind, Megan invited Gram to Saturday afternoon tea at her condo. "Or I could come to your place if you'd rather."

"No, I need to get out," Gram said. "I've been holed up here too long."

"I'll make up a pot of that tea you like and some chocolate chip scones."

"Sounds wonderful."

Megan tried not to feel guilty for not telling her grandmother that she also planned on talking to her about Buddy. It's not like she was scamming her or anything.

Meanwhile, that gave her a few days to figure out what she was going to say to convince Gram. Megan reminded herself that she should also be trying to convince herself that getting involved with Logan was trouble in capital letters. The week passed by quickly with work taking up most of her time, both in the library and at home. She had to bring professional journals home to try and keep up.

The upcoming holidays were always crazy times at the library. They'd made it through Halloween okay. Next up was Thanksgiving. It didn't escape Megan's notice that this was a time for families, which made her situation with her mother all the more poignant. She'd lost track of how many times she'd stared at the photos of her mother at Woodstock. What was Astrid doing right now? Was she thinking about the holidays? Was she even in the country?

Thinking about it too much drove her crazy, so she instead concentrated on work. There was plenty of that to go around, especially regarding the ALA committee she was a member of.

Saturday came fast enough with no further contact from Logan. She should have been relieved. Reminding herself that she wasn't going to dwell on him, she got the scones in the oven and then tidied her condo. Smudge knew all this cleaning was a sign company was coming and didn't really approve. When Megan got the vacuum out, Smudge gave her a dirty look.

"Maybe I should get one of those Roomba automatic vacuums. I saw a YouTube video of a cat sitting on one of those, happy as a clam. Would you like that, Smudge? Would you like to ride around on a Roomba?"

Smudge stuck her nose in the air and marched down the hall into the bedroom.

"Apparently not. Obviously you think that vacuum riding is beneath you. How about a little dusting with that lovely tail of yours?" she called after her. "I wouldn't mind a little help with the housekeeping."

Smudge kept going, sliding under the paisley Shabby Chic bedskirt and disappearing from sight.

Megan waited until that moment to turn on the vacuum. This was a regular ritual. She wouldn't admit it to a living soul, but there were times when she'd put off vacuuming because Smudge was basking in a pool of sunshine and Megan didn't have the heart to disturb her. Only another cat person would understand. And even then only one who was as polite as she was.

By the time Gram arrived, the place smelled of baked goods. All the loose papers had been tidied and books put back in their places on the floor-to-ceiling bookcases that lined one wall of her living room.

"Something smells good," Gram said as she entered. "I brought you some of those Swedish mints you like so much."

"You didn't have to do that."

"I wanted to. I also gave some to that nice doorman of yours. What's his name again?"

"Danny. Danny Boone."

"That's a nice name. He's so polite."

"Yes, he is."

"So where's that cat of yours? Taking a nap again? I swear, that kitty sleeps all day long."

"It's officially catnap time."

"Hmmph. If I don't take naps, I don't see why she should. You know, you were brave to adopt a black cat."

"There was nothing brave about it."

"I'm just saying that some people are superstitious."

"You know I always speak up for the underdog. Or undercat, in this case."

"Yes, you do. That's one of the things I love about you. And you even apply that to teacups, collecting the orphaned ones from thrift shops."

"It's true. I don't have the heart to leave them by themselves, abandoned. It's all your fault, you know. You're the one who got me hooked on serving tea. You invited

Faith and me to tea parties as little girls. Faith might be the huge Jane Austen fan, but I'm the huge tea fan. I brewed a pot of Earl Grey, by the way. I hope that's okay?"

Gram nodded her approval. Tea bags were frowned upon in her view. "It's true that you took to the concept of serving tea more than Faith did. And I got my love for it from the time I spent with my parents in London, when I was a teenager and they were working at the consulate. It's rewarding to think that I've passed that ritual on to the next generation."

"You certainly have. As for the teacups and saucers, I only get the ones that call to me. This one, for example." Megan had set the rustic farm dining table with two teacups from her collection along with a white teapot and matching sugar bowl and creamer. "I loved the red leaves on this one, and the other one has a fall harvest design."

"And they both go with the carved wooden Dala horse from Sweden I got you. Clever of you to use it as a centerpiece." Gram nodded appreciatively. "You have a real eye for that kind of thing. Design. Colors. Displays."

"I do the displays at the library. The current one is on holiday recipes from around the world."

"Did you include Sweden?"

"Of course I did. And I have a surprise for you." She went into the kitchen and returned with a plate of cookies. "*Chokladbollar* cookies. I had some in the freezer and I let them defrost a bit." The no-bake cookies were favorites of both Megan and her grandmother. "Remember how you taught me to make these when I was a little girl?"

"Yes. The fact that they are ready really fast was always a good thing. Not that you were an impatient little thing, because you weren't. You had such a long attention span even at a very young age. You got that from your father."

"I wonder what I got from my mother."

"She did not like cooking." Gram took care of pouring the tea, as she had for as long as Megan could remember. "She didn't like much aside from mathematics."

"Did she not like me?" Megan asked quietly.

"What makes you think that?"

"Because she left me. Gave full custody to my father, who paid her."

"Who told you such a thing?"

"He did."

Gram's face reflected her confusion. "But he did not have much money in those days. The company hadn't become as big as it is now. We were still struggling."

Megan had to admit she hadn't thought of that, putting the timeline together that way. She offered Gram a scone before saying, "Maybe he continued to pay her to stay away."

"I thought you talked with him about this."

"I tried talking to him but he didn't say much. He claims he did what he did because he loves me. That he was trying to protect me."

"You don't believe him?"

"I don't know what to believe," Megan said.

"I know the feeling."

"You're thinking of Buddy, aren't you?"

Gram nodded.

"I don't think he lied to you on purpose, Gram."

"He lied by omission. By not telling me about his second marriage."

"It didn't last very long. What did he say . . . forty-eight hours?"

"It just makes me wonder what else he hasn't told me."

"Yeah, I wonder about that with my dad as well."

"We make quite a pair, don't we?"

Megan squeezed her grandmother's hand. "Yes, we do. A fine pair."

Gram gave her an innocent look as she asked a naughty question. "So you and Logan really haven't had sex?"

Megan nearly spewed her tea all over. As it was, she choked, forcing Gram to pat her on the back. "Gram!" she gasped.

"What? You were choking so I hit you on your back. What's wrong with that?"

"I wouldn't have been choking in the first place if you hadn't asked me that question."

"Which you still haven't answered."

"No, we did not have sex. I haven't known him that long." Megan couldn't believe she answered her grandmother's question. Where was her backbone? Her resolve?

The call from Danny the doorman was a welcome relief. "Miss Megan, your cousin Faith is here to see you. I sent her on up. And please thank your grandmother again for the mints."

The instant Faith walked in, Gram said, "Megan seems upset that I asked her if she and Logan had sex. We Swedes are more liberal about such things," she added matter-of-factly. "Sex is nothing to be ashamed of as far as we are concerned."

Megan slapped her hands over her ears. "I don't want to hear this."

Faith pulled Megan's hands away. "So what did you tell her?"

"That she hasn't had sex with Logan because she hasn't known him very long," Gram said on Megan's behalf.

Megan and Faith shared a look, both knowing that Faith and Caine had done the deed after their first week together.

"Before I forget, I want to talk to you girls about Thanksgiving," Gram said. "You know, it's next Thursday, and we usually celebrate at Jeff and Sara's."

Megan nodded. She was dreading the holiday given the awkward situation with her dad and uncle.

"This year we're having it at my house," Gram said. "It's neutral ground. And since everyone always brings their specialty dish it's not much work. You'll still bring your cranberry Waldorf salad, right, Megan?"

Again she nodded.

"Faith, you'll bring your lemon-glazed sweet potatoes?"

Faith followed Megan's lead and nodded in agreement.

"Excellent. We've got that settled then." Gram checked her watch. "I've got to get going. I've got a meeting concerning global warming to get to. You do know that Swedes are responsible for the refrigerator and vacuum cleaner, right?"

Even though she didn't see the connection between vacuum cleaners and global warming, Megan again nodded obediently before hugging Gram and seeing her out.

"Did Gram ask you that kind of question about having sex with Caine?" Megan asked Faith once they were alone.

Faith grabbed a cookie before replying, "I don't remember, but if she did, I'm sure I managed it better than you did."

"No way."

"You blush. It always gives you away."

"Like you don't blush too?" Megan scoffed.

"Yes, but I'm a much better liar than you are. My PI training helped with that."

"Maybe you should teach me how to be a better liar."

"Why?"

"Because Logan is an outstanding liar. He told me so himself. It's a requirement in his line of work."

"Your face is too expressive."

"I can fix that." Megan schooled her expression.

Faith laughed. "Now you look like Botox gone bad."

Megan sighed and sank onto the couch. "My dad is great at lying. I mean, the man lied to me for over twenty years and I never had a clue. Did you have any luck yet finding my mom?"

"Not yet, but I have some promising leads."

"Logan thought it was suspicious that there was so little information about her in the databases."

"It's all in knowing where to look."

"You mean like searching for her overseas? Do you think she went back to Germany?"

"It's a definite possibility. And she could have remarried there. She could have more kids."

"I hadn't really thought about that as a possibility."

"I know you haven't. That's why I'm bringing it up. To get you used to it just in case. She may not want you to contact her."

"Is this part of your worst-case scenario philosophy?"

Faith nodded.

"I thought Caine cured you of that."

"He did, where love is concerned. But where investigations are concerned . . ."

"Anything is possible," Megan finished for her. "Do you think she's even still alive?"

"I don't know."

"She was alive ten years ago for the high school reunion thing."

"I know. You told me."

"This not knowing is driving me crazy."

"I'm sure it is." Faith sat beside her on the couch and hugged her. "Hang in there."

"I'm trying to."

"Meanwhile, maybe having sex with Logan would distract you."

Megan pulled away.

"What?" Faith laughed at Megan's outraged expression. "It was just a suggestion."

"A dumb one."

"He would be one sexy distraction."

"I don't do distractions," Megan said.

"Maybe it's time to start. If I didn't do distractions, I wouldn't have met Caine."

"You're different."

"No, I'm not."

"I've only had two serial long-term relationships. One with Bryan all through college."

"I know. And you broke up right after graduation when he got a job in London."

"He dumped me."

"You told me the breakup was a mutual thing."

"I lied. See, I can lie if I have to."

"What about Andrew?"

"Another four-year relationship," Megan said. "And it took me a while to get over Bryan and get involved again."

"But you did with Andrew."

"Yes, I did."

"Don't tell me he dumped you too."

Megan nodded. "Because I refused to audition for that TV show *Amazing Race* with him."

"Wow." Faith blinked. "I don't know what to say."

"Okay, it wasn't just the fact that I didn't want to do that reality show, or any other reality show for that matter. It was a bunch of things. We grew apart. He didn't want kids. I do. He pretended to like Smudge, but he really wanted me to get rid of her and for him to get a Rottweiler."

"Yeah, I can see how those things would be deal-breakers."

"Whenever I asked him where he saw our relationship going, he'd put me off. As time went on, he'd act like he was encouraging me, but would really be putting me down in a subtle way. So subtle I didn't even get it for a long time. I mean, I didn't recognize it."

"Neither did I."

"He wouldn't say anything in front of others, but when we were alone he'd say things like, 'Oh you don't really want to do that.' Or, 'Why do you need to get more books when you already have so many?'"

"Uh-oh."

"I mean, it's not as if he didn't like reading too. But once he'd read a book he got rid of it. That was just his way. Which is fine, until he tried to make his way my way."

"Yes, but Logan isn't anything like either Bryan or Andrew. Come on, you have to admit they weren't men of action. They were pretty much geeky brainiacs."

"I like geeky brainiacs."

"I know you do."

"Logan isn't stupid, if that what you're insinuating."

"I wasn't. I wouldn't."

"But he's not geeky."

"I didn't think Caine was, but I've seen him get his geek on to go undercover when we were investigating his dad's death."

"I'm sure Logan could do 'geek' if he was working a case. He wanted me to talk to Gram about Buddy," she added. "Which I tried to do today. I'm not sure how good I was at it though. You know Buddy better than I do. You worked with him investigating Caine's dad's death. You should talk to Gram."

"Buddy's not the one who needs convincing. It's Gram. And you know her as well as I do."

"Yes, but you could sing Buddy's praises better

because you know him better," Megan pointed out. "You could list specific things about him to remind Gram of why she loves him."

Faith shook her head. "Don't go trying to palm this off on me. I've already got my hands full."

"I know, I know. You're already helping me in the search for my mother and I'm really grateful for your help. It's okay. I'll keep trying to convince Gram."

"And keep in touch with Logan. I'm just saying that maybe you should give the chemistry between the two of you a chance. Find out if it's real or not. Don't let your fears hold you back."

"It's hard not to."

"You still don't trust him?" Faith asked.

"It's not that as much as it's me not trusting myself. Getting involved with a cop . . ." Megan shook her head. "I don't know. It takes a strong woman to do that. It wouldn't be easy."

"Hey, I never said it was easy. But we're librarians. We don't give up just because it isn't easy. We like challenges. We live for them."

"I wouldn't go that far."

"So how are things going at work?"

"I've got a big presentation at the library next Monday night. I've got an outside speaker coming in. You remember how I told you about Julia Maguire? She's a librarian from Serenity Falls, Pennsylvania, who served on an ALA committee with me, and we became friends. Anyway, a good friend of hers, Emma Riley-Slayter, has written a book. A couple books, actually. *Taking Chances* and her latest, *Loving Risk Takers*."

"I read her first book and really liked it."

"Emma is on a book tour and our library branch is her final stop. We're lucky to have her."

"Maybe she can give you some pointers," Faith said.

"About?"

"Loving a risk taker like Logan."

"That would be a stupid move."

"Talking to Emma?"

"No, loving Logan. Who said anything about *love*? I thought you were talking about chemistry." Megan's voice rose.

"Hey, calm down. Here, have some more tea." Faith got up and filled Megan's cup.

"I can barely cope with the chemistry. What makes you think I can deal with loving a cop?"

"Because you don't give your body without your heart being involved. You're too nice that way."

"You're as nice as I am." Megan's words were not a compliment but rather an accusation.

"No, I'm not," Faith said. "You're nicer."

"I am not!"

Faith just grinned. "You feel guilty if you don't go out of your way to hold the elevator for someone."

"So do you."

"So the bottom line is that we're both too nice," Faith said.

"Nice but tough," Megan said.

"Absolutely. Nice but tough," Faith agreed.

"Maybe we should be tough but nice. I like that better," Megan decided. "Yeah, that's us. Tough but nice." She sighed. "I may need to work on that."

• • •

"I thought you were tough," Ria told Logan in a crowded bar on Saturday night.

"I am tough."

"Then why that face?"

"I hate karaoke."

"Yes, but this is cop karaoke. Songs cops like."

"Like the Police's 'Every Breath You Take'?"

"It's by the Police," Ria said. "Get it?"

"It's a song about a stalker," he retorted. "Get it?"

"Geez, talk about a buzzkill. You are such a party pooper. If you keep this up, I'm gonna be forced to show you photos of my Precious." She whipped out her cell phone.

Ria waved her photo of her pet snake in front of Logan.

"And when Precious gets hungry, Ria has to feed him live mice," fellow officer Andy Jablonski said as he joined them.

"They're feeder mice," she said.

"Just like that famous opera *Feedermice*," Andy said.

At Logan's and Ria's blank looks, he explained, "There's an opera by Strauss called *Fledermaus*. Actually it's an operetta. Get it? *Feedermice, Fledermaus*?"

As their blank looks continued, Andy said, "Philistines."

"Hey, we can't all have opera-singing mothers the way you do," Logan said.

"Ignore him," Ria told Andy. "He's just in a bad mood because he's got woman trouble."

"No. I'm in a bad mood because I'm in a karaoke bar," Logan said before pulling out his iPhone to answer a call, hopefully one to get him out of here. "Doyle."

"This is Megan." She paused. "Is that music in the background? Is this a bad time?"

"It is a bad time caused by bad karaoke."

"You're singing in a karaoke bar?"

"Not in this lifetime."

"Not a fan?" she said.

"No. How about you?"

"Doing karaoke? Not in this lifetime."

"Yet another thing we have in common."

"I talked to Gram about Buddy this afternoon," Megan said.

"And?"

"And I didn't make a lot of headway. But I haven't given up."

"No, you're not the kind to give up easily. Listen, I needed to talk to you anyway. Are you home?"

"Yes."

"I'll be right over," he said.

"Where are you going?" Ria demanded. "Esposito is gonna sing 'YMCA.' And Jablonski is gonna do 'Danny Boy' after that."

"Haven't you heard?" Logan said. "Torture is illegal."

"So much for being tough."

"Everyone has their limits. And Esposito singing 'YMCA' is mine."

Logan ignored the taunts and catcalls as he quickly made his way to the nearest exit.

• • •

Megan was waiting for his knock on her front door. She opened it instantly. "Did you find out something about my mother?"

"No."

She frowned at him. "But you said you needed to talk to me about something."

"I do. Have you ever heard of the Leonids?"

"The meteor shower?"

"That's right. Where's your coat?"

"What?" She blinked in confusion.

"Your coat? Where is it?"

"Why?"

"Because I'm taking you to see the Leonids," he said. "You've got to get away from the city lights to see them."

"That's the plan."

"You think you can just show up here out of the blue and take me to see a meteor shower?"

"Yeah. Do you have a problem with that?"

She glared at him. "Yes, I have a problem with that. You kiss me, you sweet-talk me and then you disappear for days."

"You could have called me any time."

"I called you tonight," she pointed out. "You didn't call me."

"I was trying to be good. You don't like cops."

Her mouth dropped open.

He gently closed it with his index finger before cupping her cheek with his hand. "I know you've got reservations. So did I. But I want to kiss you again. I want to explore every inch of your body. I want to take you to bed and keep you there for days. But before I do that, I need to convince you that it's okay to be with me. So we're going to see the meteor shower so you can wish on some shooting stars. Get your coat."

"I'd be crazy to go with you," she muttered.

"You've been crazy before and you had a good time with me."

"Is that all I am to you? A good time?"

"No." He threaded his fingers through her hair before pulling her close for a hotly intimate kiss that said what he hadn't or couldn't. That he wanted her as badly as she wanted him. That he was as confused by their chemistry as she was. That he couldn't resist her any more than she could resist him.

His groan when her tongue tentatively met his told her that she had power over him. Their kiss was their way of acknowledging that something worth exploring was going on here. She couldn't blame him for not saying the words. She couldn't say them either.

He pulled away from her to rest his forehead on hers. "Coat?" he said huskily.

"Right." She stepped back and retrieved her coat, hat and scarf. She had a pair of gloves tucked in the coat pocket.

"It's not real cold out and it's clear so we should have a good view."

An hour later, Megan found herself out in one of the many forest preserves ringing the suburbs. They officially closed at sunset but that didn't stop Logan from parking his Ford Explorer.

"I can't believe you brought me all the way out here to wish on a shooting star. I think it's really sweet."

"Sweet?" He rolled his eyes.

"Nice?" she said.

He rolled them again.

"Sexy?"

He grinned. "That's better."

He pulled a couple sleeping bags out of the back of his SUV and set them on top of a picnic table.

"We need to lie down to do it properly," he said.

"Do what properly?" she asked suspiciously, her heart racing a mile a minute at the erotic images that came to mind.

"Watch the meteor shower. Why? What did you have in mind?"

Megan knew damn well what he'd wanted her to think. She smacked his arm, which had little effect through his leather jacket. He spread out one sleeping bag for them to lie on and another to cover them. "You'll be snug as a bug in a rug, as my granddad would say."

Logan helped her step up onto the tabletop. A few minutes later she was tucked against his warm body, her face turned to the skies.

"Remember the sky in Last Resort?" he asked.

She nodded.

"There! Did you see that!"

She nodded again. A streak of light across the night sky. A shooting star.

"Make a wish," he said, turning her face up to his.

The next thing she knew, she was kissing him. He was just too damn tempting. And he tasted so damn good. He unbuttoned her wool peacoat and slid his hands beneath her sweatshirt to find her front-fastening bra, unfastening it with ease.

She tugged his shirt from his pants and slid her hands beneath it to touch his bare chest. His skin was hot beneath her fingertips.

He cupped her breasts in the palm of his hands, rubbing the ball of his thumb over her nipples. And all the while he kept kissing her. Deep, wet kisses that made her moist between her legs.

His hands were on the move, sliding around her waist to the small of her back. She shivered with delight. Then he slowly moved his hand beneath the elastic waistband of her pants and underwear to cup her bare derriere.

Rolling over, he hovered over her, still kissing her. She kissed him back and then some. He shifted his attention around her hip to the place that ached for him. She wiggled against him.

Bells were ringing. It was his phone.

"Damn." He paused, resting his forehead against her, his fingers stilling. So close . . . "It's Buddy. That's the urgent ring."

Megan knew all about urgent. Her body was humming with urgency. From the feel of his body, he was throbbing with urgency too. Yet he moved away. What was it with this guy and phones and beepers?

Logan swore under his breath as he took the call.

Chapter Fourteen

· · · · · · · · · · ·

"I need you to come to my house right away," Buddy told him. "It's your dad. He's fallen off the wagon."

Logan couldn't believe it. This was why he didn't make plans. They always got screwed up. But now it seemed that things got screwed up no matter what.

"Logan, did you hear me?" Buddy said. "Will you come?"

"Yeah, I heard you." Logan swore under his breath. His dad had been sober for five years now, and he chose tonight to fall off the wagon? So much for wishing on shooting stars bringing you good luck.

Not that Logan had made any wishes. He no longer believed in them. But he knew Megan still did, so he'd planned tonight for her. The Leonids were supposed to appear again tomorrow night. His master plan had been to call her and invite her tomorrow, but when she'd called him tonight, he couldn't resist seeing her. He'd been fighting the urge to be with her for far too long and now this latest interruption.

"Can't you manage?" he said.

"No, I can't." Buddy's voice broke.

"Fine," Logan growled. "It will take me a while to get there but I'll come." Logan disconnected the call and turning to Megan. "Sorry to cut this short, but we've got to go. That was my grandfather."

She sat up and pulled her coat around her. "Is Buddy okay?"

"He will be. It's a problem with my dad, not with Buddy."

"Was your dad shot? I mean, I know he's a police officer. Did something happen to him? If it's an emergency, I can go with you. You don't have to take the time to drop me off at my place."

"No, it's nothing like that." He gathered up the sleeping bags and tossed them into the back of his Ford Explorer. "It's personal."

"Still . . . if Buddy needs you . . ."

"They can wait for me to take you home." He held the passenger door open for her.

"Do you want to talk about it?" she asked before hopping inside.

"No." He slammed the door and went around to the driver's side.

"Right," she said as he slid behind the wheel and turned the ignition. "Because you're not a touchy-feely kind of guy."

"Damn right."

"You don't talk about your dad much."

"Right."

"The two of you don't get along?"

"You could say that."

"Were you ever close?"

"We used to be."

"What changed?"

"Life."

"Yeah, I know how that can happen. I was close to my dad as you know, and right now that's no longer the case."

"That's different."

"Is it? Why?"

"Because you're an optimist."

"I'm working on that," she muttered darkly.

"Don't. The world needs a few optimists."

"Why?"

"Someone has to believe things will get better."

"You don't believe that?"

"I don't believe much," he said.

"You must have seen some miracles along with the awful things."

"Not lately."

"How about tonight? That was pretty spectacular."

"Yeah." He remembered how she responded to his kisses.

"I was referring to the shooting stars," she said primly.

"Yeah, me too." He loved when her voice went all sexy librarian on him.

"I thought you said you were a good liar?"

"I am when I want to be," he said.

"Then how I do I know when you're telling the truth?"

"I don't lie in my private life."

"You don't? What about telling my family that Rowdy's shotgun wedding was just a joke?"

"It was a joke. I can't believe Rowdy thought they could get away with that."

"You know what I mean."

"Okay," he admitted. "I do lic sometimes."

"Then how do I know when you're telling the truth?" she repeated.

"I don't lie about important stuff."

"So the fact that you lied about me to my family means I'm not important?"

"No, that came out wrong. Look, can we not talk about this now?"

"Sure. What do you want to talk about?"

"Football. I noticed you're wearing a Bears sweat-shirt. I didn't expect you to be a football fan."

"Why not?"

"Because you like teacups."

"So?"

"And vintage clothes. Girly stuff."

"Girly stuff?" she repeated in disbelief. "Women and girls can be football fans. You can like both football and teacups."

"Maybe *you* can, but not me."

"So you don't like football? I'm sorry to hear that."

He had to smile at her quick comeback. "I like the Bears. I like them better when they win than when they lose."

"Ah, a fair-weather fan."

"Hey, they have to earn my respect. It's not like being a Cubs fan out of loyalty."

"So you don't believe in loyalty? I find that hard to believe. From what I understand of cop culture, loyalty is a very strong and very powerful element."

"That's different. You're thinking about your friend's asshole abusive ex, aren't you? What happened to him? Did he try to go after his kid? Did he ever try to hassle you to find out where she was?"

"He tried it once."

Logan felt his blood starting to boil.

"I told my uncle and he took care of it," she said.

Sensing her unrest, Logan tried to lighten the mood by teasing her. "Did he call in the Swedish mob?"

"He spoke to the mayor and the police commissioner."

"That'll work too. But it could have backfired and made him angrier with you."

"Luckily it didn't. Her ex got a job with the Houston Police Department, last I heard."

Logan noted that she still never referred to him by name, a sign that she didn't trust Logan with any details of the case. It shouldn't have aggravated him, but it did. Megan should know that she could trust him. She should know that he wasn't like the bastard who beat up her good friend.

He clammed up after that. Megan returned to talking about the Bears and carried most of the conversational load, which was fine by him. Talking was vastly over-rated, in his opinion. He was more a "just the facts, ma'am" kind of guy. That worked for him. Especially since Will's death.

The department had required him to complete a crit-ical incident debriefing after the shooting. He'd given them all the right answers, never unlocking his real feel-ings of guilt and helplessness.

He became quieter and quieter the closer they got to Megan's condo. So did she.

Finally he had to ask, "You don't really trust me, do you?"

"What makes you say that?"

"You never mention the name of the ass who beat your friend. It's like you don't trust me with that much information."

"It's not my secret to tell," she said quietly. "I prom-ised I wouldn't give that information to anyone. I take my promises seriously. I think you take your promises seriously as well, so you should understand that it's not a matter of trust. It's a matter of honoring my friend's request."

He got that now. "Understood," he said gruffly.

"I know you're in a hurry, so you can just drop me off in front of the building," she said. "That will be fine. Or on the corner. I could walk."

"Not on my watch. I'll drop you in front of the building because I know you've got twenty-four-hour doorman service."

"Protective much?"

"All the time."

She leaned over to kiss his cheek. "And who protects you?"

"My mom would say it's St. Michael the Archangel, the patron saint of police."

"I hope she's right." Megan trailed her fingers down his face before hopping out of his SUV and hurrying inside her building.

How could Logan believe that when St. Michael hadn't protected Will? He'd removed the silver St. Michael medallion that night and hadn't put it back on since then.

Logan's mood was already deteriorating by the time he entered Buddy's South Side brick bungalow. It got worse when he saw his dad sipping hot coffee at the kitchen table with his grandfather. Billy Doyle had inherited all of his father's stubbornness and then some. His dark hair had gone gray at the temples, but he had Logan's blue eyes. Rather, Logan had his dad's blue eyes. He hoped he hadn't inherited his problem with alcohol as well.

"I don't believe this," Logan said. "You stay sober for five years and now you fall off the wagon? Why?"

"I'm not drunk," his dad said.

"Yeah, right."

"He's telling the truth," Buddy said.

"You told me he'd fallen off the wagon."

Buddy shrugged. "I lied."

Logan narrowed his eyes suspiciously. "Why?"

"We needed to talk to you," Buddy said.

Logan didn't like the sound of that. Not one damn bit. "Your timing sucks," he said. "I was having a great evening."

"With Megan?" Buddy guessed.

"What's so important that you couldn't wait until morning to talk?"

"You. You're what's so important. Pull up a chair. Want some coffee?"

"No. I want an explanation."

"And you're about to get one."

"What is this? Some kind of intervention?" The look on their faces said it all. "Shit." He turned to walk out, but Buddy stopped him with a firm hand on his shoulder.

"Sit down, boy-o. It's time."

Logan glared at his grandfather but took the chair he offered. "Fine. Give it your best shot. This is about Will, right?"

"It's about you."

"So just because I don't react the way either of you would, that means something is wrong?"

"The fact that you're having nightmares a year later means something is wrong. The fact that you didn't cry at Will's funeral—one of the few times it's okay for a cop to cry—means something is wrong."

"I'll tell you what's wrong," Logan said grimly. "The fact that Will is dead. Nothing you say can make that right."

"You can't keep holding on to the pain," his dad said, taking over the role of intervention advocate.

"Sure I can."

"It will eat you up inside."

"That something you learned at AA?" Logan said.

"Don't you be disrespectful of your dad," Buddy said.

"You don't think it's disrespectful to ambush me this way?" Logan retorted.

"What are you afraid of?" Buddy said.

"Snakes. You know I hate snakes."

"You can joke around all you want, but you're staying here until you talk about this."

"About my fear of snakes?"

Buddy glared at him. Logan recognized that look. It was the same one he'd received as a boy when he'd broken a window playing baseball. He'd hung his head and slouched his shoulders a bit without even realizing it. Logan straightened up. He was no longer a kid. But he was acting like one.

"We never talk about stuff," he muttered, still acting like a kid.

"We're starting now."

"We don't do touchy-feely."

"We do now. Just this once is okay. So start talking."

"What do you want me to say?"

"I want you to tell the truth."

"You want the truth? Fine. I feel like shit. It's my fault that Will died."

Instead of being shocked by this news, his dad and granddad just looked at him with understanding. Why were they nodding like that? Did they agree that he was to blame?

"Because you were his partner and it was your job to protect him," his dad said.

"Damn right. I sensed something was up but I couldn't put a finger on it. Will was talking about his fiancée. We were serving a warrant on a guy. No prior history of violence. When I said I felt antsy, Will just laughed and said that's because he was talking about getting married.

He was standing right next to me. Then the shot came." Logan's throat tightened and he couldn't speak for a moment. His mouth was dry. "I keep seeing it over and over again in my nightmares. One second we're standing there talking . . . then he's hit. Took a bullet in the neck. Blood all over. Everything goes into slow motion. I pulled him behind the parked car next to us. Put pressure on the wound. There was so much blood." His throat tightened and he couldn't speak for a moment. "He died in my arms." His voice cracked.

Buddy and his dad gave him a moment to recover.

"What would you have done differently?" his dad asked quietly.

"Everything. I should have known. Should have trusted my gut. That was a mistake. One that cost Will his life." Logan remembered yelling, "Officer down," as the patrolmen who had accompanied them exchanged fire with the shooter.

By the time Logan pulled his own weapon out, it was all over. Will was dead and so was the shooter. "I'm not the same person anymore." He couldn't begin to describe the despair that had crept over him the instant he realized Will was gone.

"As cops we are trained to be in control," his dad said. "Trained to function in emergency situations. We are action-oriented problem-solvers. We believe we can control the unexpected. But we can't. Not all the time."

"Why Will and not me?"

"Ah, that's the question, now isn't it?" Buddy stood behind Logan and put his hands on his shoulders in a show of support. "It wasn't your time, boy-o."

"I can't accept that."

"You think you are in charge of the world but you're not. And Will's death forced you to acknowledge that."

"He shouldn't have died."

"No, he shouldn't have. But you didn't kill him. I know you'd give anything for things to have turned out different. If you could only go back and do it over, you'd trust your gut. You'd have been more cautious. But we rarely get do-overs in this life. And even if you'd been more cautious somehow, there's no guarantee the outcome wouldn't have been the same. And we plan on talking to you all night if we have to in order to convince you of that fact. So make yourself comfortable, boy-o. We're here for the long haul, and you might as well get used to it."

• • •

Megan worried about Logan and his dad and grandfather all night and all day Sunday. She didn't want to intrude on a personal family situation. She just wanted to know that everyone concerned was okay. She finally gave in by Sunday evening and called Logan.

"I can't talk now, Megan." His voice was curt. "Everything is okay. I'll call you later." An instant later, she heard the dial tone.

She tried not to be hurt by his brush-off, but it was difficult not to be. He hadn't even given her the chance to say anything before hanging up on her. And when was later? Later tonight? Tomorrow? Next year?

His record as far as calling her went was dismal.

Fine. She wasn't going to sit around and mope. She had plenty of things to keep her busy. She would kick Logan Doyle out of her mind. She was tough. She could do that.

The next morning, Megan started her Monday walk to work by appreciating the above-average temperatures making this one of those rare late–Indian Summer days when the sun felt deliciously warm against her face. It was also one of those days that tempted a person to play hooky.

But Megan couldn't do that. They were too short-handed as it was. Library support staff had been cut back by city budget issues, which meant the professional staff was called upon to do everything including reshelving library books. And it meant no playing hooky.

Besides, Megan had a special program at the library tonight. Emma Riley-Slayter was speaking. It was her final appearance on her book tour. And Megan had arranged to have dinner with her at an Italian restaurant near the library before the presentation.

Which meant it would be a long day, but that was okay. It prevented her from thinking about Logan.

She was not calling him again. Let him call her for a change. Did they even have a relationship? Okay, maybe they did. But what kind of relationship was it? A romantic relationship? A make-out relationship? The memory of his kissing her in between shooting stars made her feel all hot and bothered.

Getting hooked up with him was a recipe for disaster. She already had enough mayhem in her life with the news about her mother being alive. Did she really need more complications?

Yeah, if that complication could kiss the way Logan does. He made her feel good all over. As long as she didn't dwell on him being a cop with lousy communication skills. So she didn't. At least for today.

Megan smiled at the street musician on his customary corner and dropped her usual donation into his guitar case. She even paused to listen to him complete his song before continuing on. Today she'd decided to listen to music for the remainder of her walk instead of a professional workshop podcast and had chosen Owl City's upbeat "Ocean Eyes" album on her iPod.

By afternoon her day had definitely gone downhill. The slide started when she was working the reference desk, where library patron Wally Hunt delivered his weekly rant. "There're too many do-gooders in the world. That's the problem. And it's getting worse."

Personally Megan thought the problem was that Wally was a pain in the heinie, as Tori would say. Actually Tori would probably be much blunter than that.

Megan wondered if Wally would consider her to be a do-gooder. Were optimists do-gooders? Probably. They were more likely to try to make a difference than a pessimist who thought it wasn't worth making an effort because it would fail.

She remembered Logan telling her the other night that the world needed more optimists. She couldn't help thinking that the heart of an optimist beat somewhere deep inside that sexy pessimist body of his. Otherwise, why would he continue to fight the bad guys and try to right wrongs?

"This day couldn't get any worse if someone set my tampon string on fire," Tori proclaimed as Megan joined her in the staff room.

"Another Southern saying? I'll bet that one isn't from your uncle Bo."

"No, it's not."

"I'm sorry your day is going so badly. You could perk it up by attending the program this evening with our guest author."

"Or I could go home and eat a carton of chocolate–chocolate chip ice cream."

"Or you could come to the program tonight," Megan repeated.

"Are you afraid no one is going to show up?"

"Not really. A large number of people signed up. But there's always the chance they won't show."

"And there's a chance the planet will get hit by a giant meteor. Hello? Reality calling. You can't live that way."

"On second thought, maybe that ice cream option would be a better one for you," Megan said.

"I agree."

Megan spent the rest of the day working the reference desk, where she got more vague questions than usual. "I saw this book. It had a blue cover and was set somewhere in the south."

Not a lot to go on. "Do you remember anything else about it?"

"Yes. That I wanted to read it."

"Do you remember what part of the south?"

The patron shook her head.

Some might give up and say they'd need more information. But Megan prided herself on not doing that if she could help it.

"The author had three names. Or two first names. Something like that. And the book title had a city name and two words."

Megan went online and pulled up Amazon's website. "Was it *Savannah Blues*?"

"That's it! Do you have it?"

Megan changed screens to her branch's collection. "We do and it's on the shelf. You might want to check out *Savannah Breeze* and *Blue Christmas* as well. They include the same characters."

No sooner had that patron left than she was replaced with another one. "There's this book . . . I don't remember the author but the title had sugar in it. It's fiction."

This time Megan took a wild guess. Sometimes that worked. "*The Sugar Queen* by Sarah Addison Allen?"

"That's it!"

Again Megan checked the database and found the book for the patron. "You rock!" Aisha said as she walked by, pausing to give Megan a high-five.

Megan had a few minutes left before she had to meet Emma for dinner so she spent the time checking the status of the various book displays. The one she'd done on Novel Writing Month needed replenishing. The Arab Heritage Month display also needed some additions; she took care of both before heading out.

Megan had chosen an Italian restaurant near the library to meet Emma for dinner. Faith was joining them too as well as Emma's two sisters, Sue Ellen and Leena.

Once they were all seated and had placed their orders they started talking like old friends. Megan immediately related to Emma, who wore smart-girl glasses and a tailored black pantsuit with simple pearls.

"We decided to meet up here in Chicago for a girls' weekend," Emma said.

"We left the men behind to take care of our darling children," Sue Ellen said. Unlike her sister Emma who seemed a quiet academic type, Sue Ellen appeared to be one of those people who gobbled life in large bites. She was wearing purple knit pants and top with a matching purple jacket. Emma's other sister, Leena, was wearing a gorgeous outfit that suited her curvaceous body wonderfully.

"Yes, we left the kids back in Rock Creek, Pennsylvania. I've got a daughter, Annelise," Leena said.

"And I've got a boy Donny Jr," Sue Ellen said.

"They were born a few months apart."

"My sister has to copy everything I do," Sue Ellen said with a knowing grin at Leena.

Leena ignored her sister's teasing comment and spoke to Megan instead. "I like your cloche. It's an August Hats design, right? And that's a great vintage sweater."

"Leena is a former plus-size model," Emma said. "Fashion is her thing. She's now an advocate for improving womens' and girls' self-esteem. She has a wonderful website and is working on a book now about body image."

"It can be challenging being a size sixteen in a size-zero world," Leena said. "I'm all about changing people's views on the real definition and diversity of beauty."

"You'll have to have Leena speak at your library when her book comes out," Sue Ellen said.

"Let's finish this book tour first," Emma said with a laugh. "We head home tomorrow for the opening of my husband's environmentally friendly sports resort next weekend."

Megan knew from reading Emma's bio that her husband was Jake Slayter, a former extreme sports athlete who'd nearly died in a climbing accident in the Andes Mountains.

"I read your book *Taking Chances*," Megan said.

"I did too," Faith said. "And I was just telling Megan the other day that the two of you have something in common. She's seeing a Chicago cop."

"He's a police detective," Megan said, almost as if that somehow made him less of a cop, which was ridiculous.

"Which is a risky job, as I'm sure you can imagine," Faith said.

Megan had been imagining that entirely too much lately. Avoiding it didn't seem to be helping.

"So I thought maybe you could give my cousin some pointers in dealing with falling for a guy who is a risk taker."

"Sometimes it's riskier for us, the women who love them," Emma said. "They get the adrenaline rush from the risks. We don't. We just get the adrenaline rush from being with them. Which, I have to admit, is a pretty powerful rush."

"You can also get that same rush from being with a sexy veterinarian," Leena said. "Like my husband, Cole."

"And I get the same rush from my husband, the sexy owner of Smiley's Sewer Service," Sue Ellen said. "It's all about being with the man you love. That's where the rush comes from. And our husbands face risks too, you know. Sewers aren't always safe. And Cole could get attacked by a mad dog or something."

"Putting those happy thoughts aside," Emma said with a roll of her eyes. "Getting involved with a cop has a special set of emotional demands."

Megan nodded. "Yes, I know. They see physical and verbal intimidation as ways of getting the job done."

Emma frowned. "Has this cop of yours shown any sign of that with you?"

"No. He just rolls his eyes at me."

"That's not all he does," Faith said. "He took her to see the meteor shower the other night so she could wish on shooting stars."

"Aww," Emma and her sisters said in unison.

"Says the woman whose husband proposed to her at a White Sox game." Emma and her sisters looked at Megan blankly. "Faith is a big fan," she explained. "Her husband is a former Force Recon Marine."

"Another man accustomed to taking risks for the completion of the mission," Faith said.

"Why do we love the men we do?" Megan said.

"Because they're our soul mates," Faith said.

"I agree," Emma said. Leena and Sue Ellen both nodded.

"Not that I'm falling in love with Logan," Megan quickly added. "I just wanted to clarify that."

"Right." Emma and her sisters gave her an eye roll.

"No, really. I'm not," Megan insisted. "No way."

"Give it up, sweetie," Faith said. "You're not convincing anyone."

Megan didn't care about convincing them as much as she was determined to convince herself, hoping that the more she said it, the more she'd believe it.

Chapter Fifteen

. . . .

As Megan approached her building after work the night before Thanksgiving, she saw someone standing there. It wasn't Danny the doorman as she first thought. It was Logan. He had this way of just appearing, just as he had a way of not calling her.

The only reason she didn't kick him to the curb was that he looked like he'd already been through hell. Sure, he had that sexy stubble thing going on, but he also had dark shadows under his eyes. "Are you okay?"

"Yeah," he said gruffly. "Can we talk? I just wanted to explain what happened when I was called away by Buddy the other night."

She sighed. She could make him stand out here in the cold or she could have him come up to her condo. She chose the latter option, telling herself it was because she was on the verge of having her teeth chatter. That didn't mean that she wasn't tough. "Come on in."

Logan didn't say anything in the elevator on the way up to her floor. He didn't speak until they were in her living room and she'd invited him to sit on her couch. Instead he was pacing back and forth.

Megan tossed her keys into the carved wooden bowl she'd gotten at the Gold Coast Art Fair and leaned down to pet Smudge before straightening to face Logan. "So what happened? You don't look like you've gotten much sleep lately."

"A case I've been working on. I've been putting in a lot of extra hours. I'm sorry I haven't been in touch."

"Is everything okay?"

He shrugged. "Buddy told me that my dad had fallen off the wagon after being sober for five years."

"I'm so sorry."

"It was an intervention."

"For your dad?"

"No. For me."

She frowned. "You have a drinking problem?"

"Not a drinking problem. I have nightmares, as you know."

"Lots of people have nightmares."

"Exactly. I tried to tell them that."

"So why did they feel you needed an intervention?"

He shifted from foot to foot. "Have you heard of PTS?" he said abruptly.

She nodded. "Post-traumatic stress."

"They thought I had it."

"Do you?"

Another shrug. "My partner Will was killed in the line of duty a year ago. That's what the nightmares are about."

"I'm sorry."

"He died in my arms."

Megan didn't know what to say.

"The shot hit him in the neck. I sensed something was up beforehand, but I was too late."

"So you felt guilty?"

Emma had touched on survivor guilt in her presentation at the library. Her husband, Jake, had survived a horrendous climbing accident that had killed his good friend.

"Will was like a brother to me," Logan said.

"Have you talked to someone about this?"

"I'm talking to you."

"I meant a professional."

"Cops don't do that."

"Why not?"

"It's a good way to get stuck with desk duty."

"So you're saying it might be perceived as a sign of weakness."

"Right," he said.

"Because a cop would never ask for help. For some backup."

"This is different."

"So knowing you wouldn't ask for help, Buddy and your dad offered you some."

"They didn't try to drag me to a shrink or anything. They made me talk about that night."

"You sound aggravated about that."

"I am. They ambushed me."

"They were trying to help you," she said.

"Yeah, well your dad was trying to help you when he lied to you about your mother."

"That's different. Your family wasn't lying to you. They were making you face the truth."

"Which is?"

"That you weren't guilty of causing your partner's death."

"How do you know that?"

"Because I know you."

"Do you?"

When he glared at her like that, she wasn't quite as sure. But she knew guilt when she saw it. "Did you shoot him?"

"Of course not."

She shrugged. "You could have shot him accidentally."

"I don't shoot people accidentally." He'd gone from aggravated to irritated. "Don't you get it? I sensed something was up and I didn't take evasive action."

"You *sensed*? Like ESP or something?"

He growled.

"I'm just trying to follow what you're telling me," she said.

"A civilian wouldn't understand."

"What about your dad and Buddy? Did they understand?"

"I don't know."

"I thought they staged an intervention. Didn't you all talk?"

"Yes."

"And did they make you feel better?"

"This isn't something that goes away overnight."

"I don't imagine it would. It's something that would stay with you the rest of your life. We've done presentations about PTS at the library over the years."

"And that makes you an expert?"

"No. I'm just saying that I think talking to your dad and Buddy was a good thing. I'm glad they intervened."

"Well, I'm not."

"Why not?"

"I don't like being ambushed." He headed for the door. "I've got to go."

"What is your problem? Every time you show up, you take off suddenly. I'm starting to think that I'm not the one afraid of our relationship, if you can even call it that. I think you're more afraid than I am. That's why you kiss and run."

"I do not kiss and run." He turned to glare at her.

"Yes, you do." She glared right back.

"I didn't kiss you tonight."

"And you're not going to."

He came closer. "Aren't I?"

"Don't even think about it," she warned him. "If you think you can ignore me for days and then just show up unannounced and kiss your way . . ." she sputtered.

"Kiss my way where?"

"Anywhere." She put her hand out, stopping him in his tracks. "Go home. Get some sleep. And listen to what your dad and grandfather told you."

"There you go. Being bossy again."

She grabbed a handful of his shirt, intending to push him away. Instead she yanked him closer and kissed him. She was clearly certifiable. He'd driven her over the edge. She should be booting him out of her condo, not licking his bottom lip and devouring his mouth like a wanton.

He definitely wasn't protesting. Instead there was a mutual battle for domination as he tried to take over the kiss and she fought to maintain her advantage. Their dueling tongues engaged in an erotic dance as old as time.

What was she *doing*? Eventually the question seeped through the sensual haze. He was a cop. Used to issuing orders and having them blindly obeyed. Refusal to comply was a punishable offense. Was that why he thought he could take her for granted? Just show up and the mousy librarian would melt at his feet?

She pulled away. Her lips throbbed and the rest of her body wanted more. "Go home," she repeated.

This time he did.

• • •

"The woman is certifiable," Logan told his brother Connor as they watched a football game awaiting Thanksgiving dinner at their mom's house. The air was filled with tempting smells from the kitchen where their mom and grandmother were busy doing their magic. "Totally certifiable."

"So you've told me a dozen times." Connor had come in from Ohio for the holiday weekend.

"It bears repeating."

"So does that play." Connor pointed to the TV. "I can't believe they stopped the ball where they have."

"She's been impossible from the moment I met her. Yanking me out of the wedding at the Venetian."

"I'm sorry to have missed that."

"And then demanding I help her."

"Knowing you're a sucker for damsels in distress."

"She made me take her to a brothel."

Connor sat up. "Okay, now the story is getting interesting."

"And then we got marooned in this podunk town in the middle of nowhere."

"Wait, go back to the brothel part."

"Nothing happened there."

"Too bad. Are you having erectile dysfunction?"

"No."

"Hey, I'm your brother. You can tell me."

"Watch the game," Logan growled.

"Believe me, I'm trying to."

A minute later, Logan said, "I'm just saying that she's the one who is being unreasonable. She said I kiss and run."

"Of all the nerve. Was she right?"

"I was called into work."

"Right."

"It's the truth."

"I'm sure it is. Hold on a minute. I thought you said nothing happened. So what's with the kiss-and-run shit?"

"Watch your language. You know if Mom hears you . . ."

"The shit will hit the fan?" Connor grinned.

"Easy for you to say. You live in Ohio and fly into town for a day or two and then disappear."

"To my podunk town, right?"

"I don't know if your town is Podunk. I've never been there."

"The town is called Hopeful."

"It has more than three inhabitants, right?"

"Right."

"Then it's bigger than Last Resort, where I was marooned with Megan."

"Wait, start over. I wasn't paying attention."

Logan threw a pillow at him.

Connor grabbed it midair. "Interception!"

"You boys better not be playing football with my couch pillows!" their mom yelled from the kitchen. "Don't make me come out there."

Logan and Connor sank back onto the couch, laughing.

"What are Dad and Gramps doing today?" Connor asked. "Going to the Aunts'?"

Logan nodded. The Aunts was a special label for their dad's four sisters, all of whom lived in the Chicago area. They usually presented a united front, which is how they got their name as a group rather than as individuals. "Unless Dad and Gramps decide to come over here and stage another intervention," he grumbled.

"I heard about that," Connor said. "I thought it was a good idea."

"So did Megan."

"I had a feeling we'd get back to her."

"I thought she'd see my point of view. Foolish on my part, I know."

"Downright stupid, I'd say."

"She could have been more understanding."

"About you kissing and running? You're not going to find many women who'd be understanding about that."

"Yeah, but *she* kissed me last night and then kicked me out of her condo."

"Good for her."

"Are you even listening to me?"

"Not really."

"You're a big help."

"That's my goal in life."

"You're my brother," Logan said. "You're supposed to have my back."

"Only if someone is threatening you. Not if you're just acting stupidly."

"I'm not acting stupidly."

"So you're saying this Megan, the smart librarian, is the one who is stupid?"

"How do you know she's a librarian?"

"Gramps told me. If you're not interested in her, maybe I should give her a call and see if I can hook up with her this weekend. I wouldn't kiss and run."

"Don't make me shoot you," Logan growled.

"I'm just saying if you don't appreciate her, maybe I would."

"Who says I don't appreciate her?"

"Your actions say it. You don't call her. You said she's certifiable."

"And that makes you want to hook up with her?"

"You're a sucker for damsels in distress. I'm a sucker for certifiable women who'll grab me and kiss me."

"In your dreams."

"Are you staking some kind of claim on her?"

"She's not a gold mine."

"Isn't she?"

"Fine. You want me to call her, I'll call her." He grabbed his iPhone. "Watch me."

"Do I have to?" Connor groaned.

"Damn. I got her voice mail."

"So leave a message."

"Uh, Megan, this is uh, Logan. Happy Thanksgiving." He quickly disconnected.

Connor shook his head in mocking awe. "You are such a romantic sap. That was sheer poetry. I don't know how any woman could resist you."

Logan reached for another pillow.

"Dinner," their mom yelled from the kitchen. "Come in here and help us with this heavy turkey. I can't carry it by myself. First one in the kitchen gets the wishbone."

Logan hopped over the back of the couch and raced his brother into the kitchen, jockeying for position the way they had as kids.

"I thought you didn't believe in wishes," Connor said.

"I don't," Logan said. "I believe in winning."

• • •

"Was that your phone?" Faith asked Megan in between coughs.

"I let voice mail pick it up. You sound horrible."

Faith coughed some more. "It's just a little cold."

"Then why are we out here? We should be inside."

Faith put a hand on Megan's arm. "I have news."

"About my mother?"

Faith nodded. "I found her."

Megan's breath caught. She was shaking inside. "Where is she?"

"In Washington, D.C. I e-mailed you her contact info. She works at a think tank there."

"Is she doing some sort of top secret government work?"

"I'm not sure."

"How did you find her?"

"I told you I was good."

"Was the fact that she works at this think tank the reason there wasn't any information about her?"

"I don't know. I do know she doesn't drive or own a car so there were no DMV listings. And she doesn't own a home or have a mortgage. So nothing there. And she doesn't seem to have a bank account or credit cards. These are all signs of someone trying to disappear. Are you going to call her?"

"No. I need to see her in person."

Faith looked worried. "Don't do anything impulsive. Wait and I'll go with you. We'll talk to her together. But I think it would be best to touch base with her ahead of time."

Megan shook her head. "She could just tell me not to come. I can't take that chance."

"You need to think this through before you go and do something crazy. Pinkie swear you won't do anything foolish."

"I pinkie swear. Now come on, let's go back inside before you get pneumonia or something."

"It's almost sixty out today. Remember that year we had snow on Thanksgiving?"

Megan nodded as she held the back door open for Faith. They entered the kitchen, where the delicious smells made Megan's mouth water. Faith's mom was busy concocting her maple Brussels sprouts specialty. She'd been avoiding direct eye contact with Megan, who'd done the same. Faith's mom had known the truth but had not revealed the lie, which made things awkward. But not as awkward for Megan as being near her dad, although she was actually more afraid of her uncle rocking the boat. Gram gave her a reassuring smile, silently communicating the fact that she'd warned everyone involved that a truce was in place today.

Which was fine with Megan. She hugged the knowledge to herself that she now knew where her mother was located. "You did a great job with the Thanksgiving centerpiece again this year, Megan," Gram said. "I especially liked the way you spread a few maple leaves in with the pair of little gourds and pumpkins."

"I pressed the leaves last year in the pages of an old dictionary between sheets of waxed paper."

"That was clever of you. And the wooden candlesticks with creamy beige candles go together wonderfully."

"Thanks."

The oven timer went off, which galvanized Gram into action. "The bird is ready."

Ten minutes later, they were all seated around Gram's large table, with all the side dishes and the turkey. Gram had gotten out the good Swedish china that she usually only had out for Christmas, when she did her traditional *julbord*, or Christmas smorgasbord. That multicourse extravaganza included ham, meatballs, smoked salmon, pickled herring with boiled potatoes and hard-boiled eggs, pickled cucumbers, cabbage rolls, beetroot salad and Gram's favorite, dried codfish. Gram was the only one who ate that last one, while Megan's favorite were the Swedish meatballs. But today's meal was all-American. Faith brought the sweet potatoes, Megan brought her cranberry Waldorf salad, Aunt Sara did her maple Brussels sprouts. The turkey had two kinds of stuffing—sausage and apple at one end and hamburger and celery at the other end.

"Hold hands and say what you're thankful for this year. I'm thankful Aunt Lorraine is taking a spa vacation in Mexico for Thanksgiving," Faith said. "And I'm thankful I married a wonderful man like Caine."

"Notice I get second billing after Aunt Lorraine," Caine said before adding, "I'm grateful Faith is my wife."

"I'm grateful to have my family all around me," Gram said before giving a meaningful glance to her sons.

"Yeah, I'm grateful for that too," Megan's uncle said.

"Me too," Megan's dad said.

"Same here," Aunt Sara said.

"I'm grateful that we get to eat all this great food now," Megan said. "Dig in."

The only discussion following that was how great everything tasted. Although Megan kept her eyes on her plate for the most part, she was very aware of her family around her. For the first time, there was a gap, something missing. *Someone* missing. Her mother. She'd always felt her absence growing up, but this was different. Now she had a way of filling that gap.

After dessert of pecan pie, the men headed to the kitchen to wash up, another family tradition.

Gram pulled Faith's mom upstairs to consult about some top secret Christmas gifts, leaving Megan and Faith alone. "How's Logan doing?" Faith asked. "Is he spending the holiday with his family?"

"He didn't tell me his plans. The man just shows up," Megan said in exasperation.

"Caine used to do that too."

"What did you do about it?"

"I married him."

"That seems a little drastic."

Faith grinned and shrugged. "Works for me."

"Works for me too," Caine said as he joined them.

"Don't tell me your work in the kitchen is done."

"You family didn't like my suggestions."

"Marines don't give suggestions. They give orders.

I better go check things out." She got up and headed for the kitchen, snagging a bottle of cough medicine from the sideboard along the way.

Caine took the chair his wife had just abandoned. "You know, it occured to me that we have something in common. Both our dads never remarried."

"Yes, but your mother really was dead." Megan hung her head. "I'm sorry. That sounded cold-hearted and I didn't mean it that way."

"Faith told me about the situation with your mom."

"What about the situation?" Megan asked suspiciously. Faith had promised not to tell a soul about her search for Megan's mother. That included telling her sexy husband.

"She told me that your mom isn't dead. Why? Is there more?"

Megan quickly shook her head. "That's enough."

"I know you're angry with your dad now, but as someone whose dad is no longer with us, I just want to say that you shouldn't dwell on your anger. Trust me, I know how anger can eat you up inside."

"I know you do."

"And I know about family complications."

"I'm sure you do." Megan knew the story of Caine's dad being falsely accused of a crime he hadn't commited and Caine blaming Faith's dad for botching the investigation and causing his dad's apparent suicide. "Things weren't the way they seemed in that case."

"No, they weren't. My dad was murdered by the real criminal. Faith's dad apologized for his part in missing critical evidence and clues. I could have held a grudge, but I didn't. It wasn't easy. In fact, it was damn hard. But I knew it was the right thing to do."

"The right thing to do would be for my dad to tell me the truth about his reasons for lying all these years. But he's not willing to do that yet."

"Be patient," Caine said.

"How did that work for you?"

"I usually suck at being patient."

"Yeah, me too," she admitted.

"But in my case it paid off. I think it will in yours as well."

What had paid off was Faith's diligence in tracking down Megan's mom.

No, Megan wasn't good at being patient. Which is why twenty-four hours later she was in Washington, D.C., standing outside an apartment. Her mother's apartment. Her hand shook as she pressed the buzzer. She was afraid she'd have to talk her way past a doorman but the security at the building was lax.

The door opened. And her mother stood there. Despite the number of years since the last photograph Megan had seen, she recognized her. Her hair had turned gray and was blunt cut at her shoulders. She wore a crabby expression and no makeup. Her icy-blue eyes were paler than Megan's and made her seem cold. The flannel shirt she had on was faded and well washed, as were the khaki pants. "Whatever you're selling, I'm not interested."

"I'm not selling anything. My name is Megan West. I'm your daughter."

Chapter Sixteen

. . . .

Megan wasn't sure what she expected but in none of the many scenarios she imagined had she come up with one where her mother just stared at her with no sign of emotion. "What are you doing here?"

"I came to see you."

"Why?"

"Because you're my mother."

"What do you want?"

"Nothing. I just . . ." Megan's mouth was so dry she could barely speak. "Can I please come in so we can talk?"

Her mother grudgingly opened the door farther to let her in.

Megan noticed that the combination living/dining room was done in minimalist furnishings. No paintings on the wall. No photos anywhere. No tchotchkes. The table was filled with two laptops and papers.

"I'm sorry if I interrupted your work."

Her mother didn't say "that's okay" or any of the polite comments that most people would make. Instead she just stood there, arms crossed, her expression devoid of anything—surprise, happiness, sadness.

Megan tried not to panic. She stuck her hands in the pockets of her jacket to hide the fact that they were trembling. She'd dressed carefully in black pants, a white top and a knit berry-colored jacket. She'd added one of her favorite necklaces, a delicate hand-carved cameo that Faith had bought her in Italy. She'd needed the self-confidence that looking good was supposed to provide. She wanted her mother to be proud of her.

Now she just wanted her to say something to break this excruciating silence.

Megan cleared her throat. "I, uh, probably should have called first."

Again no response.

"I, um, I just found out that you're not dead. I didn't know. I've been trying to find you for a few weeks now. I even tracked down someone you knew in high school. Do you remember Fiona? You went to Woodstock with her. She gave me copies of some photos of you there. I brought them with me." Megan reached into her bag and pulled them out to show them to her.

She held them out for her mother to take, who merely gave them a cursory look.

"Maybe you want to see some identification for me," Megan said. "Prove that I am who I say I am. I mean, the last time you saw me I was two years old. I've changed since then. Here." Again she dug into her purse. It distracted her from staring at her mother's impassive face. She opened her wallet. "Here's my driver's license. I still live in Chicago. I'm a librarian there. So is my cousin, Faith. I don't know if you remember her." Hell, Megan didn't know at this point if her mother even remembered Megan. "Do you want to see it?" She held out her license.

Her mother gave it an even briefer look than she had the Woodstock photos. She didn't actually touch it or touch Megan.

Still no expression. No comment. Nothing.

"If this is a bad time, maybe I should come back later?" Megan said.

"No."

Okay, finally a verbal response. That meant her mother wanted her to stay, right? That was a good sign.

"Okay, so now you know that I really am Megan West, your daughter." She put her wallet away. "Like I said, I've been trying to find you for a few weeks now. Ever since I found out at Faith's wedding that you were still alive. Well, it was the reception actually. Not that you care about that."

At this point her mother didn't seem to care about anything. Maybe she was in shock? "I know my dad gave you a large sum of money to stay away from me."

"I wouldn't call it a large amount."

"Are you afraid of him? Did he or my uncle threaten you if you tried to contact me or if I found you?"

"Of course not."

"That's good to hear. I'm relieved."

Her mother didn't seem relieved.

"Are you okay?" Megan asked.

"No."

"You're surprised to see me. I get that." Maybe a blank face was her mother's way of expressing surprise. It could happen. Megan, ever the optimist, was frantically trying to find a silver lining. "And I've been babbling since I got here. Usually Faith is the one who babbles when she's nervous. She was going to come with me to D.C. but she's sick and I couldn't wait to meet you. She's the one who tracked you down. She's a librarian, like I said, but she has a PI license too. Because her dad and mine own West Investigations. But you know that already. I'm still babbling. Sorry." Megan looked down at the Woodstock photos she still held in her hand. "Do you still have the jeans?"

"What?"

She pointed to the group photo. "The jeans you wore to Woodstock."

"No."

"But you and Fiona promised you'd keep them."

Her mother shrugged. "It was a stupid promise."

"You've probably moved around a lot since then and that made keeping the jeans difficult. Or have you been in D.C. since you left Chicago?"

"No."

"Fiona said she thought you might have been in Europe several years ago."

"She talks too much."

"She wasn't gossiping or anything," Megan defended her. "She knew I'm your daughter and she was trying to be helpful."

"That was a stupid thing to do."

"What was? Her talking to me or me talking to her? Why all the secrecy? Are you involved in something with national security at the think tank?"

"As if I'd tell you if I was."

"Right. Good point." Again Megan stared at the photo before looking back at her mother, searching for some sign of the young woman she'd once been, the one who'd flashed the peace sign at Woodstock. She found none. She only saw a blank detachment. "Fiona will be disappointed that you didn't keep the jeans. She did."

"Like I said, it was a stupid promise."

Her indifference was getting to Megan, which was why she said, "Were your wedding vows a stupid promise?"

She gave Megan a haughty look. "That's a personal question."

"You're my mother. This is all personal."

"For you, maybe. Not for me."

Her mother's words hurt. But she wasn't done yet.

"I have no interest in being a mother," Astrid continued. "Then or now. I had your father tell you that I was dead because I didn't want you trying to track me down someday."

The words hit Megan like weapons and left gaping wounds. "I didn't . . . I didn't . . . know. He didn't tell me. I shouldn't . . . I shouldn't have come."

"No, you shouldn't have."

"I won't bother you again." Megan blindly headed for the door. She couldn't get out of there fast enough. Astrid stood aside to let her pass, placing the final nail in the coffin of Megan's wish for a mom of her own.

Megan was too numb to cry. She felt icy cold. As cold as her mother . . . she corrected herself. As cold as Astrid.

Even Faith's worst-case scenario couldn't have anticipated this situation. Megan had been so full of hope at locating her mother. The holidays were a time for family and reunions. Possibilities. Redemption. Instead, she felt a despair unlike anything she'd ever experienced before.

Megan was so lost in a blurred world of shocked pain that she had no idea how she made her way back to her hotel. How could she have been so stupid? What made her think her mother would welcome her with open arms? She'd already tried via her BlackBerry to get a flight back to Chicago tonight but nothing was available.

As the hotel room door closed behind her, Megan saw the vintage purple suitcase Pepper had given her in Las Resort sitting beside the bed. Megan had thought her mother might be able to spend the holiday weekend with her, so she'd packed enough to stay until Sunday if necessary. That certainly wasn't the case.

Today was the day after Thanksgiving. Black Friday. The name suited Megan's experience as never before. It had turned out to be a black, utterly dismal Friday.

Megan was so cold she didn't know if she'd ever warm up again. When someone knocked at her hotel room door a few moments later, she automatically went to open it before pausing at the last minute to look through the peephole to see who it was.

Logan stood there.

Megan opened the door. Logan took one look at her and stepped into the room to take her in his arms. "Are you okay?" he said gruffly.

Megan shook her head. She didn't know if she'd ever be okay again.

Her teeth were chattering, making speech difficult but she managed to say, "What are you doing here?"

"Faith sent me. She was worried about you. When she couldn't reach you on your cell, she was sure you'd come looking for your mother on your own despite something called a pinkie swear not to do anything foolish."

"I didn't think it was foolish. But I was wrong. Very, very wrong." Being held in his arms warmed her, reassured her, comforted her. But it didn't erase the pain.

"What happened?"

"She said she'd wanted my dad to tell me she was dead so I'd never try to find her." Repeating the words brought tears to Megan's eyes.

Logan swore under his breath.

"What's wrong with me that my own mother doesn't want me?" Megan half sobbed.

"There's nothing wrong with you. There's definitely something wrong with *her*."

"I'm going to cry," she warned him. "A lot."

"Go ahead. I can handle it."

And he did, patting her back and making soothing noises that she would never have expected from a tough guy like him. She'd thought that crying might send him running for the hills but no, he stood there and took it. He let her cry on his shoulder. And not just cry, but downright sob.

When she finally stopped, he leaned back slightly and smoothed her hair away from her tear-streaked face. "Feel a little better now?"

She nodded but felt embarrassed by her outburst. Stepping away from him, she reached for the tissue box on the nearby desk. She winced as she caught a glance of herself in the mirror. "I'm sorry about that. I don't usually fall apart like that. I know you might not believe me because this is the second time I've lost it with you."

"I don't mind if you lose it with me," he said.

"My nose is all red," she muttered, blowing into the tissue. "I look like Rudolph."

"I could say that you have a nice rack, but I'm a better man than that."

She couldn't help it, she had to smile at his stoic expression. "I can't believe you came all this way to see me. Wait a second, how did you know where to find me?"

"Faith checked your credit card records. She saw the flight you booked and the hotel. I had to make sure . . . you know . . . see for myself that you were okay. I had the weekend off anyway, which is rare. But I've been putting in a lot of overtime. All those calls that interrupted us before," he reminded her.

"Right."

"I can't get called into work from D.C."

"Really?" she teased him. "Are you sure the president won't need you for some emergency?"

"He's got the Secret Service, the FBI and CIA. I'm sure he can manage without me."

Megan wasn't sure she could manage without him. "Your shirt is all wet. I'm sorry."

"Don't be. I brought another shirt." He pointed to the duffle bag he'd dropped by the door before unbuttoning the denim shirt he wore.

"Let me." She moved closer and took over the unbuttoning duties.

Tilting up her chin, he looked deep into her eyes. She was a goner. Somehow she started kissing him. Or he started kissing her. She wasn't sure who made the first move. She only knew that having his lips on hers was as close to heaven as she could be.

Passion flared between them. She practically ripped his shirt off while he slid her jacket off her shoulders and let it fall onto the floor. She backstepped toward the bed, tugging him with her.

When the mattress hit the back of her knees, she yanked the bedding out of the way before tumbling backward onto the ritzy sheets. He came with her, kissing her deeply, sliding his hand beneath her top to undo the front fastening of her lacy bra. He cupped her bare breast in the palm of his hand as he brushed his thumb over her taut nipple. The need to join with him pulsed through her entire body.

She gently pushed him away in order to remove her top. He watched her and huskily said, "Are you sure?"

"Yes."

"You're upset."

"Because you're not kissing me."

She couldn't cope with another rejection, but the hot desire blazing in his eyes told her how much he wanted her. So did his kiss as he quickly lowered his head to consume her mouth. Eventually he moved on, lowering his lips to her breast, where he teased her with his talented tongue until she arched her back and shivered with delight.

Threading her hands through his hair, she shifted his attention to her other breast, which pouted at being ignored. With every pull of his mouth she experienced a mirroring tug deep within her womb. She'd never felt this way before. Never been so consumed with pleasure and desire.

Things moved rapidly after that as they disposed of items of clothing—her black pants, his jeans. Their embrace and caresses became more intimate. Megan moaned with pleasure as he slid his fingers beneath her lacy underwear to seduce her with his erotic touch. She was spinning out of control by the time he removed her underwear and his.

"Condom?" she whispered.

He leaned away to remove one from his wallet. "I was a Boy Scout. We're trained to be prepared."

"You thought you'd get lucky?"

He stared at her. "I didn't come to D.C. to have sex with you," he said bluntly. "We can stop this . . ."

"No, we can't," she said fiercely. "We've been fighting this forever." She cupped his erection, full and hot, in her hand. "I'm done fighting. Make love, not war."

He rolled on the condom. She reached for him and guided him into her. He rocked against her, sending her to a new level of sensual bliss. Her pleasure increased with every thrust he made until she reached the pinnacle and flew over the edge.

His ensuing shout of satisfaction brought a smile to her lips. She was too steeped in sexual delight to speak for several minutes.

"Was that your stomach growling or mine?" she asked.

"They don't feed you on the damn planes anymore."

"We better order room service. I have a feeling you're going to need to keep up your stamina." She placed her hand over his lips. "And don't say that's not the only thing you need to keep up."

He nipped her finger before licking the center of her palm. "As if I'd say such a thing."

"How many condoms did you bring?"

"Not enough. Order more when you order room service."

"I'm pretty sure condoms aren't on the menu."

"I suppose I could go down to the gift shop and get a box."

He rolled away from her and put on his briefs and jeans. He pulled a plain black T-shirt from his duffle bag. She sat up, tugging a sheet around her. "Don't be long."

He returned to kneel on the bed and kiss her senseless. "Don't worry, I'll hurry."

He did. He was back in time for them to make love again before the room service she'd ordered arrived.

She'd taken a quick shower while he dealt with the hotel employee who brought their meal. "Steak," he said approvingly.

"Protein for your . . . stamina."

"Strawberries and whipped cream."

"For dessert."

"I can hardly wait."

They shared their food, Logan offering her a taste of his steak while she offered him a taste of her asparagus. But dessert was the most fun of all. He dipped a strawberry in the bowl of whipped cream and offered it to her. She took a bite. So did he. Then he kissed the fruity juice from her lips before scooping her in his arms and dumping her on the tousled bed. "I'm a detective. I interrogate people for a living. I detect that you make this sexy kind of little gasp when I touch you right here. But I need to know more. Does this feel better?"

"That feels so good it should be criminal."

"How about this?" He reached for the bowl of whipped cream and placed a dollop on the tip of her breast. She shivered at the chill followed by the heat of his tongue lapping at her.

Later, when they were both nude, she returned the favor by placing a generous bit of whipped cream on the tip of his penis. His groans of pleasure made her feel powerful as she seduced him the way he'd done her.

The next morning, Megan sat on the straight-backed chair and nibbled on the fresh fruit they'd had brought to the room. She was wearing a blue cotton shirt of his and nothing else. The hem of his shirt hit her above her knees but that didn't stop him from leering at her.

"What is it with you and loose shirts?" she asked. "Most guys like tight T-shirts, preferably wet, tight T-shirts."

"You don't have to flaunt what you've got. I prefer to explore your . . . riches on my own."

"So you're an explorer now, hmm?"

He stood her up and backed her against the wall. He held her wrists above her head with one hand, which lifted the hem of the shirt she wore, giving him easy access. "An explorer and a miner. Searching for gold." He slid his index finger into her, brushing her most sensitive places. "I think I found it. A very rich vein."

She tilted her head against the wall as orgasmic tremors consumed her body.

"Should I stop . . . or explore more?" he murmured.

"More," she whispered.

"Hmm. Which way to go? Is there more gold here?" He brushed his thumb over her clitoris. "Or here?"

Every nerve was singing with divine bliss as he continued having his very wicked way with her.

By the time they left D.C. on Sunday morning, they had made a sizeable dent in the box of condoms. Megan fell asleep during the flight, with her head on Logan's shoulder.

She woke up a few minutes before they landed. "I was dreaming about your grandfather," she said. "You should thank Buddy for caring enough about you to do that intervention."

"If I do, do you promise to wear that oversized I LOVE D.C. T-shirt I bought you at the airport?"

Megan smiled her best vixen smile. "I promise."

• • •

Logan entered his grandfather's house to find Buddy sitting on the couch, watching the Bears game.

"How was D.C.?" he asked Logan.

Logan helped himself to a beer from the fridge and joined Buddy before replying. "D.C. was good."

"You and Megan do a lot of sightseeing?"

"None at all." He took a sip of beer from the can. "What's the score?"

"That's what I'm trying to find out," Buddy grumbled. "But you're not cooperating much."

"I was referring to the football game."

"It's seven to fourteen."

"Who are we playing?"

"The Redskins. You know, that team from D.C."

Logan grinned. "They're actually in Maryland. Interrogate me all you want, I'm not saying anything more about my trip."

"You don't have to. I can tell by the look on your face that things are good with you and Megan."

Logan let his grandfather's comment go without responding.

"Fine," Buddy grumbled. "If you won't confide in me, then do me a different favor."

"Depends what it is."

"Put that St. Michael's medallion your mother gave you back on. Don't look so surprised. I know, even if she doesn't, that you took it off when Will was killed. But you need to put it back on now. It's time."

Logan didn't know what to say.

"Promise me," Buddy insisted. "Put it on today."

"Fine. I'll put it on."

"Good. I'm glad to hear that. And I'm glad to hear that you and Megan had a good time in D.C. So you're a couple now, right?"

Logan didn't answer, instead focusing on the game and the pass interference call that was called on the Bears' defense. He waited for a commercial before hitting the mute button on the remote and stealing the last potato chips from the bowl between them. "About the last time we got together . . . I know I was grumpy at the time, but I appreciate what you did. With that intervention. I needed help and you gave it."

"You come by your grumpiness honestly," Buddy said. "And I'm glad you realize that you needed help. Even the toughest people have their limits, you know."

"Does that include you?"

Buddy nodded.

For the first time, Logan noticed how pale he looked. "Hey, are you okay?"

"Sure now, boy-o." He stood up and grabbed the bowl to get more chips. "Don't you be worrying about me." Then he collapsed.

Chapter Seventeen

· · · · · · · · · · ·

"**Gramps!**" Logan caught him before he fell to the
floor.

As he held his grandfather and lowered him to the
ground, Logan was instantly hit with the memory of
holding Will the same way. Panic knifed through him
before he shoved it aside. He was trained to expect the
unexpected. He could do this.

He automatically checked his grandfather's pulse with
one hand while calling 911 with the other. Buddy's heart
was still beating, thank God. His breathing was shallow,
though, and his color wasn't good. He'd lost consciousness but Logan kept talking to him anyway until the
EMTs arrived. He also kept giving updates to the emergency dispatcher. The ambulance arrived in less than five
minutes. The fire station was only a few blocks away.

His grandfather used to joke that's why he'd bought

the house: to be close to an ambulance should he ever need one. It was no joke now as Logan watched the paramedics working on Buddy.

"What medications is he on? Any medical conditions? A pacemaker? Heart trouble?" they asked.

Logan answered as best he could. He handed them the list of medications that the Aunts had insisted Buddy post on the freezer door after they'd read an article about senior safety. "He had triple bypass surgery about ten years ago. No trouble since then though."

Buddy didn't regain consciousness until they loaded him on a gurney. He removed his oxygen mask. "Ingrid," he gasped. "Get Ingrid!"

• • •

"You sound better," Megan told Faith as she entered her cousin's condo with a care package. "I brought you homemade chicken soup and your fave mac and cheese from the Comfort Café."

"Do you think you can bribe me with food?"

"Bribe you?"

Faith nodded. "So I'd forgive you for breaking a pinkie swear."

"I pinkie swore not to do anything *foolish*. I didn't consider what I was planning to be foolish. I know better now."

"Ya think?"

Megan hung her head.

"I was worried sick about you. Well, I was already sick, but you know what I mean. I couldn't go after you myself. I couldn't send your dad since I promised I wouldn't tell him anything about the search for your mom." Faith grabbed the bag of food from her and curled up on the couch with a comfy microfiber throw. She opened the soup container and used the spoon provided by the café to start eating. "Mmm, this is soooo good. It's a variation on chicken soup. It's more like a stracciatelli soup with eggs, orzo and finely grated Parmesan cheese." She paused to close her eyes in epicurean delight. When she opened them, she said, "Okay, there's a chance I'll forgive you but only after you tell me everything that happened. All you said on the phone was that it didn't go well but that you were okay. Are you really okay?"

"I'm better than I was."

"And did a sexy Chicago cop named Logan have anything to do with that?"

"I couldn't believe he flew all the way to D.C. to check on me. He said you sent him."

"I just asked him if he'd heard from you and shared my concerns about you going on your own. He had me check your credit card records, and the second we found out you'd charged a ticket and a hotel room, he was off to rescue you. We had no way of knowing if things were going well or not with your mom. Logan said if it went well, he'd celebrate with you. Luckily he had the weekend off, because he'd been putting in so many extra hours. And he has a cousin who works for the airlines."

"Yes, he told me."

"Tell me what happened with your mom first, then I want to hear every detail about Logan making you feel better. What did your mother do to make you feel so badly?"

"The bottom line is that she didn't want me looking for me. She told me she was the one who told my dad to say she was dead so I wouldn't go after her someday."

Faith's eyes widened in disbelief.

"Those were her words. She didn't tell me that until after I'd made a fool of myself, going on about how I'd been searching for her after only recently discovering she was alive. I even brought the photos I got from Fiona of them at Woodstock. She looked at them without any sign of emotion. She showed no emotion the entire time I was there. I thought at first maybe she didn't believe that I was who I said I was so I showed her my driver's license. That didn't really help."

"Oh, Megan, I'm so sorry. I'd hug you but I don't want to give you any germs I may still have."

"You did try to warn me."

"Yes, but to actually say that she was the one who concocted the story that she was dead." Faith shook her head. "I don't know how to respond to that."

"I didn't know how to respond either. I apologized for bothering her and got out of there as fast as I could."

"You must have been devastated. Here." Faith handed her the unopened container of mac and cheese. "Have some of this. It will make you feel better. Here's an unopened plastic-covered fork."

"Thanks." Megan took a bite and chewed slowly. "I think the reason she was so hard to locate was that she didn't want me finding her." She put a hand to her throat as emotion gripped her. She set the food on the coffee table. "That's pretty hard to take, you know? What does it say about me that my own mother couldn't love me?"

"That you had a rotten mother."

"She deserted me when I was two years old."

"Look at it this way. Would it have been better if she'd stuck around and constantly made you feel unwanted? Instead, you were raised by your dad, who loved you to bits and still does."

"If he'd only told me that she didn't want to see me . . ."

"Would you have believed him?"

"Maybe not," Megan admitted. "I was pretty swept up with the idea of having a mother of my own."

"Besides, he didn't even know you were looking for her."

"She didn't keep her Woodstock jeans," Megan said abruptly.

Faith blinked. "Huh?"

"She and Fiona had promised to keep their jeans forever. The ones they wore at Woodstock. Fiona kept hers. Astrid didn't. She said it was a stupid promise so I asked her if her promise in marrying my dad was stupid."

"Wow. What did she say to that?"

"That it was a personal question. I told her this was *all* personal. She didn't see it that way. She was so cold. Detached."

"Good riddance to her. You're better off without her. I know you don't think that yet, but you will. Enough about her. Let's get back to Logan."

"I was pretty upset when he showed up."

"I can imagine."

"I felt numb."

Faith grinned. "I'll bet he cured you of that feeling."

"He was really understanding about it all."

"And?"

"And he was patient when I cried."

"And?"

Megan smiled. "And we didn't leave the hotel room until we headed back here."

"Really. You didn't go sightseeing?"

"Not of D.C."

"Oh ho. So you were sightseeing and touring one Logan Doyle, eh? You're blushing. A lot. It was that good, huh?"

Megan nodded.

"So something good came out of something bad," Faith said.

"What do you mean?"

"I mean that the something bad obviously was the meeting with your . . . with Astrid," she automatically corrected herself. "That woman is no mother. And the something good is Logan."

"It's not that simple."

"Of course it's not. Relationships rarely are."

"I'm in a relationship with Logan," Megan said with a sense of awe.

Faith laughed. "That's only just now occurring to you?"

"I was distracted before."

"And you claimed you didn't want to be distracted. I told you that distraction can be wonderful. So now that you know that, what are you going to do about it?"

"Do about it?"

"Where do you see things going between you and Logan?"

"I see us going to bed a lot. I don't know what will happen. You need to be tough to be in love with a cop."

"We already had this discussion. You're tough but nice."

"Yes, but am I tough enough to handle him being in such a dangerous profession? I don't know. Being bold and brave aren't the first things that come to mind when I think of my strengths."

"You don't think it was bold and brave to take off on your own to D.C.?"

"Look how well that turned out."

"But you survived. What doesn't destroy you strengthens you. You've got the T-shirt with that Nietzsche quote."

"You got it for me."

"Because it's true."

"For you, maybe."

"For you, for sure," Faith said.

"I'm not the one who took off on my Italian honeymoon on my own."

"No, you're the one who took off on a road trip with a sexy cop in the middle of the night from Vegas."

"I didn't think it would turn into a road trip."

"You don't give yourself enough credit," Faith said.

"The fact that Astrid rejected me might have something to do with that."

"Don't let her do that to you. Don't give her that kind of power over you. Focus instead on the way Logan makes you feel."

Megan smiled slowly. "He makes me feel pretty damn awesome."

"Yeah?"

Megan nodded. "His detecting and interrogating skills are remarkable."

Her BlackBerry vibrated. She checked caller ID. "It's Logan."

"My grandfather collapsed and is in the ER," he said. "He wants Ingrid."

"Is he going to be okay?"

"They don't know yet. Can you bring her?"

"Of course." She got the name of the hospital. "We'll be there as fast as we can."

"What's going on?" Faith asked.

"Buddy collapsed and he's in the hospital asking for Gram."

Forty minutes later, Megan accompanied Gram into the ER. She found Logan in the crowded waiting room. He was pacing. "How's Buddy?" Gram demanded, her voice strained. "What do the doctors say?"

"They think it's his heart," Logan said, "but they're still running tests."

"Can I see him?" Gram asked.

Logan shook his head. "Not yet. They're not letting any of us in to see him right now."

"He's not going to die, is he?" Tears welled in Gram's eyes. "Tell me he's not going to die."

"My dad is too stubborn to die," an older man said. "Not gonna happen. Not on my watch."

"Are you a doctor?" Megan asked.

"I'm Logan's dad."

"And Buddy's son," Gram added. "Where are the Aunts?"

"On their way."

Megan moved closer to Logan. "Are you okay?"

He nodded. "I was with him when he collapsed."

"That's good. At least he wasn't alone."

"I'm telling you, he's too stubborn to die," Logan's dad repeated. "I'm Billy Doyle, by the way. You must be Megan."

She nodded. Now that she took a closer look, she recognized the similarities between Billy and Logan. He had Logan's eyes.

"I've heard a lot about you," Billy said.

"You have?"

"Buddy thinks very highly of you."

Megan wondered about Logan. Did he think highly of her? Had he talked to his dad and grandfather about her? Then she chastised herself for such selfish thoughts. She should be focusing on Buddy's well-being.

The wait seemed endless but it was actually barely an hour later when a nurse came through the doors to the waiting room. "Buddy Doyle's family?"

They all stood. Except for Logan, who had yet to sit in the first place.

"He's being admitted to the cardiac unit," the nurse said. "Which one of you is Ingrid?"

Gram stepped forward. "I am."

"He's been asking for you. Come on back."

"Did he have a heart attack? Is he going to be okay?" Gram asked.

"We'll know more in a few hours. For now, he's stable."

"Thank God," Billy said as he sank onto a chair.

Logan showed no outward sign of emotion, but Megan could sense he wasn't as calm as he seemed. "Does this bring back memories of your partner's death?" she asked quietly.

"Will died before he got to the hospital."

"I'm sorry." She slid her hand in his. She was prepared for him to pull away but instead he threaded his fingers through hers. "Is there anything I can do?"

"Just be here." He paused to take a deep breath. "You know how Buddy gave up swearing."

"Right."

"I never told you why he did that. He'd made a pact with God that if he survived his heart surgery a decade ago, he'd never swear again. And he kept that pact until I went to Vegas and told him he was still married."

"You better not even be thinking about blaming yourself for Buddy collapsing. Look at me." She took his face between her hands. "This is not your fault."

"He collapsed while I was talking to him."

"About what?"

"I'd thanked him for that intervention," Logan said.

"And that upset him?"

"No, he was pale when I got there."

"My point exactly. You didn't do anything to cause his collapse. You don't run the world, you know," she said. "You just think you do."

Gram's return prevented Logan from answering. "He looked so pale," Gram said. "And he has tubes and wires connected to him."

"One of the tubes is probably oxygen and another would be connecting him to an IV for any meds. The wires are to monitor his heartbeat and blood pressure," Megan said. "A good friend of mine's mom had heart trouble a few months ago and I saw her in the hospital. She's fine now though."

"You have a good memory to recall all those things," Billy said.

"She's very smart," Gram bragged. "She's a librarian."

"Yes, I know."

Logan eyed his dad carefully. "Do you want me to get you some coffee or something?"

"When Dad had his bypass surgery a decade ago, I was still drinking. It helped dull the pain and the worry. I don't have that option this time."

"Do you need me to call your sponsor?" Logan asked.

"No, but thanks for the offer."

"And thanks for butting in with Gramps the other night."

"You're my son. It's my job to butt in. I may not have been the best dad in the world for you in the past, but that can change."

"It already has," Logan said.

• • •

Megan didn't return home until the wee hours of the morning. By then, Buddy had continued to improve and was even demanding to be released. Gram was staying in the room with him, keeping him manageable, she said. Before Megan had left, Gram had taken her aside outside the hospital room and shed a few tears of relief before saying, "Time is precious. Not just for Buddy and me. For everyone. You think there's all the time in the world—to get angry, to make up. But there isn't. All we have is the here and now. This was a real wake-up call. The doctor said stress contributed to Buddy's collapse. His blood pressure was high and he wasn't remembering to take his medicines. That's going to change."

"So you two are back together?"

Gram nodded. "We can work out the details of his annulment later. For now, the important thing is that

Buddy is going to be all right and that the two of us are going to be together because life isn't open-ended. Don't ever forget that."

Megan thought of nothing else the next day at work. She went through the motions—answering reference questions, showing a patron how to use the public computers, attending a staff meeting, working on a speech she was supposed to give at ALA Midwinter in January—but her thoughts remained consumed with what Gram had said.

Which was why she called Logan during her afternoon break. "Do you think you could stop by my place after work? Unless you're going to the hospital to see Buddy?"

"I stopped by on my lunch break and he seems to be doing just fine. Your grandmother is keeping him in line."

"I'm glad to hear that. If you come over tonight, I'll make you a home-cooked meal."

"Are strawberries and whipped cream on the menu?"

"Absolutely."

"I'll be there," he said. "Around seven okay?"

"Fine. See you then."

When Megan got home with groceries from the nearby food market, Megan noticed that Danny Boone was not on duty. She hadn't seen him that morning either, it now occurred to her. The temp replacement, an old guy with a comb-over trying to hide his baldness, said Danny was on vacation in Tennessee with his family for a few more days.

In addition to the strawberries and a can of whipped cream, Megan got salmon steaks, which would be easy to grill once Logan arrived. But her mind wasn't on the menu or even what erotic things could be done with that can of whipped cream. No, her focus was on the decision she'd made to tell Logan she loved him.

Gram was right: Time was precious.

A knock at her front door a few minutes later had her heart beating fast. Logan was a little early. No problem. The temp doorman hadn't called ahead to warn her someone was coming up. Impatient to see her, Logan probably just flashed his badge at the guy.

She eagerly opened it to find Astrid standing there.

Megan could hardly believe her eyes. "What are you doing here?"

"I came to see you."

"Why? What do you want?"

"Can I come in so we can talk?"

As Megan grudgingly allowed her in, she realized that the brief conversation they'd just had was similar to the one they'd had in D.C.—only now the roles were reversed. Megan doubted that Astrid was experiencing one-billionth of the nerves that Megan had a few days ago, however.

"How did you know where to find me?" Megan said.

"Your address was on your driver's license. You showed it to me."

"Only for a few moments."

Astrid shrugged. "I have a photographic memory."

She seemed willing to forget me fast enough, Megan thought.

"I'm in Chicago for a conference," Astrid said.

Goodie for you. Megan was tempted to say the words aloud but was too nice to do so. Instead she said, "I'm expecting company shortly."

"I didn't like the way we left things," Astrid said. "I don't think I expressed myself well."

"You were pretty clear about not wanting anything to do with me."

"I didn't want you growing up thinking I abandoned you. You shouldn't have to suffer just because I couldn't be a good mother. It wasn't you. It was me. Anyway, I brought you something. I lied about the jeans."

"The jeans?" Megan repeated in confusion.

"The jeans from Woodstock. I did keep them. I thought you might want them. Here." She practically shoved them at Megan.

Megan was speechless. In that moment of stunned silence, Smudge meandered into the living room, where the cat paused to stretch and yawn before noticing Astrid. Smudge instantly arched her back and hissed before turning and racing out of the room.

"You have a black cat," Astrid said. "Interesting."

"What's that supposed to mean?"

"I was just making polite conversation. I'm not very good at it. I'm not a hugger or a joiner. But I did have a black cat when I was growing up. Her name was Kinder. It's German for child."

"Do you speak German?"

Astrid nodded. "I moved back there after the divorce for several years. I also worked on mathematical analysis at CERN—that's the European Laboratory for Particle Physics located near Geneva, Switzerland. I don't know if you're aware that a scientist at CERN invented the World Wide Web in 1989."

"I wasn't aware of that, no."

"I did wonder if perhaps you'd gone into the field of mathematics, considering both your parents are in the field. But you told me you're a librarian, correct?"

"Yes."

"Your father's sister-in-law was a librarian, yes?"

Megan nodded. "That's right."

"She seemed like a hugger. She didn't approve of our plan but agreed to stay silent."

"You said it was *your* plan. That you didn't want me bothering you, so you said to tell me you were dead."

"I explained that. I didn't want you to suffer because I couldn't be a good mother. It's not like I left and had other children. I realized I was no good at it. I lacked the skills."

"You could have learned the skills."

"Perhaps I used the wrong word then. I couldn't learn the ability. I lack it. People tell me I'm detached and they're right. I can deal with mathematical equations. Not people."

"My father can deal with both."

"Which is why I gave you to him. Wasn't he a good parent to you? Didn't he show you love? Didn't he hug you?"

Megan nodded. "More times than I could ever count."

"There you go then. I did the right thing."

"I don't know that I'd go that far."

"I don't want to undo all his good work. I never meant to hurt you. Quite the opposite. I was trying to do the right thing. Not just for me, but for you as well. I'm sorry if I failed at that."

"So what now?" Megan asked.

"I'm not sure. What are your thoughts on the matter?"

"I'm not sure either."

"We could maybe . . . stay in touch?" Astrid said tentatively.

"Via the World Wide Web?" Megan teased.

"Ah, you have your father's sense of humor. That is a good thing. Does he still carve the symbol for pi on the pumpkin at Halloween?"

Megan nodded.

"He's a good man."

"Did you break up because of me?" Megan had to ask. "Because you had a baby?"

"No."

"But you didn't want children."

"I didn't know what I wanted. I don't regret having you. I regret that I couldn't be the mother you wanted and needed. If I'd stayed, I would have messed you up—not intentionally, but it would have happened. I'm sure of it. I couldn't do that to you. My parents messed me up, always telling me that everything was my fault. They loved me in their own way, I suppose, and I loved them in mine, but it wasn't a good thing."

"Did you love my father?" Megan asked.

"I did at the time."

"But you loved mathematics more?"

"I felt more secure with mathematics. It was not risky."

"I have trouble with risk as well where emotions are concerned."

Astrid looked surprised. "Yet you took a huge risk coming to see me the way you did."

"I know."

"I'm sorry I'm not the huggable mother you were searching for."

"I'm not the only one who took a huge risk. You took a risk coming to see me today. I could have turned you away."

"The way I did you."

"You didn't slam the door in my face."

"Not literally, perhaps. I'm aware I was not welcoming. I don't do welcoming very well," Astrid admitted.

"Maybe I could help you with that. If you want me to."

Astrid paused a moment before nodding slowly. "That could be . . . educational. I must get back to the conference now."

"I understand."

Astrid looked at her. "I think you do. Thank you for that. I'll be in Chicago for a week. Perhaps we can do this again?"

"Do you want my cell number? Or do you prefer e-mail?"

"I have them both. Fiona gave them to me."

"You contacted Fiona?"

Astrid nodded. "For old times' sake."

"Did you tell her you had the Woodstock jeans?"

"I did. And I told her I planned on giving them to you. She thought that was a good idea. I thought it might be too sentimental . . ."

"No. Trust me, you can't be too sentimental with me."

"Thank you. That's good to know. I look forward to learning more."

"Same here," Megan said.

Astrid eyed her warily. "You're not going to hug me, are you?"

"Not today, no."

"Good. I appreciate that."

"I can't say that I'll never ever hug you," Megan said. "But if that day ever comes, I'll give you plenty of warning ahead of time."

"Fair enough."

After Astrid left, Megan glanced at her watch. Logan should be arriving any second. Wait until he heard about this latest development with her mother. Megan wasn't sure what to make of it, but it seemed like a positive step.

It appeared that risk aversion ran in her family, at least where her parents were concerned. But Buddy's collapse and Gram's words had made Megan see that time shouldn't be wasted. She couldn't wait to tell Logan she loved him. She didn't expect him to say the words back to her. At least not right away.

She realized he'd been burned in a bad marriage. He'd known more than his fair share of pain. It wasn't easy for him to open up. But she knew that beneath his tough exterior beat the heart of a good man.

She was still leaning against the door when someone knocked. This had to be Logan! She yanked the door open.

Her father stood there.

Chapter Eighteen

. . . .

"**Faith** just told me that you met with your mother in D.C."

Megan ushered him in. "You just missed her."

"Your mother was here?"

"Yes."

"I don't understand," he said. "I thought you went to meet her in D.C. and that it didn't go well there. I dragged that information out of Faith while she was woozy from cold medicine. So maybe I misunderstood?"

"No, you didn't misunderstand. I did go to D.C. and my first interaction with Astrid did not go well. Why didn't you let me know that she was the one who suggested you tell me she was dead? Is it true?"

He nodded slowly. "That's not something you tell your child."

"I'm not a child any longer."

"You'll always be my little girl."

He said it so tenderly that Megan had to blink away the tears, and she had to hug him, she just *had* to. He hugged her back so fiercely that she almost cried. He was her dad—the one who loved her, who'd held her when she broke her toe at age six, who'd sat in the front row and videotaped every single one of her ballet recitals from age eight through eleven, who'd proudly took her photograph for her first high school prom. Her dad was the person who had always been there for her no matter what. That was the bottom line here.

Megan finally stepped away and blinked away the dampness in her eyes. "I'll always be your little girl, but not hers."

"Why did she come here today? What did she want?" he said suspiciously. "What did she say to make you cry?"

"It's not her, it's you."

He looked stricken.

"No." She reached for his hand. "I'm crying in a *good* way because you've been the best dad in the universe to me. Astrid told me that's why she left me with you— because she knew she couldn't be a parent. She was lacking something inside. But she knew you'd be awesome, and you have been."

"I've made mistakes."

"So you're not perfect. Neither am I."

"Astrid isn't an evil person."

"I realize that now. She's even interested in continuing a dialogue with me. Not a mother-daughter relationship but a person-to-person one."

"I should have told you sooner."

"I understand now why you didn't. You didn't want to tell me she was avoiding me, that she didn't want me contacting her at any point. Did you know she was at Woodstock when she was a teenager?"

"No, I didn't know that."

"She kept the jeans from that weekend all these years. She and a friend had made a pact to keep them and Astrid did. She brought them to Chicago and gave them to me."

He looked confused as she showed him the jeans. "Muddy jeans? Why?"

"For sentimental reasons."

"Are you going to wash them?"

"I don't know. I don't think I'm going to wear them. They represent a time when the world was filled with possibilities for Astrid."

"You're using her first name."

"Because she never was a mother to me and never will be. And I think I'm finally okay with that," she said slowly.

"I'm glad. Listen, I have some news about Buddy's second wife. Faith couldn't go visit him today because she's still fighting that cold. So she did some digging, got some info from Logan about the woman's name and date of the marriage in Vegas. Buddy's pride wouldn't let him accept Faith's offer of help when she got home from her honeymoon. But when she heard the doctor say stress played a factor in Buddy's collapse, she went ahead anyway. You know Faith is awesome at finding information."

"I know. I might not have found Astrid if it weren't for her."

"Well, it turns out the woman died in some out-of-the-way place in Utah. Faith called me on the way over here."

"Which means Buddy is free to marry Gram now. That's good news. I talked to her this morning; she said Buddy should be released from the hospital tomorrow morning."

"So it looks like everything is working out in the end," her dad said.

Megan smiled, thinking of Logan on his way to be with her, and the can of whipped cream she planned to use on him later. "Yeah, everything is working out," she agreed. "Hold on a second, that's Faith calling now." Megan answered her BlackBerry. "Hey Faith, Dad and I were just talking about you."

"Do you have the TV on?"

"No."

"Turn it on." Faith's voice was strained.

"Why? I'm expecting Logan for dinner any minute—"

"He's going to be late."

Megan frowned. "What do you mean? How do you know that? Did he call you?"

"Are you sitting down?"

"Faith, you're scaring me."

Are you okay? her dad mouthed.

Megan shook her head. "Turn on the TV. Channel Five."

Her dad reached for the remote, and a second later Megan saw a special report news segment with one of the local female reporters saying, "We're here live at police headquarters. It's still very early in this situation, so we don't have a lot of information at this point, just that there's been a shooting here. The building is currently in lockdown. We don't know how many are injured or how serious those injuries might be. We have confirmation of one officer down, perhaps two. We also don't know if it's a single gunman or multiple shooters. We're getting word that there may be a hostage situation going on here as well, but that is still unconfirmed as of yet."

"Logan works there," Megan whispered, sinking onto the couch.

"I know," Faith said.

"Maybe he already left. He could be on his way here. I've got to call his cell." Megan hung up and hit speed dial. It went directly to Logan's voice mail. "You know the routine. Leave a message."

"It's Megan. Please call me. I hope you're okay." She

had to keep her message short because she was afraid her voice would start cracking if she spoke any longer.

"Don't panic," her dad said as he joined her on the couch and put a comforting arm around her shoulders. "Maybe he stopped at the hospital to visit Buddy."

A phone call to Gram, who was in Buddy's hospital room visiting him, disproved that theory. "Is Logan with you?" Gram asked.

"No," Megan said, her stomach dropping to the soles of her feet. "I was calling you to ask the same question."

"Buddy says he's sure Logan is okay because Logan is wearing his St. Michael medallion again."

"The patron saint of police officers," Megan said.

"That's right. I know what's on the TV now is scary, but hang in there, okay? And let us know when Logan calls you."

"Same with you, okay?"

"Absolutely."

"Buddy and Gram haven't heard from him," Megan told her father.

She shoved her fear down deep so it wouldn't overwhelm her, but it refused to be managed. "I don't know if I can do this," Megan said with tears in her eyes.

"You don't want to spend the rest of your life thinking about a chance you didn't take. I don't regret taking a chance on Astrid even though it didn't work out."

"You don't?"

"No. Do you want to know why?"

Megan nodded.

"Because loving her gave me you." He reached out to cup her cheek. "And you are definitely the best and brightest thing in my life."

"Oh, Daddy." She held back a sob.

"You haven't called me that since you were twelve," he said gruffly.

"I know."

"Can I get you anything?" he asked with concern. "Some tea? Wine?"

"I'll get it." She brought the bottle of Argentinean Merlot that she'd offered Logan the first time he'd come to her condo and they'd shared a pizza. She brought two wineglasses and filled them both.

Meanwhile the local station had resumed normal broadcasting. Megan channel-surfed but she couldn't find any more coverage on the situation. A tense two hours later, Logan finally called in.

"I'm sorry I'm late," he said. "Something came up."

"Yes, I heard. It was on the TV."

"I'm on my way now." He paused. "Or is it too late?"

Was it too late? Would she be able to hide her fear from him? Could she bounce back from the nervous wreck she'd been for the past few hours? She'd have to. "No," she said unsteadily. "It's not too late."

"Good. I'll be there in about five minutes."

Megan's dad and Logan crossed paths in the hallway. Megan kept her door open as she pulled Logan inside. He was wearing his customary work attire of black pants and blue shirt with a dark tie. She removed his black leather jacket and tossed it aside.

"Are you okay?" She ran her hands over his arms and chest as if searching for possible injuries.

"I'm okay." He took her hands in his. "The media exaggerated the situation. The suspect was the one shot. The police officer down actually tripped and broke his ankle. No weapon was involved except maybe for his own shoelaces, which he tripped over while trying to apprehend the suspect."

"Were you in danger?"

"I was in danger of missing a date with you and some whipped cream," he murmured huskily.

"I'm serious."

"So am I. Let me show you how serious."

Logan didn't want to talk about it. Okay, Megan got that. She also got that he was using sex as a distraction, but she didn't care. She wanted to be distracted by him. She wanted to be taken to new heights of ecstasy by him . . . and she was.

But after they'd made love and Logan fell asleep, Megan sat and stared at him for hours. She saw the medallion around his neck and touched it as if to reassure herself that it was still there. He'd taken it off when they'd had sex but she'd insisted he put it on again afterward. She wanted him protected. She *needed* to have him protected.

The bottom line was that Megan was spooked. She told herself she just needed some time to recover. For the next two weeks, she threw herself into holiday preparations and spending time with Logan. He helped her decorate her tree and didn't mock the teacup motif of the ornaments she was using this year. She rewarded him with whipped cream, which she now kept stocked in her fridge at all times.

She made love with him whenever she could but didn't tell him she loved him. Not yet. She was still trying to work up her nerve.

Meanwhile she carried out her customary holiday traditions, like lunch with Faith and Gram at the Walnut Room in the former Marshall Field's store. Afterward, Faith stopped at Megan's condo.

"This is your first Christmas as a married woman," Megan noted as she handed Faith a cup of hot cocoa. "How's Caine holding up?"

"He's the best. He took such good care of me when I was sick. He even went to stand in line for Do-It-Yourself Messiah tickets for me. You know, legend has it that when Handel's 'Messiah' debuted in Dublin in April 1742, the ladies were asked to attend sans hoops in their skirts and gentlemen sans swords because they expected the audience to be huge." Her expression turned dreamy.

"Thinking about Handel gives you that goofy look on your face?" Megan teased her.

"No. Thinking about Caine and his sword does."

Megan laughed and took a sip of tea before saying, "Did I tell you that I got an e-mail from Fiona yesterday?"

"Fiona of brothel fame?"

Megan nodded. "She asked if I'd gotten the Woodstock jeans from Astrid. She also wrote that Pepper Dior e-mailed her asking for my address. Fiona didn't know if she should give it out, so Pepper included a message for Fiona to forward on to me. I told you about Pepper from Last Resort, right?"

"The one you got all those vintage outfits from."

"Right. Anyway, it turns out that that storage room where they tried to hold Logan and me had some unexpected treasures in it."

"Like what?"

"Like a remarkably preserved Native American blanket worth . . . are you ready?"

"Yes."

"$100,000."

Faith almost spewed her hot cocoa over Smudge, who was curled up on the couch beside them.

"There were several antique quilts and other items worth money as well," Megan said. "They're going to use the funds for improvements to the café and motel. Pepper wrote that if I hadn't been locked up in the storage room and found the teacup I liked, they wouldn't have thought to look through the stuff."

"What teacup?"

"This one." Megan held it up.

"Is it worth a ton of money too?"

"Only to me." She ran a finger over the Wedgwood design. It seemed like a lifetime ago that she and Logan had been marooned in Last Resort. So much had happened since then.

"Tell me again why she wanted to lock you and Logan up in a storage room?" Faith said.

"It was their version of a jail."

"Right. The shotgun wedding scheme. So tell me, what's up with you and Logan these days? Things are pretty serious, huh? Have you told him how you feel about him yet? Has he told you?"

"No to both questions. What's the rush?"

"Didn't you tell me when Buddy was in the hospital that Gram saying time is precious really hit home and made you realize life is short?"

"Okay, you're right. I'm not making sense. But I'm scared."

"Of what?"

"Of everything."

"Well, that narrows it down."

"What if he doesn't love me? What if this is just a fling for him? What if he *does* love me, and something happens to him? What if I can't cope with the stress of his job?"

"What if you drive yourself nuts by asking too many what-ifs?" Faith said.

"Don't try telling me what Jane Austen would do. That doesn't work for me."

"What *does* work for you?"

"Logan."

"There you go then. Just have faith and go with that. See where it takes you."

"What if it takes me right off a cliff?"

"Then a parachute would come in handy."

"Yeah. Know where I can get one of those?"

"It's all about taking chances, isn't it? You read Emma's book *Taking Chances*. Risk versus reward. Is the reward worth the risk?"

When Megan was with Logan, the answer to that question was yes. The problem was that when she wasn't with him, the doubts and fears set in.

But Gram was right. Time was precious and life was short.

That was still the case when Logan picked her up to go to the ice rink Sunday afternoon. When she'd mentioned that she'd always wanted to go to the McCormick Tribune Plaza and Ice Rink on the western edge of Millennium Park, he'd insisted that he'd be happy to take her skating. She'd visited in the summer, when the rink was turned into an outdoor café with the awesome view of the Michigan Avenue skyline, but never in the winter. The skyline was just as impressive and was hands down one of the best views in Chicago. She, however, was not one of the best skaters.

Megan was a reference librarian, so naturally she'd done her research beforehand, especially refreshing her knowledge on how to fall and get up again on skates. She'd also read all she could about police psychology and police families. Much of it she already knew, at least where the police stuff was concerned. The skating stuff was tied in because at times she felt like she was skating on thin ice. Especially when she almost fell on her fanny the second they got on the rink.

Logan kept her upright and kept his arm around her. "Relax. Trust me, I'm a professional."

"A professional cop, not a professional ice-skater," she said, tugging her angora knit hat down lower on her head with one hand while clutching his arm with the other.

"I'll have you know that you're hanging on to a guy who played four years of hockey in college and could have played for the Blackhawks."

"Really. The Chicago Blackhawks?"

"The Berwyn Blackhawks."

"I doubt there even is such a team."

"You doubt me?" He loosened his hold on her to give her a reprimanding look with those sexy eyes of his.

She grabbed his arm as one of her skates almost slid out from under her on the slippery ice. "This is much harder than it looks."

"And that's just my arm. You should feel the rest of my body."

"Logan! There are kids here."

"I love when you use your scandalized librarian voice on me."

"Behave yourself. As for your four years of hockey, I had four years of ballet in middle school."

"Hockey trumps ballet any day."

"Ha!" She was more determined than ever to show him some moves. She'd been deliberately underplaying her talent. Okay, maybe it didn't rank as talent per se, but she wasn't as klutzy as she seemed. She released his arm and did a pirouette on ice. "I did it!"

"I love you," he blurted out.

"What?" She almost fell on her fanny with shock.

"You heard me."

"Are you blushing?"

'No," he growled. "Keep skating."

"Wait. Did you mean what you just said?"

"I don't say things I don't mean."

"You love me?"

"Yes."

"You don't look very happy about it."

"I planned on telling you in a more romantic setting." He glared at a group skating by. "Without all these people around."

"You can still do that."

"Yeah, but it won't be the first time I tell you."

She unzipped her jacket as the sound of Gloria Estefan's "Let It Snow, Let It Snow, Let It Snow" filled the air around the rink with its sassy brass section.

"What are you doing?" Logan demanded.

"You'll see." She lifted the hem of her red sweater.

"Are you going to flash me in public?" He appeared pleased by the prospect.

"No. Look." Beneath the sweater was the I LOVE D.C. T-shirt he'd given her. She'd put masking tape over D.C. and wrote on it so it now read I LOVE LOGAN. "I was going to tell you somewhere private too."

"Really?"

She nodded. "I don't say things I don't mean."

"You didn't really say it yet. Are you sure you're okay with me being a cop?"

Here was the pivotal moment. Time to go forward and take chances instead of falling back in fear. Sure, there would be times she'd fall down, but as long as she knew how to get up again, she'd be okay.

She was tough. She was brave. She was bold. She could cope with the stress of his job. She couldn't cope with the regret she'd have if she never even tried.

She'd been spooked by the realization that loving Logan was an emotional hazard that could end up breaking her heart. But she had the strength now to take that risk instead of playing it safe as she always had in the past. And so she said, "Yes."

"Yes?"

"Yes, I love you. Yes, I'm okay with you being a cop."

He dragged her sweater down and fastened her coat. "Let's go."

"Where?"

"Someplace quiet, private and romantic."

"My bedroom?"

"That works."

It not only worked, it proved to be an incredible night filled with love, laughter, sex and whipped cream.

Who could ask for anything more?

• • •

One year later . . .

It was a terrible day for a wedding in Chicago. The city was in the midst of the worst blizzard in years with wind-chills below zero. Luckily, Megan, Logan and most of their families were in sunny Las Vegas at the Venetian.

Their guests at the ceremony included Astrid, who insisted she was there as "an interested bystander" and not as mother of the bride, which was fine with Megan. Also present were Last Resort residents Pepper, Rowdy and Chuck as well as Fiona from the Butterfly Ranch. Connor acted as Logan's best man while Faith was Megan's matron of honor.

"Are you sure you don't mind me using the same wedding venue that you did?" Megan asked Faith.

"For the thousandth time, I'm sure," Faith said. "And I appreciate you choosing an Empire-style matron of honor dress that not only hides the fact that I'm four months pregnant, but also is a gorgeous burgundy color. Now let's go out there and be the bold women we were born to be."

"My little girl is about to get married," her dad said

as they prepared to walk down the aisle to where Logan stood waiting. "You look so beautiful."

"Thanks." Megan loved her wedding gown. The white dress was new although in a vintage princess style with a strapless satin bodice and a satin-lined tulle full skirt.

"Logan is a lucky man and he knows it."

She blinked away the dampness in her eyes. "Don't make me cry, Daddy."

"Don't make me cry, either," he said with an unsteady laugh. "Are you ready?"

"Yes," Megan said firmly. "Absolutely."

She and Logan had selected music from the final verses of the song "Chances" for this part of the ceremony. Slowly walking down the aisle with her dad, Megan flashed back to Logan formally asking her dad for her hand in marriage last Valentine's Day, right before Buddy and Gram got married.

"Too bad the Swedish mob couldn't attend," Logan had teased the happy couple.

"They're very discreet," Buddy had said.

Megan smiled at the memory. Her Art Deco filigree-style engagement ring flashed on her finger. Logan's actual proposal to her had taken place later on Valentine's night in her bedroom, when he'd taken off her clothes and slipped on her ring. He'd gotten down on one knee beside the bed and simply said, "Please marry me."

She'd cried and simply said yes. She'd never forget the love in his blue eyes.

Her breath caught as she saw the way Logan was staring at her now. He'd communicated his feelings for her in so many ways—by talking to her about the things that mattered to him, by opening his heart to her, by sharing his thoughts. None of that was easy for a cop trained to control his emotions, but he'd done it . . . for her. He looked incredibly sexy in a dark suit, crisp white shirt and black tie.

The minister, the same one who'd officiated at Faith's wedding, eyed the couple warily as he went through the short ceremony.

"The bride and groom want to say a few words," the minister said.

"Here we are," Megan said, holding on to both of Logan's hands with both of her own. "Returning to the scene of the crime, where you stole my heart. And a good part of my sanity as well." Their families laughed. "But I'm not just crazy in love with you, I love you for the incredibly strong and caring man you are."

"I was in a dark place back then," Logan admitted. "And trying to hide it from the world. But you brought me back into the light." He touched her cheek with their joined hands. "I'm so lucky to have you and your love."

"Luck had nothing to do with it," Pepper called out. "It was destiny!"

"I now pronounce you husband and wife," the minister hurriedly declared.

Logan took Megan in his arms and kissed her as the sound of "Let It Snow, Let It Snow, Let It Snow" and white confetti snowflakes magically filled the air.

Luck or destiny, Megan knew deep in her heart that she'd made the right choice in loving Logan. Sometimes taking a chance was definitely worth the risk because the reward was totally awesome.

Turn the page for a preview
of Cathie Linz's next romance

Tempted Again

Coming soon from Berkley Sensation!

Chapter One

. . . .

When in trouble, seek shelter. Marissa Bennett had learned that lesson at an early age. She'd had to. Seek shelter from the storm. And there was no safer haven than her hometown of Hopeful, Ohio.

Or so Marissa hoped. Not that hoping, wishing or even praying had helped her out much lately. The bottom line was that her life had completely fallen apart over the past year. And now here she was, heading back home in a used and dented lime green VW Bug. The eyesore of a car was a necessity, not a choice.

Hopeful hadn't changed much since Marissa had left to go to college over a decade ago. As she traveled along Washington Street, the main highway into town, she drove past the oak tree–filled campus of Midwest College. The ivy-covered brick buildings glowed in the May sunshine. It was Saturday afternoon, so the campus wasn't as bustling as a weekday when classes were in session, but groups of students sat out under the trees, enjoying the fine weather.

Her father was a history professor at the college and had been for years. One of her earliest memories was of him carrying her on his shoulders to touch the abundance of crab apple blossoms in the trees lining the entrance to Birch Hall, where he had his office.

Marissa's parents had wanted her to stay and attend Midwest College, but Marissa had had her heart set on attending Ohio State. She'd been eager to spread her wings and fly, excited about the world of possibilities open to her.

No, Hopeful hadn't changed much . . . but Marissa had. Divorce and disillusionment did that to a woman. Knocked the stars from her eyes and turned her dreams to dust.

How different would her life be right now if she'd stayed in her hometown instead of leaving?

She wouldn't have met and fallen for Brad Johnson. Wouldn't have married him. Wouldn't have caught him in their bed with another woman.

The humiliating memory cut clear through her so Marissa shoved it out of her mind for the time being. She'd been doing that a lot lately. Shoving thoughts away and locking them up somewhere deep inside her as if they were radioactive waste. It was the only way for her to cope with the fact that she'd lost the life she'd built. Living a mere hour outside of New York City had given her the best of both worlds—the culture and excitement of the big city and the suburban lifestyle. But that was all over now. Gone.

Infidelity had ended her marriage. Budget cuts had ended the job she had loved at the local library. The divorce had ended her ability to stay in the compact English-style cottage home of her dreams she'd shared with her husband. Her situation had started to seem hopeless before she'd been given this second chance in her hometown.

"What makes you want to return home?" library director Roz Jorgen had asked during Marissa's interview at the Hopeful Memorial Library several weeks ago.

The fact that my life is a mess was not a suitably professional response so Marissa had come up with an alternative statement about not realizing the value of something until you were away from it for a while.

Marissa must have said something right during the lengthy interview with Roz and the library board, because they eventually offered her a job, and in doing so, offered her a lifeline when she desperately needed one.

So now she had a position at her old hometown library, where she'd gone to Story Hour as a kid and worked as a page shelving books while in high school. She slowed as she drove past the library building on the corner of Washington and Book Streets.

There were so many memories here. Her father had taken pride in telling her that the white Doric columns guarding the library's front entrance were the same style found on the Parthenon in Greece. She wondered if her dad was proud of her now that she'd returned home after messing up so badly. Beyond the words, "Good luck," he hadn't said much when she'd come for the library interview several weeks ago.

Marissa had felt so stupid and useless after the divorce. Signing the divorce papers on her one-year anniversary hadn't helped. She couldn't even stay married for twelve months. How lame was that?

"You are *not* falling to pieces," she fiercely ordered herself. "Not in front of the library's book drop. It's been six months. Your falling-to-pieces days are done. You're starting over. Focus on that. Your new life. New job."

Yes, the pay was low, but it was a job and Marissa was grateful to have it. And yes, she'd have to stay at her parents' house for a week or two until she got her act together and her first paycheck. But there were worse things, right?

The threat of tears came suddenly and intensely as it often did since walking in on Brad in their bedroom doing the nasty with a female intern from his office. Blinking frantically, Marissa turned onto Book Street and found an empty parking place along the curb. Needing a moment to collect herself, she put the demon VW into park. She missed her Ford Five Hundred, but she hadn't been able to afford the car payments so she'd had to trade it in. This rust bucket was the only thing in her price range. She'd told the car dealer, "Any color but green." Yeah, right.

"Beggars can't be choosers," Marissa muttered, glaring at the rusty lime green car hood.

"Are you lost?" The question came from a woman leaning on the open passenger window. "Do you need help?"

Yes, Marissa wanted to reply to both those questions.

"Marissa, is that really you?" the woman asked.

That was the question. Was Marissa really sitting there staring at her high school guidance counselor, Karen Griffith, who always described her as "smart and perky"? Or had Marissa fallen into some alternative universe? Was this all just a bad dream and she'd wake up to find herself in her sleigh bed with her husband . . . her totally committed, non-adulterous husband?

Not gonna happen, her inner voice told her.

"Are you okay?" Karen was staring at her with concern. In high school, she'd always invited the students to call her by her first name, and she cared about their well-being.

"Yes, I'm okay." Marissa wished she sounded a little more confident.

"Are you sure? You look a little pale."

"I'm sure." Not really, but Marissa had become a fairly good liar. Sometimes she could even lie to herself. "Are you still working at the high school?" She'd learned that diverting attention away from herself was a useful tactic.

"Yes. I saw your mom at the grocery store the other day, and she was bragging about how you're coming home to work at the library. I remember you were an avid reader in school. You always had a book in your hand. You knew early on what you wanted to do with your life. You had a plan. Not many students do."

Yes, Marissa had had a plan but it certainly hadn't included a failed marriage or ending up broke.

"Well, I'd better get going. It was nice to see you again. Welcome home." Karen waved and walked away.

Before Marissa could put the car in drive, her cell phone rang. The ringtone of Bon Jovi's "Livin' on a Prayer" let her know her mom was calling. At fifty-two, Linda Bennett was a huge Bon Jovi fan and a self-confessed worrywart. She'd called Marissa every hour since she'd set out very early this morning from just west of New York City, her former home.

"Where are you?" her mom demanded.

"On Book Street by the library."

A souped-up Camaro pulled alongside her VW with rap music blaring at rock concert decibels, making it hard for Marissa to hear what her mom was saying. "What?"

" . . . go around the barricade."

"What barricade?" Marissa asked.

No answer. Marissa's phone was dead. She'd forgotten to charge it last night before heading out. No big deal. She was only a few blocks from home . . . her safe haven.

• • •

Connor Doyle surveyed the crowd gathered for Hopeful's Founders' Day Parade. As the town's sheriff it was his job to make sure that things remained peaceful. Not that Hopeful was a hotbed of trouble or crime. Coming from Chicago, where he'd been an undercover cop in the narcotics division, he knew all about trouble and the worst that humanity had to offer. The brutal murders, the gang violence.

Connor had been a third generation Chicago cop. His grandfather, his dad, his brothers—all Chicago cops. Well, his younger brother, Aidan, had recently moved to Seattle, but he was still a big city cop. Connor's family didn't understand why Connor had left Chicago two years ago for "a hick town." Their words, not his.

Connor had his reasons, and they were nobody's business but his. No one expected him to spill his guts. That wasn't the way his family worked. It certainly wasn't the way a cop worked.

The bottom line was that his years working undercover had left a mark on him. A permanent mark. Connor absently rubbed his left shoulder where a jagged scar remained to remind him of a knife fight that had almost ended his life.

Connor's older brother, Logan, had once told him that undercover cops were great liars. They had to be.

Connor had certainly been damn good at his job. So good that the lies had nearly consumed him.

His gaze traveled over the crowd. He knew most of the people he saw. The six Flannigan kids, all age eight and under, were present with their parents front and center. The kids had dripping ice-cream cones in their hands. The only exception was the baby still in the stroller, who was reaching for her sister's cone, her face screwed up on the verge of a hissy fit.

Farther down, the older generation was well represented by a group from the Hopeful Meadows Senior Center. The women outnumbered the men by ten to one today.

Beside them was Flo Foxworth in her folding chair. Flo always reserved a curbside front row seat for every city event—from parades to concerts to fireworks. She worked in the post office and knew who subscribed to what magazines, although she didn't share that knowledge with many. Not far behind her was Digger Diehl, the best plumber in town, who proudly wore his "Drain Surgeon" T-shirt with his denim overalls.

The mayor, Lyle Bedford, wore his customary red vest with his suit as he walked at the head of the parade with the Girl Scout troop holding the large Founders' Day Parade banner in blue and gold. Looking at him now, you'd never know that the guy had had open-heart surgery six months ago. A lifetime resident of Hopeful, Lyle had been mayor for nearly two decades now, and his popularity showed no signs of decreasing. Lyle loved Hopeful and the town loved him back.

Behind him was a Brownie troop, and then a group of Boy Scouts. Then came one of the town's shiny red fire trucks with Connor's buddy Kyle "Sully" Sullivan at the wheel, followed by the fully decorated Chamber of Commerce float.

Next came the Hopeful High School Marching Band playing the theme song from *Star Wars*—playing it badly but with a lot of enthusiasm. The teenagers' faces were already hot and sweaty from the above-usual May temperature, which was already in the low eighties. At least the predicted storms had held off for the parade.

The arrival of the perky cheerleaders waving their pom-poms was greeted with cheers from the men at the senior center—both of them. The football team was met with cheers from everyone for their impressive winning record last season.

Connor looked away to check the crowd. A second later he heard a murmuring among the parade watchers.

Turning back to the parade he was surprised to see a rusty lime green VW Bug crawling along the parade route at about three miles an hour, blaring some rock song he didn't know.

He expected to see some rebel teenager at the wheel, someone who'd pulled this stunt on a dare. Instead he saw a woman. Not a senior citizen who might have gotten confused, but a fairly young woman. Her smile was a little strained as she held up her hand and waved at the crowd as if she were royalty. Her face was flushed and she wore no ring on her left hand.

There were no markings on the car to indicate that it was part of any city organization or group.

Who is she?

Connor didn't realize he'd said the words aloud until the woman beside him turned to answer him. "That's our new librarian," library director Roz Jorgen told him.

"Is she part of some library entry in the parade?" he asked.

"The teenage pages and members of Friends of the Library are participants in the book cart drill team . . ."

"That VW may be small but it's no book cart."

Roz shrugged sheepishly. "I don't know what to say."

"No problem. I know what to say."

Connor walked around the barrier and headed for the rowdy VW with the out-of-state license plates. "Stop your vehicle, ma'am," he said.

"What?" she yelled.

"Turn down the music."

"I can't. It's broken. It turns off and on by itself."

"Green Day," a teenager yelled from the sidewalk. "'Boulevard of Broken Dreams.' Awesome song."

"Pull off at the next intersection," Connor ordered the librarian, shouting so he could be heard over the music.

She flashed her brown eyes at him, startled by his

bossiness perhaps. She shouldn't be. He was a cop, after all. Giving orders went with the badge. And he was in uniform, complete with sunglasses, so there was no mistaking who he was.

Several things about her startled him. Her eyes, for one thing. They weren't just brown, they were a light brown that reminded him of fine whiskey. Her shoulder-length brown hair was loose around her face.

He moved a barricade so she could turn off the parade route onto a side street.

Putting the car in park, she hopped out of the car before turning to face him. "If you can figure out how to stop the music, I'd appreciate it."

He reached in and twisted the keys in the ignition, turning the car off.

"I should have thought of that. But then I'd be stuck in the middle of the parade and I didn't want to do that." Her smile was a little wobbly. "I wasn't expecting a police escort."

"I wasn't expecting an unauthorized rusty VW to appear in the parade," he said.

"Are you going to give me a ticket?"

The dread in her voice made him curious. Not that most folks were eager to get a ticket. But there was something more in her case.

"Since you're new in town, no," he said.

"What makes you think I'm new?"

"Aside from the out-of-state plates, you mean?" he said.

She nodded and nervously twisted a strand of her hair before tucking it behind her ear.

"Most local folks would know better than to crash a parade," he said. "And Roz told me that you were the new librarian."

"She saw me in the parade?"

He nodded, watching as a blush covered her face. She looked good all hot and bothered. "License and registration, please," he said.

"Of course. Um, do I take them out of my wallet or just hand you the wallet?"

"Have you ever received a ticket before?"

"No, of course not!"

She seemed upset that he'd even ask such a question.

As she reached for her wallet he noticed the paleness around her left ring finger.

According to the New York driver's license she handed him, her name was Marissa Johnson. She was born in 1983 and was five foot six.

"Well, Ms. Johnson, welcome to Hopeful. I'm Sheriff Connor Doyle." He removed his sunglasses to give her one of his trademark reprimanding don't-mess-with-me stares. Did he imagine her startled recoil just then? Hell, on the don't-mess-with-me scale, the look he'd just given her barely rated a two. He could be much more intimidating without even breaking a sweat. "You really do need to pay attention to the barricades and other traffic signals in town."

The signals he was getting from her abruptly changed from nervous uncertainty to downright irritation. He wondered what caused the transition. He'd let her off with a warning and even welcomed her to town. What more did she want? Why was she eyeing him as if he was rodent shit all of a sudden?

Connor's expression remained impassive as he slid his sunglasses back on. "You could have caused an accident. Could have hit someone in the parade," he said.

She remained silent. She was biting her lip, which strangely enough made him want to reach out and save her lush lower lip from such abuse.

He definitely had not imagined the change in her

attitude. Maybe she had a thing against cops? Then why had she acted all sweet and polite in the beginning? No, he was willing to bet it wasn't all cops, it was something about him in particular that got her all riled up.

Connor was used to riling up women. His brothers often kidded him that he was the womanizer in the family, which was bullshit because the truth was none of the Doyle men had trouble with the ladies. No trouble finding them, that is. Definitely some trouble keeping them. Connor's older brother, Logan, and his dad were both divorced.

Connor had lost track of how many times his dad had hopped on the marriage-go-round. Logan had recently remarried and hooked up with a librarian. Connor had been the best man at their Las Vegas wedding in December. That hadn't changed his personal aversion to getting hitched, however.

Connor eyed Ms. Johnson carefully before contacting dispatch to run a check on her plates and license. The response came back negative. Clean record. Not even a parking ticket.

He returned her license to her. She made a point of avoiding touching him as if they were in first grade and he had cooties. What was her problem?

"What are you doing to my daughter?" a woman demanded as she marched toward them. "You don't think she has enough trouble, losing her job and her house and her husband? She could be having a nervous breakdown."

"Mom, what are you doing here?" Marissa said.

"Flo called to tell me you'd been arrested."

"I was just giving her a warning," Connor said. "If she's unstable, however, she shouldn't be driving."

He knew it was the wrong thing to say the instant the words left his mouth.

The librarian turned into an infuriated woman-warrior

ready to do battle. "I am not unstable," she growled at him. "And you have no right saying that I am."

She stood there, in her white shirt, jeans and sandals a good six inches shorter than his six-foot frame, and dared him to say something else.

Of course it was a dare he accepted. "And you have no right crashing a parade," he said.

"I didn't crash it. I was very careful not to hit anything. It was a mistake, that's all."

Connor was starting to think it was a mistake not to ticket her for giving him a hard time.

He had the feeling that things in Hopeful were about to get much more interesting with her arrival. He wasn't sure if that was a good thing or not.

• • •

Marissa couldn't believe it. Of all the cops in all of Ohio, she had to be pulled over by this one. Connor Doyle. The guy who'd taken her virginity back in high school.

Okay, so he hadn't "taken" it. She'd willingly given it to him. Practically thrown herself at him. She'd been a high school senior and he'd been a freshman at Midwest College. An out-of-towner from Chicago. A sexy bad boy with a romantic streak. He'd followed his high school sweetheart to college but they'd broken up halfway through the school year.

Marissa had been working beside Connor at the popular Angelo's Pizzeria for five months by then. She'd gone by the nickname of "Rissa" in those days and had dyed her short hair ink black. She'd had a humongous crush on him from day one.

When she'd heard Connor was available, she'd been thrilled. Not that she was the only girl to try and catch his eye. But she had the advantage of having known him for months—knowing what made him laugh, knowing his favorite songs, the way he thought.

So she'd screwed up her courage and "Rebel Rissa" had kissed him one night as they'd left the pizzeria. He'd pulled her closer and kissed her back.

"You taste like tomato sauce," he'd murmured against her mouth.

"So do you," she'd murmured back.

They'd done a lot of murmuring in those days. A lot of kissing. He'd introduced her to the art of French kissing and she'd become hooked. They were a couple. Not that she went around bragging about it and not that she told her parents. What she and Connor had shared was too fiery and intimate to talk about. Their actions spoke louder than mere words.

And their actions had escalated with every heated embrace or tongue-seducing kiss. She'd wanted him to make love to her and he had. She hadn't told him she was a virgin because she didn't want him to have second thoughts.

Her first time had been awkward and a bit painful, but he'd been so tender and loving afterward that she'd fallen even deeper in love with him. Her second time was much better and her third time was awesome. So were the multiple times after that. She was on the pill and he used a condom, so they were being careful. But she hadn't been careful with her heart.

So she'd been totally blindsided when their three-month relationship ended at the end of the school year. He'd dumped her and gone back to Chicago. No explanation. Nothing.

She was starting to see a pattern here. She'd been blindsided by her first love and blindsided by her last love, her husband, Brad. Men sucked.

292 · Cathie Linz

How dare Connor show up here in her hometown. This was supposed to be her safe haven. And, despite the badge he now wore, there was nothing safe about Connor Doyle. Not one solitary thing. He still had those hard-to-define blue-green-gray bedroom eyes, broad shoulders and lean build. Age hadn't seemed to do anything but improve his looks.

No, there was nothing safe about Connor. He was trouble she didn't need.

When in trouble, seek shelter. But how the heck was she supposed to do that when the trouble was right here in her own backyard?

Enter the rich world of
historical romance
with Berkley Books.

Lynn Kurland

Patricia Potter

Betina Krahn

Jodi Thomas

Anne Gracie

Love is timeless.